RECKONING

MADALYN MORGAN

Storm

To request permissions, contact the publisher at rights@stormpublishing.co

Ebook ISBN: 978-1-80508-231-6
Paperback ISBN: 978-1-80508-233-0

Previously published as *Chasing Ghosts*

Cover design: Debbie Clement
Cover images: Arcangel, Shutterstock

Published by Storm Publishing.
For further information, visit:
www.stormpublishing.co

ALSO BY MADALYN MORGAN

Foxden Acres

Destiny

Betrayal

Redemption

Legacy

Reckoning

Confessions

Reckoning is dedicated to my mother and father,
Ena and Jack Smith.

OXFORD, ENGLAND

DECEMBER 22, 1949

ONE

Claire turned the key in the lock on the front door. It swung open and she stumbled over the threshold. The late afternoon light crept into the house behind her, casting a gloomy shadow on what was already an unhappy homecoming.

'Excuse me, ma'am?'

She stepped to the side to allow the young sergeant who had driven her from Brize Norton aerodrome to pass. He carried two large suitcases, which he placed in the alcove under the stairs in the narrow hall. Returning to Claire, he took the holdall out of her hand and the small vanity case from under her arm and set them down next to the suitcases.

'Thank you,' she whispered. Dropping the house keys on the hall table next to the telephone she pushed open the door to the sitting room. It felt cold.

'Is there anything else, Mrs Mitchell?'

Claire turned and, grateful for the help he had already given her, said, 'No, thank you.'

The airman hovered for a couple of seconds before standing to attention. 'If there *is* anything, ma'am?'

'I'll telephone the base. Thank you, Sergeant.'

Claire closed the door behind the young airman and, ignoring the luggage, went into the sitting room. Dust and the musty smell of a room several months without heating filled her nostrils. She switched on the light, walked over to the window and stared out. Thick low-level grey clouds covered the sky, blocking out what was left of the pale winter sun. The day had almost gone. It would soon be dark. Shivering, she drew the curtains to shut out the onset of the cold night.

She yawned. The flight from Canada, which had taken longer than the estimated ten hours because the aircraft had landed to pick up military personnel in several cities en route, had taken its toll. The endless and repetitive questions that followed during a three-hour interview with her husband's base commander when she arrived at Brize Norton, had exhausted her. She knew the questions were to enable Commander Landry and the Canadian Air Force to help her – and, more importantly, to find and help Mitch. All the same, she felt as if she had been put through a full-scale interrogation.

She dropped onto the settee shivering. Thank God she had left her daughter with Mitch's grandmother. At least Aimée would be warm. And Esther always had plenty of food in.

She looked at the clock above the fireplace. It had stopped. Of course it had. It hadn't been wound-up during the three months she had been in Canada. She pulled back the sleeve of her coat and glanced at her wristwatch. Ten past six. Esther would have given Aimée her tea by now.

Claire wondered if her neighbour had remembered to buy her a pint of milk and a loaf of bread. She had telephoned her from the airport, before she and Aimée had been hustled through passport control and bundled onto an aircraft bound for England.

Tears fell onto her cheeks. What had happened to him? He knew the time of the flight to England – had known it for weeks – so why did he miss the plane? Did something unforeseen happen, like an accident? Or was he absent without leave by choice, as the sergeant from St Hubert Airbase in Montréal had intimated? If he had chosen to stay in Canada, was it to be with the woman he dreamed about, who he talked to in his sleep? The woman called Simone?

Claire was driving herself mad. She took a handkerchief from her pocket and wiped her tears. Surely if Mitch was having an affair she would have known, sensed something was wrong with their relationship. She took a sharp involuntary breath. Was Simone one of the nurses at the hospital where he'd been having treatment? No, she couldn't be. Mitch had said her name in his sleep months before they went to Canada. But, Claire recalled, he had been to Canada on military business several times in the last couple of years. Perhaps he had met her on one of those occasions. If Simone was the reason Mitch had stayed in Canada, she must mean a lot to him, for him to abandon his daughter. Mitch was as devoted to Aimée as she was to him. Questions whirled round in Claire's head until it ached. There were no answers.

She caught her breath. 'Damn!' she said out loud. When the plane landed at Brize Norton and she was told by Commander Landry that Mitch was officially AWOL she had been so worried that she'd forgotten to let her sister Bess know that she and Aimée were back in England. She ought to telephone her, not only to let her know that they had arrived home safely but also to tell her that they would not be joining the rest of the Dudley family at the Foxden Hotel for Christmas.

Claire wiped the tears from her face with the flat of her hand, hauled herself off the settee and lost her balance. Nausea swept over her. She felt light-headed. Her stomach lurched and the pulse in her temples began to throb. She took a couple of slow deep breaths. She needed to eat something and hobbled out of the room. Ignoring the telephone in the hall, she went into the kitchen. She opened the door to the

larder and found a bottle of milk, a loaf, half-a-pound of
butter, six eggs, and a greaseproof paper parcel, which she
assumed contained bacon. Her neighbour had not only
remembered the bread and milk, she had bought Claire a small
feast.

Dying for a cup of tea, Claire filled the kettle and lit the gas.
Too tired to cook but knowing she needed to eat something to
settle her stomach, she took the bread from the larder and cut a
thick slice. While the kettle boiled she built a fire, speared the
bread on the toasting fork and held it close to the crackling
kindling. When she had made the tea, she buttered the toast
and returned to the sitting room, where she sat on the rug in
front of the fire and ate.

Armed with a second cup of tea she went upstairs and took
off her outdoor clothes. In the bottom drawer of the tallboy was
an old pair of winceyette pyjamas. The knees were worn and
they were frayed around the ankles, which was why she hadn't
taken them to Canada. They felt cold to the touch. Claire
hoped they weren't damp. She didn't have the energy to go
downstairs and air them by the fire, or to sort through her suitcase for a dry pair, so she put them on. Swallowing the last of
her tea she climbed into bed and pulled the eiderdown up to
her chin. She was soon asleep.

'Where is my husband?' Claire looked around the vast airport
concourse. 'Where is Captain Alain Mitchell? I can't see him.
Aimée, don't wander off, darling. We'll be leaving as soon as
Daddy gets here.'

'Excuse me, Mrs Mitchell, you need to board now. The
plane is about to take off.'

'But my husband isn't here.' Claire turned her back on the
man. 'Where did Mitch say he was going?' she asked her
father-in-law.

'As far away from you as possible.' Alain Mitchell Snr. snarled, his mouth gaping open to show a black toothless void.

'What's happening? I don't understand. Mitch?' Claire shouted. 'Alain?' Aimée began to cry. Claire reached out to her, but her daughter backed away. 'Aimée, darling?' Claire called. 'Don't you leave me too.'

'I'm sorry, Mrs Mitchell, but if you don't board now the plane will go without you.'

'Then let it go! You don't seem to understand that my husband, Captain Alain Mitchell, isn't here and I am not leaving without him! And,' Claire looked around, 'where is my daughter? I only turned away from her for a second. Aimée!' she shouted. 'Aimée, where are you?'

Claire spun round and glared at the official. 'What have you done with her? I am not leaving Canada without my daughter and my husband.'

One man grabbed Claire by the arm while another wrapped a thick winter coat around her shoulders. Together they marched her away from Mitch's sneering father. She struggled to look over her shoulder; to say goodbye to him, but he was no longer there. Instead, Aimée stood in his place.

'Aimée?'

'Goodbye, Mummy.'

'You can't stay here, Aimée.'

'I'm waiting for Daddy.'

'But he isn't here, darling. Let me go!' Claire screamed at the airport officials. 'I need to get my daughter. Please,' she pleaded, first to one and then the other of the men. Neither took any notice. 'Aimée?' she called again, 'Aimée? Come to me, sweetheart.' Claire shook herself free of the men's grasp and tried to run, but the coat was too heavy. It weighed her down. She couldn't move. She gasped for breath, as the collar of the coat tightened around her throat.

'Get it off me!' she screamed. Clawing at her neck, she

threw off the coat that threatened to strangle her and turned to her daughter. She wasn't there. First Mitch had disappeared and now Aimée.

Somewhere far in the distance she heard a shrill incessant ringing. She rolled over, arms flailing to free herself from the tangle of sheets and blankets that had been the restraints in her nightmare. She pushed the counterpane from her face and opened her eyes. She lay on her back, disorientated. Staring at the ceiling she squeezed her eyes shut, opened them, and exhaled. 'Bess!' she said aloud. 'It's the telephone. It'll be our Bess.'

Dragging herself out of bed, Claire grabbed the eiderdown, threw it around her shoulders and left the bedroom in a bundle of bedding. Barefoot, she ran downstairs to the hall and snatched up the receiver. 'Hello?'

'Claire, it's Bess. Thank God you're there. You were going to ring me when you landed. When you didn't, I began to worry. Is everything all right?'

'No, Bess, it isn't.'

At that moment Claire heard knocking on the front door. 'Someone's at the door,' she said. 'It's probably Esther bringing Aimée home. Can I ring you back, Bess?'

'Yes. I'll wait for your call... Claire?'

'I'm still here, but I must answer the door. I'll ring you when Esther has gone.' Claire put down the telephone and unlocked the front door.

Aimée ran into the house ahead of her great-grandmother. She put her arms around Claire's waist and clung to her but didn't speak.

Esther entered carrying a large cardboard box. 'Father Christmas wasn't sure whether you'd be back from Canada in time for Christmas. So, as he didn't know your address over there, he left these gifts for you, Aimée, and Alain, with me.'

Claire forced herself to smile. 'Thank you.'

Aimée let go of her mother and, showing no interest in the box Grandma Esther was holding, ran upstairs to her bedroom.

Esther went into the sitting room and Claire followed. As she turned to close the door she heard Aimée's bedroom door slam.

'Shall I go up to her?' Esther asked.

'No,' Claire said, 'I'll go.'

'And while you're up there, dear, why don't you get washed and dressed?' Esther said as Claire left the room.

When she returned half an hour later, Claire could smell bacon cooking. 'Can I do anything?'

'Not in here, but you could take a look at the fire. Make sure it hasn't gone out, will you?' Esther shouted. 'I'll be with you in a jiffy.'

The warm smoky scent of wintergreen and vanilla met Claire as she opened the door. Crouching down she warmed her hands before the cheerful yellow flames of the burning logs. 'The fire's fine. The room is quite warm,' she called to Esther, who she could hear opening and closing drawers and clanging pots.

'Breakfast,' Esther sang, entering the sitting room with a plate of bacon and eggs on a tray. She put the food on the dining table.

'Thank you, Esther, but I'm not hungry,' Claire said.

'Maybe not, but you need to eat. Come on!' Esther might have been a great-grandmother, almost eighty now, but she still considered herself in charge. She pulled out a chair from under the table and waited for Claire to saunter over and sit on it. 'Now, young woman, eat this food or you will be ill. And that won't do, not with Aimée to look after.'

Esther was right. Claire did as she was told and began to

eat. When she had finished, Esther refreshed the teapot and sat at the table with her.

'How was Aimée?'

'Tearful. She's worried that she'll never see her daddy again. I reminded her that when she was a baby, when we lived in France with Grandma Édith, Daddy went away but he came back to us. I promised her he would come back to us again.'

'And?'

'She sniffed and nodded. She said she remembered. I'm not sure she does, but I wasn't going to argue with her.'

'Is she coming down?'

'No. By the time I got upstairs she was undressing. She said she was tired, put on her nightie, and climbed into bed. I was worried that her nightgown was damp, but it felt fine. I think my neighbour must have had a couple of fires going while we were away. I filled a hot water bottle and slipped it into the bed by her feet. I looked in on her when I'd washed and dressed. She was asleep with her thumb in her mouth.'

'She hasn't sucked her thumb for years, has she?'

'No,' Claire said, 'I thought she had grown out of it. She has never gone to bed in the day, either. You know yourself, she'll do anything to delay going to bed at night.'

'Poor lamb.' The two women sat in silence for some minutes. 'What are your plans, dear?' Esther asked, pouring them both another cup of tea. Claire looked into Esther's kind blue eyes and slowly shook her head.

'You must go back to Canada!' Esther said, with such conviction there was no room for discussion. 'Find Alain and bring him home. But first you need to give Aimée a Christmas. A couple more days without your husband won't hurt you, but not having a Christmas *will* hurt Aimée.'

'What about you?' Claire asked. 'What will you do?'

'I shall spend Christmas Day with my friend Dorry, who would otherwise be on her own. On Boxing Day two friends who make up our bridge four will join us. If you need me here to look after Aimée, they can come to me. Aimée might not have as much fun with four old fogeys as she would at Foxden with her cousin Nancy but she won't go short on love and attention. With no family of her own Dorry spoils Aimée at every opportunity.' Esther shook her head and laughed.

'So?' she said, looking at Claire over the top of her glasses, her voice taking on a serious tone. 'What's it to be?'

'All right. You win,' Claire said, pleased that Esther had forced her into making a decision. 'I'll telephone my sister and tell her we're coming up to Foxden tomorrow. That is if the car starts.'

'I'll have no excuses, young lady. If your car doesn't start, I shall drive you to the station.'

'Thank you, Esther,' Claire said, unable to stop her tears.

Mitch's ever-practical grandmother reached into her handbag at the side of the chair and took a clean handkerchief from it. 'Wipe your eyes, child,' she said, pushing the hankie at Claire. 'If Aimée sees you've been crying when she comes down, she'll be even more upset.'

With Esther's help, Claire unpacked the suitcases. Between them, they made three piles of clothes. A clean and ready to wear pile, a pile that was clean but needed ironing, and a pile to be washed. While Claire ironed, Esther fitted the water pipe to the tap and filled the washing machine. She dropped in the whites, added a cup of Persil and turned it on. While the rhythmical wave of suds sloshed from side to side, Esther filled the sink with clean water ready to rinse. She then sorted through the coloured clothes to put into the machine when she had taken the whites out and the water had cooled.

'I'm hungry, Mummy,' a little voice said at the kitchen door.

Claire stood the iron up on the ironing board and went to

her. 'Did you have a good nap, darling?' she asked, bending down and hugging her daughter. Aimée shook her head and put her arms around her mother's neck. 'How about I make your favourite lunch?' Aimée let go of her mother, took a step back and gave her a questioning look. 'Spam fritters and a yokey-egg?' Aimée shrugged her shoulders and turned her nose up at the suggestion. 'But you loved fritters with an egg that you dip your bread and butter into when we were in Canada.'

'And if you eat it all up, there's sponge cake with butter-cream and jam for afters,' Esther added. 'That is if you want cake?'

'Yes, please!' Aimée shouted.

'I spotted a cake tin in the box Father Christmas left with me, so I took a peek. I know I shouldn't have looked, but I don't think he'd mind. And I'm sure he wouldn't mind if you eat some of the cake today. Especially as you won't be here on Christmas Day.'

Claire looked at Aimée, waiting for her to jump for joy because not being at home meant she would be at Foxden with Grandma Dudley, her aunts and uncles and her new cousin Nancy. 'Aimée?'

'But Daddy won't be there. How can we have Christmas without Daddy?'

Esther went to her great-grandchild, put her hands on her shoulders and walked her into the living room. 'Because that is what your Daddy would want,' she said. Esther sat on the settee and patted the cushion next to her. When Aimée sat down, she said, 'Your Daddy wouldn't want you to stay here and be sad. He'd want you to be happy and have fun at Christmas.' Aimée looked down at her shoes, kicked her heels against the sofa and rocked back and forth.

'Before you went to Canada you told me you were worried that you wouldn't be home in time for Christmas because you wanted to go to Foxden.'

'Yes, but that was before I knew Daddy wasn't going to be with us. What if he comes home and we're not here?' Aimée looked up when her mother came into the room. 'What will he do all on his own?'

'He won't stay here on his own, darling, not if we're not here. Daddy knew we'd planned to have Christmas with Aunt Bess and Uncle Frank at Foxden, so he'll come up to us.' Aimée didn't look happy. 'I know,' Claire said, 'we'll leave him a note reminding him that we've gone to Foxden and ask him to come to us as soon as he can. How's that?' Aimée nodded, but Claire could see she wasn't won over by the idea.

After tea Claire cleared the table and washed the dishes. Esther rinsed the washing, put it through the mangle, and hung it on the clotheshorse.

'Right! It's time I made a move,' Esther said. Heading to the hall, she put on her coat. 'I'm not keen on driving in the dark at this time of year, the roads can be icy once the sun's gone down. Besides, I haven't packed my case yet.' She laughed. 'I daren't be late getting to Dorry's tomorrow. She's expecting me for lunch. If I'm not there by one o'clock she'll think I've had an accident and start telephoning round the hospitals. She is a worrier.'

After walking Esther down the icy path and seeing her safely into her car, Claire returned to the house. She closed the front door and locked it before joining Aimée at the living room window. Together they waved Esther off. When the car was out of sight, Aimée resumed her drawing and Claire went into the hall, picked up the telephone, and dialled her sister Bess's number in Leicestershire.

'Hello, Bess, it's Claire. Aimée and I will be coming to Foxden for Christmas as planned.'

CANADA – THREE MONTHS EARLIER

SEPTEMBER 1949

TWO

Aimée was excited on the flight to Canada. It was the first time she had been on an aeroplane and she asked her father a million questions. She watched with awe as the stewardess demonstrated how, in the event of an emergency landing, passengers were to stay calm and exit by the nearest doors. Aimée beamed her best smile at the stewardess and when she had finished demonstrating the emergency procedures, said, 'Excuse me, please? How does the aeroplane stay in the air?'

Looking surprised the young stewardess said, 'That's a good question.' Leaning across the seat next to the aisle, she pointed out of the window. 'You see the big engines under the wing?' Aimée nodded. 'Well,' the stewardess said, 'they draw in air and the air mixes with fuel, which burns and pushes the aeroplane forward.'

Aimée frowned as she tried to understand what the young woman was saying. 'And then the pilot who is flying the aeroplane, the Captain, controls how fast and how high the aeroplane flies.'

'My Daddy is a captain,' Aimée said, proudly. 'He flies aeroplanes too, don't you, Daddy?'

'I used to, honey. It's been a while,' he said to the stewardess.

'In the war, Captain?'

Mitch nodded.

Later, the same stewardess was serving drinks. When she had taken Mitch and Claire's order she asked Aimée if she would like to visit the cockpit and meet the pilot?

Aimée caught her breath. 'Yes please.'

'Good. I'll see you later when the plane has stopped climbing. The pilot is usually free for a while then.'

By the time Mitch had told Claire and Aimée about Canada; what the weather would be like when they arrived, how beautiful the fall is, and how it snows for several months in the winter, the stewardess had returned.

'Captain Duval, the pilot, is free now, Aimée.' Wide-eyed, Aimée looked from her father to her mother. Both nodded and she scrambled out of her seat.

The stewardess brought Aimée back in time for the evening meal. She chatted on about the dials and buttons, how she had sat in the co-pilot's seat and driven the aeroplane. She was so excited with the experience, she told the stewardess who came to take their evening meal order. She stood and listened patiently, although she must have heard the story hundreds of times before, Claire thought.

When Aimée had finished chattering, Mitch ordered Canadian bacon with asparagus and sliced tomatoes, French fries and a bread roll, followed by pancakes and maple syrup.

'The same for me, please,' Aimée said.

'I don't think you'd like the bacon, honey. It isn't like the bacon we have at home in England. Why don't you have junior roast chicken and fries?' Aimée said okay – so long as she could have tomato sauce on her fries.

'Ketchup,' Mitch explained. 'Honey?' He passed the menu to Claire.

'I'd like roast beef,' she said, 'and apple pie and custard for dessert.'

'All the trimmings with the beef, madam?'

Claire glanced down the menu and read: *Yorkshire pudding, roast potatoes, carrots, peas and gravy.* 'Yes, please,' she said, 'and a glass of red wine.'

'Make that two wines, and...' Mitch looked at Aimée. 'Cola for you, sweetheart?'

Aimée nodded. 'And chocolate,' she said, 'for pudding.'

'I think an apple would be better after your dinner,' Claire said. Aimée stuck out her bottom lip.

'I know,' the stewardess said, 'we have some juicy red grapes.' Aimée said yes to the grapes and, happy with the compromise, sat back in her seat and looked out of the window.

'Grapes?' Claire laughed. 'I can't remember the last time I had a grape.'

'Nor me.'

'The luxury of flying, a poster in the departure lounge called this airline.'

'And it sure is. There's no rationing on this flight.'

'Is food still rationed in Canada like it is in England?' Claire asked.

'No. In the summer of forty-seven, the government took dairy products off the ration list. Canada's a big country with a good climate for farming. We grow oats, wheat, barley, every kind of vegetable, and we breed cattle. Now we don't send as much food overseas we're living better.'

While they ate their meal, stewardesses walked up and down the aisle topping up passengers' glasses with wine and soft drinks. When they had finished eating they brought round newspapers. Mitch chose the *Montréal Gazette.* Claire a Canadian magazine called, *Chatelaine,* and Aimée couldn't make up her mind between *Girls Magazine* and a copy of *Calling All Girls*, an American magazine that had been left behind on an earlier flight. She chose *Calling All Girls* because it had a picture of seventeen-year-old movie star Elizabeth Taylor on the cover, saying it was more grown up. She put it on the seat next to her with her drawing pad and crayons, leaned back and yawned.

'Are you tired, honey?' Mitch asked. Aimée shook her head.

'Are we nearly there, Daddy?'

'No, we have a way to go yet. Hey? Why don't you lie down for a while and close your eyes? Have a nap and when you wake up we'll be almost there. What do you say?' Aimée nodded, kicked off her shoes and tucked her legs underneath her. Mitch got to his feet, opened the overhead locker and took out a pillow and a blanket. Sitting down again, he plumped up the pillow and laid it across his knees. Aimée stretched out with her head on her father's lap and her feet beneath the window.

Claire lowered her magazine and watched the two people she loved most in the world making themselves comfortable. When Aimée stopped wriggling, Mitch tucked the blanket around her and picked up his *Gazette*.

Claire continued to read her magazine until Mitch put down his newspaper. She reached up and put out the overhead light. When she had settled, Mitch took hold of her hand and they spoke quietly while their daughter slept.

'Are you looking forward to your new job at St Hubert?' Claire asked.

'Yes. There aren't any rookie pilots to train now, it's all pretty much intelligence work.' A sad smile crossed her husband's face.

'What is it?'

'I was thinking about when I was training rookies before the war. It seems like a lifetime ago. It is a lifetime ago,' he sighed. 'I wish I'd been in Canada when Avro designed the XC-100 jet fighter in forty-six. I saw the plans when I was back last year. Boy, the XC-100 Canuk is some aircraft. Commander Landry told me she is ready to fly. You never know, I may get lucky and get to go up in her.' Claire hoped not. Too many test pilots had been killed during the war. St Hubert's was Defence Command Headquarters, half airport half base, with the hub of RCAF intelligence based there.

A frown crept across Mitch's face, the lines on the bridge of his nose deepening. 'I wonder what the treatment at the Louis Bertrand Hospital will be like? I shall have to juggle work and hospital visits. Thank God I'm only a day patient.'

'We'll know more when you've had your initial assessment.'

'Do you think I'm mad, Claire?'

'Of course not, darling.' Shell shock had affected thousands of servicemen who saw or experienced terrible things in the war. She squeezed his hand. 'You're one of the lucky ones. You're going to have treatment to deal with the horrors you've seen, that you've been through.'

Mitch sighed deeply and looked past his sleeping daughter to the world beyond the small round window in the side of the aircraft. Claire followed his gaze but seeing clouds below them, she felt her tummy churn and brought her attention back to her magazine – though she wasn't able to concentrate to read.

When she felt Mitch's hand relax, she looked across the table at him. He was asleep.

THREE

Claire woke to the hushed sound of Mitch's voice. He was reading to Aimée. She wriggled down in the seat, closed her eyes again, and listened to the familiar words of *The Tale of Peter Rabbit*. When she was younger, it had been her daughter's favourite book. Aimée knew it so well she could recite every word of the story, as well as the five books that followed. Hearing it now reminded Claire of her oldest sister Bess and the many times she had taken her to the lending library in Lowarth when she was Aimée's age.

Claire bit her bottom lip remembering how disappointed she had been when, after several visits, the librarian told her *The Tale of Jemima Puddle-Duck* was still out on loan. When Bess was shopping in Rugby the following week she bought *The Tale of Peter Rabbit* and *The Tale of Jemima Puddle-Duck* from a second-hand bookshop and gave them to Claire as early birthday presents. From then on, Bess bought her a book every birthday which, after reading, Claire carefully placed on the shelves of an old Welsh dresser that doubled as a chest of drawers in her bedroom. The books were still in good condition and she had passed the collection on to Aimée.

'No, Daddy,' she heard Aimée say, 'you're not reading it properly.' Claire smiled to herself. Mitch had been reading Peter Rabbit stories to their daughter since they had returned to England from France in 1945. At that time Aimée was too young to read them herself, but later, as Claire had done at her age, she had memorised every word. Mitch grinned at Claire and purposely paraphrased the next paragraph.

Aimée sighed loudly, put her hands on her hips, and, looking into her father's face, tutted. She was bright for her age and more than capable of reading books written for girls much older than herself. Mitch read to her for fun and often, as she was doing now, when he got it wrong Aimée would tell him off and make him read the passage again, properly.

A worried look crept across Claire's face. She leant her head on the headrest and closed her eyes. Aimée had grown out of Peter Rabbit some years ago, but recently she had returned to the books, reading them at bedtime. And although she was much more advanced in her reading and had brought with her a selection of books recommended by her schoolteacher, she had insisted on taking *The Tale of Peter Rabbit* to Canada, too.

Claire had wondered if it was because Aimée was nervous about flying in an aeroplane, frightened even. She said she wasn't – and she certainly hadn't shown any signs of nervousness or fear. Perhaps it was the arguments that she and Mitch had been having lately that were upsetting her and she was taking comfort from something that reminded her of a time when her parents were happy. Claire hoped it wasn't that. They had tried not to argue in front of Aimée but sometimes it was impossible not to.

Aware that Mitch had stopped speaking, Claire opened her eyes. 'She's asleep, again,' he whispered. Closing the Peter Rabbit book, he passed it across the table to Claire and she slipped it into the holdall at her feet.

'We were right to bring Aimée with us, weren't we, Mitch?'

Leaning forward, Claire looked at her sleeping daughter. 'Uprooting her, I mean. Were we right to take her out of school, away from her friends, and your grandmother? Taking a child halfway around the world is a big step.'

'Yes, we were right to bring her with us. It was what she wanted. We asked her if she would rather stay with Grandma Esther or go up to Foxden to live with Bess and Frank and her cousin Nancy, but she said she wanted to come with us.'

'I know,' Claire said. 'She thinks she's going to be spoiled by her new Grandma and Grandpa.'

'And she will be. I have no doubt about that,' Mitch laughed.

After almost a decade Claire's heart still beat faster when Mitch laughed. He had joked and laughed all the time before he became ill. She looked into his eyes. They twinkled when he laughed and the skin at the corners creased. He hadn't laughed much recently. He hadn't had much to laugh about. That will change, Claire thought, when he has had treatment for anxiety and bad nerves, which the doctor at Brize Norton had diagnosed as shell shock.

'Ladies and gentlemen, would you fasten your seat belts, please. We will be landing in fifteen minutes,' the stewardess said, repeating the instruction every couple of rows, as she walked down the aisle of the plane.

Mitch gently eased Aimée up into a sitting position before buckling her safety belt. She slipped sideways until her head rested against him again. He eased his arm from under her and wrapped it around her shoulders protectively, cuddling her while she slept. Claire leant across the table and clicked Mitch's belt into position, before gathering up magazine, newspaper and Aimée's colouring book and crayons and putting them into the holdall. She then put on her own safety belt and, with the heel of her shoe, pushed the bag under her seat so it was safely out of the way.

After the customary bumps as the plane's wheels touched down, the reverse thrust, followed by ten minutes taxiing along the runway, the plane came to a halt. Claire carrying the holdall, and Mitch carrying their sleeping daughter, they shuffled along the aisle towards the exit with the rest of the passengers.

As they reached the door, about to leave the aircraft by a set of wide metal stairs, Aimée's head jerked back and her eyes opened. 'Put me down, Daddy,' she said wriggling, 'I'm not a baby.'

Mitch lowered her onto the landing at the top of the stairs and holding his hand Aimée reached up and grabbed the handrail above the metal side of the moveable staircase. Pale from having just woken up, she beamed a smile at Mitch and Claire.

The baggage claim hall, large, bare and very cold, reminded Claire of an aeroplane hangar. After twenty minutes the luggage arrived on open trailers pulled by squat tractor-type vehicles. Mitch found their suitcases, and because Montréal St Hubert's airport was half a military airbase, and Mitch was a captain in the RCAF, they were waved through security and passport control and were in the arrivals hall before the other passengers.

'Alain? Alain?' Claire turned at the sound of Mitch's Christian name being called by someone in the roped-off public area. 'Over here!' Claire looked in the direction the voice was coming from. Searching the crowd of people waiting for friends and family from England she spotted a young woman waving frantically. 'Alain?' she shouted again. Then, pushing her way to the front of the crowd she ducked under the rope and ran across the concourse. Smiling at Claire, she threw her arms around Mitch's neck.

Almost losing his balance Mitch dropped the suitcases and picked the woman up. 'Aimée?' he shouted, swinging her round.

Laughing, he set her down and held her at arm's length. 'This beautiful young woman,' he said, turning to Claire, 'is my baby sister, Aimée.' Claire was stunned how alike the siblings seemed. Aimée was pretty and petite, Mitch tall and broad-shouldered – and they had different mothers – yet they were unmistakably a pair.

After hugging Claire and kissing her, Mitch's sister dropped onto one knee and said, 'Hello Aimée.'

Aimée, tired more than shy, swayed a couple of times and looked up at her mother. Claire raised her eyebrows and nodded encouragingly. 'Hello,' Aimée whispered.

Mitch was fond of his half-sister. So fond of her that he and Claire had named their daughter after her. She had written to him regularly throughout the war. When he returned to England after several years working with the French Resistance, and several more years in a prison, there were dozens of letters waiting for him. They still wrote to each other, though not as often now she was married and ran a business with her husband.

People coming out of the restricted area into the arrivals hall were having to stop and walk round the Mitchell family as they gathered around Aimée the aunt and Aimée the niece.

'We're blocking the way,' Claire said. Mitch grabbed the cases and Claire took their daughter by the hand. They followed Mitch's sister to the public area where they were met by a rugged-looking young man. Standing six feet tall with a healthy all-weather complexion and fair hair, he shook their hands vigorously introducing himself as Aimée's husband, Dan.

A second later, Dan had whipped the suitcases out of Mitch's hands and was striding across the airport to the main exit. 'I'll get the car,' he said, setting down the suitcases by a row of chairs just inside the door.

'I'll come with you,' Mitch said, running to catch up with Dan.

While they waited for their husbands, Mitch's sister told Claire and Aimée about Dan's logging business, in Quebec.

'Does he cut the trees down?' Aimée asked.

'He used to. But now he drives a big machine called a crawler tractor.' Aimée looked puzzled. 'It has big loading arms that Dan has to guide.' Mitch's sister demonstrated using her own arms. 'One is straight,' she said, her left arm at right angles to her body, 'and goes under the pile of logs, and one is called a claw.' She lifted her right arm, bent it at the elbow and made a hook of her hand. 'The claw goes over the top of the logs and hooks around them so they don't fall off. Then it lifts them up, drops them onto the back of a big lorry, and they're taken to the river.'

'Is that where you live?'

'Yes, but not where the logs are. They're taken to a big river called the Ottawa River. Dan and I live in a cabin upstream.' Aimée made an O of her mouth and her eyes sparkled with curiosity. 'From my kitchen window I can see the River Gatineau.'

'Are there any shops near your cabin?'

'Yes. We live on the outskirts of a town called Hull. Would you like to visit us one day and see how the logs in the forest are cut down?'

Aimée's eyes grew wider with each revelation about logs and cabins. 'Can we, Mummy?'

Before Claire had time to answer, Dan came running into the building. 'Are you guys ready?' The women quickly got to their feet and gathered their belongings. 'Sorry to rush you,' he said, 'but we can't park for long out front. Alain is standing guard with his ID at the ready in case anyone tries to move the car on.' Dan picked up the cases and led the way out of the airport.

FOUR

It was ten miles from the airport to the apartment where Mitch, Claire and Aimée would be living for the next three months. The wind, by the time they had driven into Montréal, had enough rain in it for Dan to have to put on the windscreen wipers. He pulled up as near to the apartment building's main entrance as possible. The women jumped out of the car and ran for the lobby, leaving the men to follow with the luggage.

The sitting room was neat and spacious and looked as if it had been recently decorated. Wallpaper on three walls and the fourth, which was really only two large alcoves on either side of a tiled fireplace, had been freshly painted in a pale cream colour to contrast with the richer cream and dark dusky pink of the flowers on the wallpaper. Claire took off Aimée's coat and hung it up in the hall.

'This is my bedroom,' Aimée announced, disappearing into the first room along the short corridor. 'Look, that word is Paris and that one is *bonjour* – and that's the Eiffel Tower. It's the same as Grandma Édith's ornament on top of the cupboard in her sitting room,' Aimée said, and ran out of the room.

Claire pulled back the bedspread and was pleased to see the

white sheets and pillowcase had been freshly laundered. She looked around the room. The woodwork – the door, bedside cupboard, narrow bookcase and the wardrobe had been painted in the same pastel green as the script on the wallpaper and the shade on the overhead light. Returning with her books Aimée began to place them on the bookcase that faced her bed.

'Alain and Dan are here with the cases,' Claire's sister-in-law said, poking her head around the door. 'Oh, la la,' she sang. 'I love this room.'

'It's mine,' Aimée said. 'And these are my books. I have schoolbooks in my case, too.'

Smiling, Claire's sister-in-law said, 'Shall I tell them to put the cases in the master bedroom for now, while we have something to eat?'

'Eat? Goodness I hadn't thought about food. Yes, please, Aimée. I'll be with you in a minute.' She turned to her daughter. 'Sweetheart, finish that later. You must be hungry.'

Aimée followed her mother out of her bedroom.

'Hi, honey,' Mitch said, coming out of the second bedroom. Claire took a peek as she passed. It had a double bed and was larger than Aimée's room. She'd look in detail later.

'Oh, my God!' she exclaimed, walking into the sitting room. 'Where did all this food come from?'

'We brought it with us,' Dan said. 'Aimée's been baking for days. Come, sit down, she won't be a minute.'

'Hardly, Dan,' Mitch's sister shouted from the kitchen. 'I only made the meatloaf and pickle. Oh, and the Tourtière meat pie.'

'And the Montréal bagels,' Dan added. 'You'll love them, Claire. Bagels and cream cheese. Come on, tuck in.'

'This,' Mitch's sister said, entering the sitting room with a large bowl of French fries, 'is what we call an indoor picnic. And, no indoor picnic is good without fries and ketchup. What do you say, Aimée?'

Aimée clapped her hands. 'They are like chips, fat like Nanny Dudley makes at Foxden.'

'The fatter the better,' Mitch's sister said, forking a mound onto Aimée's plate. 'Come on, Alain, Claire, help yourselves,' she said, taking her seat at the table.

When they had finished eating, Mitch and his sister washed the dishes. While Claire unpacked and hung up their clothes, Dan sat with Aimée on the settee and entertained her with photographs of him and his father standing next to tall trees, piles of logs after the trees had been felled, and trees floating like huge rafts in the river.

Claire was hanging up the last of her clothes in the double wardrobe in their bedroom when Mitch looked in. 'I've put Aimée to bed. She couldn't keep her eyes open. I told her you'd go in and say goodnight.'

'Of course. I've just finished in here.' Claire pushed the empty suitcase to the back of the large wardrobe and shut the door. 'I'll go into her now.'

'Coffee when you're ready,' Mitch said, leaving the bedroom.

'Okay,' she called, 'I won't be long.'

Claire crept into Aimée's room. She was fast asleep. A triangle of white sheet hung below the bedspread and Claire tucked it under the mattress. Aimée didn't stir. It was no wonder, she'd had a long and exciting day.

'We have something to tell you both,' Mitch's sister said, when Claire sat down with her coffee. Aimée looked up at her husband and giggled. 'It's a secret. We shouldn't be telling you until we've told Mom and Dad, and Dan's parents, but...' She held her breath, 'We're having a baby.'

'Congratulations, sis.' Mitch jumped up and threw his arms around his sister, then pumped Dan's hand.

'That's wonderful news,' Claire said, looking from Aimée to Dan. 'When?'

'Not until March. It's a long way off. We didn't want to tell anyone until I had passed the first trimester date, which was yesterday. But because we have to go home tomorrow, I thought I'd better tell you now.'

'Tomorrow?' Mitch made a sad face.

'What a shame you have to leave so soon,' Claire added.

'She has a hospital appointment on Monday,' Dan said, proudly. He took Aimée's hand and kissed it. 'We're staying with your folks tonight,' he told Mitch, 'so we'll tell them, and we'll tell mine tomorrow, as soon as we get home.'

'I'm sorry you can't stay longer,' Claire said. 'I wouldn't have spent so much time unpacking if I'd known.' Aimée lifted her hand and flicked the idea away.

'I've left my father to manage on his own. Don't get me wrong,' Dan said, 'he is more than capable. He runs the place like clockwork from the office. But this is the busiest time of year for the logging business. I don't want him going out with the men and hauling logs the way he did when he was my age.'

Aimée nodded in agreement with her husband. 'You'll come over when the baby's born? Or, better still, when she's christened. I want my big brother to be her godfather.'

'It's a girl then?' Claire said.

Aimée laughed. 'Heck, I don't know.' She laughed again. 'And I don't care. Dan's father says we should have three boys so he can retire.'

After Aimée and Dan had gone, Claire and Mitch relaxed with a second cup of coffee and listened to the wireless. Most of the stations were in French, which being fluent in the language didn't matter to Claire, but after playing with the dials, Mitch found the Trans-Canadian Network. They listened to a current affairs programme, and then Mitch tuned the wireless to the Dominion Network, poured them both a Canadian Club and after twiddling the button to get rid of a crackling noise, settled down to listen to a local station called, Montréal CFCF. The presenter announced the coming hour as one of light chat and great music from North America.

Perry Como's 1948 hit 'Because' was the first song to come over the airwaves and fill the small warm room with romantic words, followed by Doris Day and Buddy Clark singing 'Love Somebody'. 'This is the ticket,' Mitch said, as Ella Fitzgerald began to sing Evening shadows make me blue, the opening lyrics to 'My Happiness'.

When the song came to an end, Mitch switched off the wireless and put his empty glass on the table and Claire swallowed the last of her whisky. 'Shall we go to bed, China?' he said, taking her glass from her.

She stood up, looked into her husband's eyes and, smiling, offered him her hand. He pulled her to him and kissed her gently on the lips. Then he kissed her again, more passionately, and guided her to the bedroom humming, 'My Happiness'.

FIVE

Claire wore a navy-blue tailored suit with wide lapels, four buttons at the nipped-in waist, and a cream silk scarf – bought specially for the occasion. Keeping an eye on the time, she applied her make-up to look as natural as possible.

She arrived at breakfast to the voice of wireless presenter Jack Dennett talking about the state of the traffic in Montréal, Aimée tucking into a boiled egg and bread and butter and Mitch drinking coffee. He gave Claire a loving smile. 'You look beautiful, honey.'

'Mummy's pretty,' Aimée said.

'Thank you.' Claire curtsied to her daughter. Then to Mitch, she said, 'I haven't overdone it, have I?'

He shook his head. 'You look perfect.'

Nervous at the prospect of meeting her in-laws, Claire wasn't hungry but agreed with Mitch she ought to eat something. Besides, a little food would settle the butterflies in her tummy. Sitting down next to Aimée, she took a slice of toast from the rack and buttered it. As she ate, Mitch poured her a cup of coffee.

'Right,' Mitch said, when Claire and Aimée had finished

eating, 'we'd better make a move.' He cleared the table, taking their dirty dishes to the kitchen, and went into the hall. When he returned he was wearing his air force blue overcoat. 'Ready?'

The rented car, a four-door saloon, was twice as big as any car Claire had seen in England. But then the Canadian roads were twice as wide, if not wider. Mitch steered the car away from the kerb and into the traffic. Claire expected to hear horns blasting out in protest, as they would have done in England, but not a beep. With three lanes solidly packed with cars, drivers were probably used to cars pulling out in front of them.

'Darling? What do your father and stepmother call you?'

Mitch laughed. 'The old man has called me a few unsavoury things in his time. Especially when I was a kid. Poor guy. I blamed him for everything that went wrong after Mom died.'

'Be serious!' Claire said. 'Does your father call you Mitch or Alain?'

'Alain. Why?'

'Because I shall call you Alain while we're in Canada,' Claire said. 'Alain is who you are to your father and stepmother – and to Grandma Esther. Mitch is your nickname, the name you're known by at the base. It's what your buddies call you.'

'Does that mean I have to stop calling you China?' Alain said, laughing. 'I rather like China.'

'Mummy's name is Claire,' Aimée piped up from the back seat. 'It's a nice name, Daddy.'

'Okay, Claire it is.' Alain looked in the reverse mirror and winked at his daughter.

'So, *Alain*,' Claire said pointedly, 'are you looking forward to seeing your father and stepmother?'

'Yes. It's been a while.' He shot Claire a sideways glance. 'I didn't visit them the last couple of times I came over on air force business, so...'

'So I'd better not tell them you've been to Canada twice during the last year?' Alain gave her a cheeky grin but didn't reply. 'Don't worry, I won't say anything.'

Claire settled back in the passenger seat and looked out of the window. They had no sooner joined the highway than they left it for Montréal's tree-lined avenues and an area called Petite Montagne, the suburb where Alain's father and stepmother lived.

'What a pretty area,' Claire said. 'Look out of the window, Aimée. There's a big park. See all the trees? Their leaves are turning red and orange. Do you remember we saw those trees in the book we borrowed from the library?'

'They're called Sugar Maple trees,' her father told her. 'There's a lake in that park. It's real big.'

'Mm,' Aimée said, without much interest. 'Are we nearly there, Daddy?' she asked, with a sigh.

'We are, honey. One more corner, and...' Alain turned the steering wheel to the left and the car freewheeled over a dropped pavement onto a wide drive, coming to a halt at the side of a garage.

Looking out of a large bay window at the front of the house was a man in his mid-sixties, who Claire assumed was Alain's father. His arm was around the shoulders of a pretty middle-aged woman with fair hair. She waved excitedly and Claire waved back.

By the time Alain had got out of the car and opened the back door for Aimée the woman had left the house by the front door and was running towards them. Aimée jumped out of the car as she arrived and the woman put her hands up to her face. Crouching down so she was level with Aimée, she said, 'Hi, Aimée, I'm your Grandma, Marie. I am so pleased to meet you. I can't believe you are finally here,' Marie Mitchell said. Taking hold of Aimée's hand, she stood up. She looked from Alain to Claire and wiped tears from her eyes.

A second later Alain's father came out of the house. 'Alain?' he called, jogging towards his son. He held Alain's hand, then threw his arms around him and hugged him. Slapping him on the back, he said, 'It's been too long, son.'

'It has, Dad.'

Releasing Alain, his father turned to Claire and welcomed her, kissing her on both cheeks, while his wife stood on tiptoe and hugged Alain.

'And who do we have here?' Alain's father asked.

'Why, Grandpa, this is Aimée,' his wife said. Aimée's new grandparents knelt down and her grandfather shook Aimée's hand before gathering her up in his arms. 'Welcome to Canada, young lady.'

Aimée looked overwhelmed. She smiled politely and nodded but didn't speak. Her new grandmother pretended to shiver. 'I think we should go inside, don't you, Aimée?' She looked at her husband. 'It's a little cold out here in the wind, dear.'

'What? Oh, yes. Come in, come in.' Alain senior said, leading the way to the front of the house, while his wife took Aimée by the hand. Aimée turned to her parents. They nodded, and she skipped along at Marie Mitchell's side. When they were in the house, Alain's father helped his son and daughter-in-law out of their coats and hung them up. He showed them into the front room, where Aimée and Marie were already seated by the fire.

The house, like everything Claire had seen during the short time she'd been in Canada, was big. The interior was spacious, and the windows were wider and taller than the windows in most modern English family houses. Especially those built between the wars.

'Where's my sister? I thought she'd still be here.'

'They needed to get away early,' Alain senior said. He directed the reason why to Claire. 'Aimée and her husband have a logging company some miles away. And,' he beamed a broad smile at Claire and his son, 'to heck with that. Aimée is going to have a baby.'

Marie put her hands up to her mouth. 'Isn't it wonderful? A cousin for you, Aimée, and another grandchild for Grandpa and me,' she said, kneeling down and making a happy face at Aimée.

She's nice, Claire thought, and said, 'Congratulations, Marie. That's wonderful news.'

'Do you like Dan, Dad?'

'Yes, he's a good guy. The point is, your sister loves him and that's all that matters.'

It might have had something to do with the cookies and soda that Marie Mitchell gave her, but Aimée took to her new grandmother straight away. 'I have three Grandmas,' Aimée told her. 'Grandma Édith who lives in France, Grandma Dudley – she lives at Foxden – and now Grandma Marie in Canada.'

When they had finished drinking coffee, Alain looked at his watch. 'I guess it's time we made a move,' he said to Claire. 'I have to be at the hospital for eleven thirty.' Claire got to her feet and Aimée jumped up too.

'Why don't I drive you to the hospital?' Alain's father said.

'It's okay, Dad. I don't want to put you out—'

'You won't be putting me out, Son, I'd like to take you. We've got a lot of catching up to do. What do you say?'

Alain looked at Claire. 'Honey?' Smiling, she lifted one shoulder and nodded.

'Okay. Thanks, Dad.' Alain knelt down in front of Aimée. 'You be a good girl for Mummy and Grandma, won't you?'

Aimée threw her arms around her father's neck and held on tight. 'I will.'

He kissed his stepmother on the cheek and turned to Claire. 'See you later, honey,' he said, kissing her.

From the front window Claire, Marie and Aimée watched Alain and his father drive off. It hadn't occurred to Claire that she wouldn't be going with her husband for his first consultation with the psychiatrist at the Louis Bertrand Hospital. She felt anxious for him. Silly really, she chided, Alain is a grown man. Besides, not having seen his father for more than a year, it will be a chance for the two men to get to know each other again and if necessary to build some bridges.

When the car was out of sight, Claire followed Marie and Aimée to the kitchen, where Aimée helped her new grandma make a cake for their tea.

It had been a long day. Aimée was exhausted from the attention her new grandma had lavished on her and was asleep before they had left Petite Montagne. 'How did it go at the hospital?' Claire asked, as they cruised along the freeway.

'Okay, I think. The head of the psychiatric wing is a Swiss-French professor by the name of Doctor Lucien Puel. He didn't say much. But he asked a lot of questions.'

'Such as?'

'What I did in the war. He'd know I was in the air force because the RCAF is paying for my treatment. I didn't tell him I was with the SOE or the French Resistance. I said I was a pilot and was shot down over France and the Gestapo caught me at Gisoir and I was put in prison. He asked me about the prison and how long I was there. I told him I'd escaped with some other guys and that they had got away but I was shot in the leg. He asked me about the doctor who patched me up after I'd been shot – asked me if I remember his name. I told him I never knew his name, and he didn't know mine – that a no-name policy was safer for everyone. What you didn't know, the Gestapo couldn't get out of you.

'He said the cause of my anxiety and the feeling of panic,

getting angry, the bad dreams, and losing my concentration are to do with what I saw in the war, especially in the prison.'

We already know that, Claire thought, but didn't want to upset Alain by saying so. 'Can the professor help you?' she asked.

'He said he could. Through hypnosis, massage and what he called occupational therapy. He said I needed to relax. And, in a safe environment guided by someone I trust, I need to talk about my past.'

Claire looked out of the window at the traffic. When Alain wasn't in a dark mood, when he wasn't having an anxiety attack or full of self-doubt, he pushed himself too hard. The professor was right. Alain never allowed himself to relax, so telling him he must relax was good. But hypnosis? Claire didn't like the sound of that. She also wondered what occupational therapy really meant. She decided not to ask Alain any more questions. He was bound to tell her more when he began his treatment.

When they arrived home, Alain carried Aimée into the apartment and through to her bedroom. Between them, they undressed her and put her to bed. When they were sure their daughter was settled for the night they put out the light and crept out of the room.

Claire made coffee while Alain poured two measures of Canadian Club. Then they relaxed on the settee in front of the fire with the wireless on low in the background.

'Marie is a nice woman. We got on really well. She loved Aimée, of course,' Claire said, laughing. 'How was it with your father?'

'Okay, Alain said. 'He seems to have mellowed, become more tolerant in his old age.' He took a sip of brandy. 'I don't remember much about him when I was growing up. He was well respected, a great engineer, but he wasn't one of nature's born fathers. He was rarely home, and when he was he was working. Weeknights he'd disappear into his study with a pile of technical drawings, come out for dinner, and go back as soon as he'd eaten. Even at weekends he brought work home with him. He wasn't like any of my school friends' dads. They were air force too, but they made time to take their kids to the park and play baseball with them. My old man was always too busy. I envied the other kids in the neighbourhood.

'After Mom died, he worked even longer hours. He was real strict when my mother was alive, and he got worse when she'd gone. He changed when he met Marie. I think he had to. She wouldn't have put up with him the way he was.'

'That's a good thing,' Claire said. 'Was she a good stepmum?'

'Yes, she was, but I didn't give her a chance,' Alain said. 'I missed my mom and with Marie not having any kids yet, she didn't know how to handle me. I'm sorry to say I played on that. I didn't make her life easy.'

SIX

Alain left the apartment before seven o'clock, as he did every morning, to drive the short distance to St Hubert's Airbase where he worked with Canadian and American military intelligence. Like his job with British military intelligence, attached to RAF Brize Norton in Oxfordshire, his work was keeping the country secure.

'The biggest problem the world is facing according to the Americans,' Alain said, 'is communism. China has declared it's now a communist state: The People's Republic of China is official, and the Soviet Union has successfully tested its first atomic bomb, which they've called, Joe 1.'

'Joe? That sounds ominous.'

'It's more than that. Since they call the US military guys GI Joes, it's damn inflammatory. So, because Russia is the main threat to the west, we're working on an air defence system with St Hubert's engineers. Add Korea into the mix,' Alain said. 'The war divided the country and now trouble is brewing between the north and the south.' He shook his head. 'The team are working to find ways to calm the situation down before it gets out of hand, so...'

'So, you'll be working all hours for the foreseeable future?' Claire said. Alain put his arms around her and kissed her. 'Promise me you won't get so engrossed in what you're doing that you miss your appointments with Professor Puel at the hospital.'

Alain saluted. 'No, ma'am!' Claire pushed him away playfully.

Alain's stepmother was a regular visitor. Aimée had a week left of her summer holiday and, being a bookworm, had read the school books she'd brought with her from England. So Claire and Aimée treated the pre-school week as a holiday. Marie picked them up in her car each day and took them out. They went to the zoo, skating rink and ten-pin bowling.

The RCAF had organised a teacher to home-school Aimée. Claire had never heard of such a thing but agreed with Aimée's form teacher in Oxford that it would be better for Aimée to do her lessons at home, rather than travel for goodness knows how many miles to a school where she wouldn't know anyone and might feel out of place, especially if the school was more advanced than the one Aimée attended in Oxford. It wouldn't be, of that Claire was sure. But, because it was only for three months, Claire agreed to have a home tutor.

She looked in on Aimée who, after a restless evening, had finally fallen asleep Aimée wasn't looking forward to the beginning of the school term with a new teacher and had decided before she met her that she wouldn't like her. Miss Brewster, Claire had been told by the education officer at the base, was the best they had. Unlike her daughter, Claire would reserve judgement until she had met her.

Closing Aimée's bedroom door, Claire returned to the sitting room, took a pen and paper from the bureau and wrote a letter to her sister Bess.

. . .

The tall, very slender Miss Brewster – glasses hanging around her neck on a gold chain – was the epitome of a school ma'am. She arrived promptly at nine o'clock and Claire showed her into the sitting room. 'I thought you could work on the dining table in here,' Claire said, feeling as nervous as if it was her first day at a new school, not her eight-year-old daughter's first day with a new teacher.

Miss Brewster nodded. 'There's ample room,' she said, moving across to the table and putting her leather case on the nearest chair. She looked around the room.

'Is there something else?' Claire asked, nervously.

'My pupil!' Miss Brewster replied.

Aimée had enjoyed spending Saturday with Mitch's father and stepmother but had eaten too many pancakes with maple syrup, resulting in her being sick. She was better, but a little quieter than usual on Sunday. Today, however, she was playing-up a sore stomach to avoid meeting her teacher. 'Of course!' Claire laughed. Miss Brewster kept a straight face. She obviously didn't see the funny side of Claire forgetting her pupil. 'I'll go and fetch her. When she's reading she gets lost in the story, and—' Claire felt her cheeks flush with embarrassment and cut short the excuse for her daughter not being there. 'I'll get her.'

'Aimée?' Claire called, mounting the stairs. 'Come on, darling, your teacher is here.' Aimée was sitting on the windowsill gazing out. She wasn't reading. 'What's the matter?' Aimée shrugged. She swung one leg off the sill, bending the other leg at the knee until she was in a half standing half sitting position. 'Come on, darling, Miss Brewster is very nice.'

'Why can't you teach me?' Aimée said, in a sulk.

'Because I am not a teacher.' Aimée sighed, loudly, and jumped down.

'I know it's difficult for you. It is for me too, and Daddy, but we've got to make the best of it.' Aimée picked up her exercise books and sauntered over to the door. Claire pushed a stray curl out of her daughter's eyes. 'Ready?' Aimée nodded and followed her mother downstairs.

Aimée, being purposely uncooperative, stood in the doorway of the sitting room leaning on the doorframe. 'Aimée this is Miss Brewster. She is going to help you with your school-work so you don't get behind while you're in Canada.'

Aimée looked at Miss Brewster who was taking books from a square leather bag. She didn't speak. Claire scowled at her daughter and nodded in the direction of her teacher.

'Good morning, Miss Brewster.'

'Good morning, Aimée.' Miss Brewster pretended not to have noticed Aimée's petulance and plunged straight in with, 'Would you help me find a book for you to read? I think it would be best if you told me where you're up to with your read-ing, don't you? The letter I had from your headmistress in England said you were bright for your age. Is that true?' Aimée lifted and dropped her shoulders as if she didn't know. Miss Brewster carried on, 'I don't want to give you anything that's too difficult. Perhaps this book to start,' she said, taking a book from her case that had 'For six to seven-year-olds' written on the front.

'I'm almost nine,' Aimée said, indignantly. She went to Miss Brewster and began looking through the pile of books.

'Oh!' The teacher feigned shock. 'Well clearly that one won't do, will it?'

'I haven't read this one,' Aimée said, picking up a copy of *Anne Of Green Gables* by L M Montgomery.

'Good choice, Aimée,' Miss Brewster said. Claire saw a glint of pleasure in Aimée's eyes and she exhaled with relief.

· · ·

'Simone?' Mitch sighed. 'Simone?'

Claire woke from a shallow sleep and opened her eyes. Mitch sat up and said again the name that she had heard him say in his sleep several times since they'd been in Canada. At first Claire thought the woman in his dreams might be a nurse at the hospital. If so, her husband had got to know her intimately in a very short time, judging by the way he said her name.

Claire had told Mitch he talked in his sleep. She'd also asked him about Simone. He had looked shocked and said he didn't know anyone by that name. If he did know someone called Simone, and Claire was sure he did, he must have been lying. She closed her eyes. There was nothing she could say or do if he refused to talk about her.

'Simone!' he called again, suddenly, making Claire jump. 'Forgive me. I'm sorry.'

Claire laid her hand on her husband's arm to comfort him. He snatched it away. 'Mitch... Alain?' she whispered, lovingly. 'Go back to sleep.'

His head jerked. His eyes opened and darted around the room, settling on the door. 'No, no, no! Come back.' He looked down at Claire with surprise, as if he was seeing her for the first time. 'Where is she? What have you done with her?' he asked, his eyes flashing with anger, his voice accusing. Then his features softened and he broke down and wept. 'Simone,' he said again, 'I am sorry.'

'Alain?' Claire said. 'Mitch?' She pushed herself up into a sitting position, put her arms around her husband and held him until his tears subsided.

With a violent shudder he caught his breath, his shoulders slumped, and he collapsed into Claire's arms. 'What the hell is going on?' he cried.

'You had a bad dream but it's over now.' Claire was mindful

that, although his eyes had been open, he was actually asleep. She knew that jolting someone out of a nightmare could be dangerous, especially when they were as troubled as her husband, and made sure she woke him slowly and gently.

Mitch lifted his head and gazed at the door again, before looking back at Claire. His body was relaxed and the frightened, staring look in his eyes had gone. He eased himself out of Claire's arms and swung his legs over the side of the bed. 'I need to go to the bathroom,' he said, making his way out onto the landing.

When he didn't return, Claire got up. Slipping her arms down the sleeves of her dressing gown and pushing her feet into her slippers, she went to look for him. He was in the sitting room listening to the commentary of an ice hockey game on the wireless. She sat on the settee next to him, tucked her feet under her and put her head on his shoulder. Mitch shifted his weight to give Claire more room and put his arms around her. Together, without speaking, they listened to the game.

Claire woke the following morning with a stiff neck. She stretched out her arm expecting Mitch to be next to her. He wasn't there. 'You're already dressed,' she said, as he handed her a steaming cup of coffee. She took a sip and made a grateful sound. 'What time is it?'

'Seven thirty. We've got to be at Dad's place for nine.'

'Half past seven? You should have woken me.'

'I'll get Aimée up, while you drink your coffee.'

Claire put the cup down on the table in front of the settee. 'I'll drink it when I'm dressed, if there's time,' she said, pushing herself up.

At the sitting room door, Claire glanced back at her husband. He looked strikingly handsome in his military uniform. He hadn't worn the uniform for a while, but today he had important meetings to attend. It was also the first in-depth session with the esteemed Swiss psychiatrist who had promised to cure Mitch of shell shock, the debilitating illness that threatened to ruin his working life and his marriage.

Ruin his marriage? Wasn't Simone – the woman her husband dreamed about, who he talked to in his sleep – already doing that? Last night wasn't the first time he had said her name while asleep. But it was the first time he had cried and begged her to forgive him. Forgive him for what? Did they have a relationship, which Mitch had ended? Claire prayed he *had* ended it. Fear of losing the only man she had ever loved tore at her heart.

Mitch was a good-looking man. Claire had taken for granted how attractive he was. If she could see it, other women would see it. And now his hair had started to turn silver at the temples he looked distinguished as well as handsome. Claire wanted to know who Simone was. She wanted to ask Mitch about her, but his appointment with Professor Puel at the Louis Bertrand hospital was in two hours. Now was not the time.

Claire was worried that Aimée was becoming withdrawn because she wasn't interacting with other children. She talked to the Education Officer about it. Perhaps Aimée could attend the base school during the week and see Miss Brewster on Saturdays and the occasional evening. The education officer was happy with the arrangement and found Aimée a place to start regular school at the end of October.

Claire had originally wanted Aimée to have a home tutor because she feared that being English, she wouldn't be accepted by the other children. Her fears were unfounded. It was because she was English that the girls of Aimée's age and younger wanted to be her friend. Aimée, soon back to full confidence, revelled in her popularity.

One of Aimée's school friends, Betty, lived in the same apartment block. Betty's father, also a captain in the RCAF, was working overseas, so with Alain working at the RCAF Airbase at St Hubert's, Claire got to know Betty's mother Naomi.

Naomi drove Betty and Aimée to school each morning and afterwards, she and Claire would go to the shops, a café or to the cinema. In the afternoons, when the two friends collected their children from school they would have tea at Naomi's apartment one day, at Claire's the next, and on the third day they would go out for a treat. And on Saturday afternoons when Aimée had finished her studies with Miss Brewster they went to the park.

Claire could see why the Canadians called autumn the Fall. Being such a large country, Canada had big spacious parks, acres of dense woodland, and great maple trees that had been shedding leaves since mid-September. The grass in the small park near the apartment where they lived, green when they arrived, was now inches deep in blazing orange, rust-red and yellow leaves in every shape and size. Only the spruces remained green. Holding hands, Aimée and Betty ran ahead of Claire and Naomi, laughing and shouting and kicking up leaves.

Autumn felt more like winter. The winds were unusually strong for the time of year, and the temperature had fallen to an unseasonal low – often below zero during the night.

By early November Mitch had been seeing Professor Puel for seven weeks and according to the professor the treatment was working. One evening Mitch came into the sitting room smiling. He took a bottle of Canadian Club from the cupboard and poured himself and Claire a nightcap. 'She's asleep,' he said, handing Claire her whisky, before sitting down with his own. 'Aimée is happy, isn't she?'

'Yes, she is.' Claire looked at her husband and smiled. She hoped her reply reassured him. He had enough to do coping with the terrible memories the psychiatrist was unearthing. 'What about you?' she asked. 'You seem more like your old self these days. The treatment must be working.'

'I guess it is,' Alain said, thoughtfully. 'Professor Puel says he's helping me to come to terms with what happened when I was in prison. I don't remember much after the sessions, so I must take his word for it.'

Not remembering much meant her husband remembered something. Claire wanted to ask him what it was he remembered. But when she met the professor he said she must not question Alain. He said questioning him would hinder his recovery. 'For many years Captain Mitchell has buried memories in a very dark place,' he said.

'I'm sorry, darling,' Claire said, 'I can't begin to imagine what awful things you suffered in that place.'

'Puel said I blocked out bad stuff. He said I have survivor's guilt.' Claire sat up in order to take in what her husband was saying. 'I escaped from the prison and survived, but deep down I knew there would have been reprisals. He said I would have known then that some of my fellow prisoners would have paid for my freedom with their lives. Because of that I buried my feelings. Puel said I have never faced up to the fact that I caused their deaths. He said the guilt I feel is so profound, so deep-rooted, that to survive in everyday life I ignore it; pretend it didn't happen. He said guilt cannot be denied forever and in time, as it has done with me, it rises to the surface and manifests in angry outbursts and nightmares.

'And you, my darling, have had to put up with it.' Mitch's eyes filled with tears. He pulled Claire to him. 'I'm sorry for all I've put you through. I shall make it up to you. All I want now is to make you happy.'

Claire inhaled deeply. 'I am happy, darling.' She looked into her husband's eyes and kissed him on the lips. 'How could I not be happy with you and Aimée to love.' She wanted to say *When you are better I shall really be happy*, but that might be interpreted as putting pressure on him. Instead, she said nothing and kissed him again.

SEVEN

It was a modern apartment. Warm air blew through grids in the walls from October to spring, changing to cold air at the end of May, keeping the apartment warm in the winter and cool throughout the summer months. The letting agent for the Canadian Air Force told Claire the cooling system was called air conditioning. It wouldn't be needed in England she thought, it is never hot enough.

She went into Aimée's bedroom. She was asleep. The nights were drawing in. Shorter days were only to be expected at this time of year – longer nights too, though Claire hadn't reckoned on there being so many without her husband.

Returning to the sitting room she drew the curtains, then poured herself a Canadian Club. She had become accustomed to a tipple after dinner with Mitch. When Aimée was in bed they relaxed, talked about their day, or listened to the wireless. She looked at the clock on the mantelshelf. Ten thirty, he hadn't come home, again. She knocked back her drink, took the empty glass to the kitchen, rinsed it under the tap and stood it upside down on the draining board. With a sigh, she scraped Alain's dinner into a bucket with a lid that they kept under the sink and put his plate in the washing-up bowl.

She switched off the lights as she walked through the apartment. After checking the front door was locked she took out the key and went to bed on her own, again.

'Good afternoon, Mrs Mitchell.' The receptionist at the Louis Bertrand hospital greeted Claire with a smile when she finally reached the front of the queue. 'How may I help you today?'

Claire was trembling with worry. 'Could you tell me where my husband is, please?' The receptionist looked confused and frowned. She scanned the names listed in the large appointment book on the desk in front of her. 'He had an appointment yesterday afternoon,' Claire said. 'He didn't go to work afterwards, nor did he come home, so he must still be here.' She watched the woman's short manicured fingernail glide across to a corresponding list on the previous day's page.

'Mitchell, Captain Alain Mitchell. Two o'clock yesterday to see Professor Puel. He won't be here now,' the receptionist said. 'The captain's appointment was for an hour. He wasn't booked in for an overnight stay.'

'No, he wasn't, but this morning the professor's secretary telephoned me to say my husband could go home.' Claire was rapidly coming to the end of her patience. 'Would you telephone the professor's secretary and find out where Captain Mitchell is, please!'

As she picked up the telephone, the receptionist glanced at the lengthening line of people standing behind Claire and smiled apologetically. Claire waited for what felt to her like an age but was probably only a few seconds, before the secretary's telephone was answered. After a brief salutation, the receptionist asked if Captain Mitchell was in the hospital, and if so,

in which ward. She spoke in French, which Claire thought was
rude considering she had asked her for help in English.

When the receptionist returned the receiver to its cradle,
Claire repeated what she'd heard her say when she confirmed
Alain's whereabouts. '*La salle d'hôpital psychiatrique aile huit?*'
she said, in fluent French. The receptionist's cheeks coloured
with embarrassment. 'Would you direct me to ward eight in the
psychiatric wing, please?'

'It is next door, madame, in the old hospital. Go out of the
main doors, turn left, and follow the footpath.'

'*Merci et au revoir*,' Claire said, curtly, and left.

Claire followed the receptionist's directions and, after
turning left onto the main drive that curved round in a broad
sweep in front of the new hospital's modern glass doors,
followed the path along the side of the building to the old
hospital at the back. It was hardly next door, Claire thought,
and it was as unpleasing to the eye as the new hospital building
was pleasing.

With its dark red and blue brick exterior, tall narrow
windows with bars across them, the original hospital, which
housed the psychiatric wing, looked more like a Victorian work-
house or an asylum. It had probably been both in its time. The
sooner she got Mitch out of the place the better.

She turned the brass knob at the centre of the heavy oak
door and pushed. It didn't open. She tried again. When it didn't
open the third time, she rapped on the door sharply. A second
later she heard a key in the lock, followed by what sounded like
a second key and the scraping of a bolt. The door opened.

'Mrs Mitchell?' Before Claire had time to answer the nurse
said, 'The receptionist rang through and told us you were on
your way. I am looking after the Captain,' she said. 'Nurse
Bryant.' She put out her hand and Claire shook it. 'Please
come in.'

'Where is my husband? Why was he kept in overnight?'

'He became upset during his treatment and had to be sedated.'

'Upset? His treatment was yesterday. Why wasn't I told?'

'I don't know. Professor Puel will explain everything to you.'

Claire followed Nurse Bryant along a short corridor into a room with several easy chairs facing a table with a wireless on it.

'Where is he? Where's Captain Mitchell?'

'He's asleep at the moment. I thought you might like to wait in here. It's more comfortable—'

'I don't want to *wait* anywhere, I want to see my husband. When Professor Puel's secretary telephoned me, she said I should come at once.'

'Ah!' The look of displeasure on the nurse's face told Claire that the secretary had no business contacting her. 'I'll take you to him right away.'

Claire had noticed wards one to six when she arrived; seven was next to the small waiting room, eight was opposite. Nurse Bryant crossed the corridor, pushed open the doors and went in. Claire followed. At first glance, the ward looked like any other hospital ward. Some beds had metal rails at the side, which, Claire thought, was to stop elderly patients from falling out. On closer inspection, she noticed leather straps across several of the beds and looking up she saw iron bars across the windows. The ward had six beds, three on each side of the room, but only one patient – her husband.

'When Captain Mitchell wakes he'll be very pleased to see you.' Nurse Bryant stood at the top of Mitch's bed, her head tilted on one side. 'Poor Captain. He kept calling for China. At first, I thought he was talking about the country, but then he said he was sorry, asked China to forgive him, and said he loved her.' The nurse looked sympathetically at Claire. 'Do you know anyone called China?'

Claire neither felt like making polite conversation nor like telling a nurse she had never met before that China had been

part of the code name she'd been given by the Special Operations Executive in the war when she and Mitch worked in
German-occupied France with the French Resistance. Not that
it would matter now. The war had been over for years.

Besides, any Canadian would be proud of the part their
armed forces had played in driving Hitler and his army out of
Europe and securing peace. Even so, her training had taught her
to be cautious. You never knew who you were talking to.

Claire could see Nurse Bryant was curious. Telling her
something would stop her from speculating. 'Yes,' Claire said,
eventually, 'it's what my husband calls me sometimes. It's his
pet name for me. It's my eyes,' she said, looking squarely at the
nurse. 'They're a similar colour blue to a well-known china we
have in England.'

'Ah... I thought it must be something like that,' the nurse
cooed. 'Oh!' she said, turning on the spot as if she had only just
noticed Claire was standing at the foot of her husband's bed.
'Let me get out of your way. Here?' She took a chair from
against the wall and placed it at the top of the bed. 'I'll fetch you
a cup of tea. Milk and sugar?'

Claire said just milk, sat down and took Mitch's hand in
hers. 'Darling, what have they done to you. Mitch? Alain? Can
you hear me?' she asked, rubbing the back of his hand with her
thumb. He didn't respond.

Sometime later, Claire had no idea how long, Nurse Bryant
returned with the promised cup of tea and a biscuit. Refusing
the biscuit, Claire took the cup and while the nurse checked
Mitch's pulse and temperature, she sipped the hot beverage.

'Good!' the nurse said, taking the thermometer from under
his arm, shaking it, and checking it against the fob-watch on her
uniform. 'Almost back to normal.' She looked at the fob again.
'He should wake up soon. When he does, I'll be at the nurse's
station.' She pointed to a table with drawers down one side and

two chairs, one in front and one behind, at the far end of the
ward. 'Give me a wave.'

'Will I be able to take him home when he wakes up?'

'Yes, if Professor Puel says you can,' the nurse said, looking
under long dark eyelashes at Claire and blushing slightly.

'Thank you.' Claire leant forward, lifted Mitch's hand to
her cheek and watched him sleeping.

Suddenly aware that a light was shining through the tall
barred window above Mitch's head, Claire looked at her watch.
It was half past five. She had been sitting at her husband's
bedside for almost three hours. She wondered if Aimée was all
right. She hadn't been without one or other of her parents since
arriving in Canada. She'll be fine, Claire told herself. By now
she'll be having tea with her new grandparents.

'China?'

'Mitch, thank God. I thought you'd never wake up.' Claire
bent down and kissed him. She turned and waved to the nurse
at the far end of the ward. She was speaking on the telephone
and at the same time reading a document by the light of a small
lamp. Claire waved again, but the nurse was engrossed and
didn't acknowledge her. 'As soon as the professor has been to
see you, I am taking you home.'

'Forgive me, Simone. I am sorry,' Mitch whispered and
closed his eyes.

'You have nothing to be forgiven for, darling,' Claire said.
She stroked his hair. He was asleep.

Releasing his hand, Claire stood up and waved to the nurse
again. This time the nurse saw her. She immediately put down
the telephone, clicked off the lamp, and walked briskly down
the ward.

'He woke up and said—' Claire didn't want to say, Simone,
'my name, but went straight back to sleep.'

The nurse bustled round to the far side of Mitch's bed, took hold of his wrist and checked his pulse. 'Normal. It won't be long before he's fully awake.'

Claire wanted to say *You said that hours ago.* Instead, she said, 'In that case, would you stay with him while I pop to the lavatory?'

'Of course. It's at the end of the corridor.' Claire looked at her husband, a worried expression on her face. Who is, or was, Simone? The nurse, misinterpreting Claire's concern said, 'Don't worry, I won't leave him until you get back.'

The bare light bulb hanging from the ceiling of the stark white concrete and tiled washroom created shadows everywhere. Claire shivered. Washing her hands she caught sight of herself in the mirror. Dark rings under her eyes made her look ghoulish. She felt tired – and worried. Mitch had called her Simone. She racked her brain. There had been no one in the Resistance cells they'd worked with called Simone. He could have known her before the war, or she could have been someone in the village where he was taken after he'd been shot, someone who had looked after him. Maybe it was a woman from the prison where he was held in France.

Or... Claire's heart began to drum as the realisation struck her. He had spent eight, maybe ten, weeks away from home on air force business during the past year. He had been back to Canada twice. Or was it three times? Her head was spinning. Could he have met Simone then? Did he have an affair with this woman, fall in love with her even, and was now asking for forgiveness?

The door opened, making Claire jump. 'Your husband is awake and asking for you, Mrs Mitchell,' the nurse said sternly.

'Thank you.' Claire pushed a rogue curl from her forehead and followed the nurse back to the ward.

She had been longer in the washroom than she had intended. When she returned to the ward Professor Puel was at Mitch's bedside talking to him. She sighed with relief. Her husband was awake. The professor, wearing a dark charcoal coloured suit, white shirt and black bowtie, was tall and slim with fair greying hair and piercing pale blue eyes. It looked to Claire as if he was saying something her husband didn't agree with or didn't know. Shaking his head, Mitch shouted, 'I don't know, I tell you. I don't remember!'

As she approached the professor raised his voice and, as if for Claire's benefit, he said, 'So, Captain, you don't remember anything of what we talked about yesterday?'

Mitch's brow creased. His eyes searched the professor's face as if what he had said the day before was just out of his reach and would come to him from some dark corner of his mind. Then he shook his head. 'No. There was something, and it was important, but it has gone. I just have a feeling of sadness; of sorrow. I felt angry when we were talking yesterday, I remember that, but I don't know why. And...' He struggled for the word, '*Remorse,*' he said at last. 'It's as if I did something shameful that I regret, which I need to put right, but I can't because I don't know what *it* is.' Tears filled his eyes.

Claire stepped between Mitch and the professor. 'My husband has had enough *treatment* for one day,' she said. 'If you have finished with him, I should like to take him home!'

'Of course, Mrs Mitchell. My secretary will telephone with the date and time of the captain's next appointment.' He saluted Mitch and offered Claire his hand. 'Mrs Mitchell?'

Claire shook the professor's hand, briefly. 'Goodbye.'

'Would you like to telephone for a taxi, or for someone to fetch you, Mrs Mitchell?' the nurse asked when Professor Puel had left.

'No, thank you.'

'I'm afraid Captain Mitchell won't be able to drive for twenty-four hours. Not until the sedative is completely out of his system.'

'Then it's a good job I'm driving,' Claire said. The nurse

looked surprised. 'I drove here, so I'm sure I'll be able to drive my husband home.' She took Mitch's shoes from under the bed and pushed them towards him. 'Close your mouth, darling, and put on your shoes.'

On the way to the car park, Mitch began to laugh. Claire glared at him. 'What?'

'You, driving. Are you serious?'

'How the hell do you think I got here, Mitch? When Professor Puel's secretary telephoned, she sounded worried. So, I jumped in your car and came straight here.'

'Where's Aimée?'

'Naomi took her to school. I asked her to telephone Marie when she got back and ask her to pick Aimée up after school and take her to her house. We're here,' Claire said, putting the key in the lock of the car's passenger door. 'Get in.'

'Are you annoyed with me, honey?' Mitch asked, when Claire slammed the driver's door.

'Not annoyed, but you shouldn't have laughed at me. It was bad enough that the nurse looked shocked when I said I was driving. You should have more faith in me. I've driven abroad before, in bigger and more powerful vehicles than this thing, or have you forgotten?'

'No, but that was different.'

'How? I don't have to dodge bombs driving in Canada. Other than that it's exactly the same, so sit back and enjoy the ride.' Claire negotiated the car out of the car park, past several badly parked vehicles and into the traffic on the three-lane free-way. 'I didn't like the way the professor spoke to you when he came to see you on the ward.'

'He said he was trying to unlock my memory.'

'And did he?'

'He said he didn't, but...' Mitch closed his eyes and massaged his temples. 'There was something... And it was important. But it's gone. This is why Puel gets annoyed. He spends an hour of his valuable time with me, and afterwards I can't remember what I said.'

'An hour? You've been in there since two o'clock yesterday afternoon. Is that why he kept you in? Because he hoped you'd remember something?'

Mitch nodded half-heartedly. 'I guess so.'

'Okay, maybe that's why he kept you in, but why did he put you in that ward?'

'It was the nearest?'

Claire threw back her head and looked to the heavens. 'I'm being serious, Mitch! The beds had leather restraints on them and the windows had bars across them. It wasn't an ordinary hospital ward.'

'I don't know! Give me a break, will you? It's frustrating for him that I can't remember, but God knows it's ten times worse for me.'

Claire bit her lip. 'I'm sorry, I shouldn't have asked.'

The first time Claire went with Mitch to the hospital, Professor Puel made it clear then that she was not to question him about his treatment. "It would be better if you don't discuss your husband's treatment at all." Part of Claire was desperate to know what had happened to him in the years he was missing, the years he had spent in prison. And although part of her wanted to know who Simone was, a bigger part of her was frightened of finding out. She let the subject drop.

FOXDEN, ENGLAND

CHRISTMAS 1949

EIGHT

Aimée was quiet on the drive up to Foxden. It was unlike her daughter but Claire didn't mind. The journey took every bit of her concentration. They had set off in what looked like an early morning mist that had become thicker in less built-up areas. As they left the suburbs of Oxford behind them they were met by patches of dense fog. It became heavier as they travelled north, suddenly lifting as quickly as it had fallen.

No sooner had the wipers cleared the windscreen and Claire had begun to relax than a blanket of fog descended again without warning. She turned on the wipers and they scraped across the windscreen. The fog had turned to freezing ice. Suddenly the rear lights of a large vehicle came into view and she slowed down again. Whatever it was, large car or lorry, it had come out of a side road and Claire was grateful for it. She followed the vehicle's back lights at a distance, keeping their red glow in view.

'Are we there yet, Mummy?'

'No, sweetheart, not yet. We're only halfway.'

Aimée sighed.

As they drove out of Northamptonshire and into Leicester-shire the fog began to disperse. The lorry that Claire had been following turned off before the town of Market Harborough – and Claire, able to see clearly now, drove on.

'Not long now, darling,' she said to Aimée. Her daughter didn't answer. She was asleep.

The drive to Foxden took another half an hour along the Lowarth Road, which was all bends. Relieved when the village of Woodcote came into view, Claire steered the car up Shaft Hill, turning off the main Lowarth road to Foxden. The lane was covered in snow. The car slid sideways and bumped the grass verge, waking Aimée up. 'Are we there yet?' she asked, sleepily.

'Yes, darling,' Claire said, with relief. 'We've arrived.'

Claire parked next to her brother-in-law Frank's car, in the car park at the back of the hotel. The drive from Oxford had taken a couple of hours longer than usual because of the weather, which changed in an instant from dense fog to freezing rain. Thankful the journey was over, she exhaled loudly and rolled her shoulders. 'Ready?' she said, looking at her daughter. Aimée nodded, pushed the blanket from her legs, but made no attempt to move. 'Come on, darling.' Claire got out of the car. The air was damp. She shivered. It wasn't as cold as it had been in Canada. Even in December, when the temperature was several degrees below zero, it wasn't damp and misty. The cold didn't seep into your bones as it seemed to do in rural England. No matter how much snow fell, or how cold it was, the air was dry and the sky seemed brighter.

She walked round the front of the car to the passenger door. 'Let's get out of the cold and into the warm,' she said, helping her sleepy daughter out of the car.

By the time Claire had taken their cases from the boot, Bess, Frank and Nancy were crossing the courtyard. Aimée ran to Frank and he bent down and kissed her. She was too big to pick up – and far too grown up. She threw her arms around her Aunt Bess, and then taking her cousin Nancy by the hand, led the way to the hotel leaving the grownups to bring the luggage.

Frank promised to take the children to collect eggs, see the animals, and give carrots to the donkey on Christmas morning, before church, 'But now,' he told Aimée and Nancy, 'you must go to bed.' Aimée pouted and Nancy copied her. 'You, miss,' Frank said, to his adopted daughter, 'take your cousin upstairs and,' he looked from Nancy to Aimée, 'both of you get ready for bed. I'll be up in ten minutes to put out the light.'

As she kissed her mother good night, Aimée whispered, 'Will Father Christmas have been to me too, when I wake up in the morning?'

'Of course he will, darling. Why would you think he might not come to you?'

'Well...' Claire could see her daughter's mind racing to give her a satisfactory reason for asking. 'I thought he might not know I was here.'

Claire pushed Aimée's hair off her face and kissed her. 'Father Christmas knows where all the good boys and girls are.'

As Aimée and Nancy left the office, Aimée said, 'That was close.'

'What was?' Nancy asked.

'I almost let slip that I know there isn't a Father Christmas. Mum hasn't had time to do any shopping since we've been home from Canada. I didn't think she'd bought me anything and I was going to say it was all right.'

. . .

After dinner, Frank checked on the children and then took over on reception, so Bess could spend time with her sister. Claire made three cups of coffee, put hers and Bess's on the low table in front of the fire, and took Frank's out to reception. When she returned to the office, Bess brought her up to date with everything that had happened at Foxden during the three months Claire had been in Canada. Nancy's adoption had gone through without a hitch, Nancy was happy and settled, and she and Frank loved being parents. Bess got up and crossed the room. Picking up the coffee and milk she went back to Claire. 'Now,' she said, refilling their cups, 'how was Canada?'

'So much has happened, Bess. Some of it was lovely, but the psychiatrist Mitch saw and the treatment he underwent.' Tears fell from Claire's eyes. She shook her head unable to speak.

Bess took hold of her sister's hand. 'Take your time, darling,' she said. When Claire had recovered, Bess said, 'From your letters, you got on well with Mitch's parents.'

'Yes. From the moment we arrived, they couldn't have been nicer or done more for us, and they adored Aimée.'

'So, what has happened? Where's Mitch? When you telephoned a couple of days ago, Mitch was with you, wasn't he?'

'No. Lord, where do I start? The day we were due to fly back to England, Mitch said he had to do something important and he would see us at the airport. And that was the last I saw or heard of him. I have no idea where he is. When the plane was ready to leave, an airport official said, if Captain Mitchell wasn't here within the next five minutes Aimée and I would have to leave without him.

'At first, I thought he'd had an accident. Then the official told me the Canadian Air Force had sent a message through to say Mitch had gone AWOL and the plane was leaving without him. I didn't believe them. It made more sense that Mitch had been delayed by someone or something when he went to do whatever it was that was so *important,* which is why we went to the airport on our own. I wasn't too worried on the plane home. I felt sure he would catch a later flight. But when we landed I was told Mitch's commander at the base wanted to see me. I was given no choice. I took Aimée to Mitch's grandmother's house and went to the base. Commander Landry questioned me for hours. I didn't know anything so I couldn't tell him anything.

'I was driven home eventually. Mitch didn't telephone, or send a telegram, which would at least have stopped me from worrying.'

'How is Aimée taking it?'

'She's upset, naturally, but she doesn't know he's missing. I told her that her father had to stay in Canada for a little while longer to have more treatment. I think she accepted that, but she misses him and keeps asking when he's coming home. She didn't want to come up here in case he came back and we weren't there. She drew him a picture of the hotel and wrote him a letter telling him we'd come up to Foxden for Christmas. His grandmother, Esther, thinks he'll be back. She said he was bound to go to her house when he gets home and when he does she'll tell him to come up here straight away.'

'And you, Claire? What do you think?' Bess asked.

'I think he has been having an affair. I think he either went back to break it off, in which case he will be home after Christmas, or he has left us for another woman and is staying with her in Canada. Esther says I should go back to Canada and find him.'

'And will you?'

'I don't know. I'll think about it over Christmas. If I do decide to go to Canada, would you and Frank look after Aimée? It's a lot to ask—'

'Of course, we will.'

There was a tap on the door and Frank poked his head into the office. 'The night porter is here. I'm going up.'

'We're coming too,' Bess said.

·   ·   ·

Claire's room in the old servant's quarters felt familiar and comfortable. She tiptoed in, sat on the double bed that she usually shared with Mitch, and watched Aimée as she slept. Her eyes moved beneath their lids. Careful not to wake her Claire quickly undressed, washed and cleaned her teeth, and climbed into bed. She switched off the light on the bedside table and pulled up the bedspread.

With one arm protectively draped over her daughter, Claire lay and listened to her calm, rhythmic, breathing. She closed her eyes but was unable to sleep. She laid on her back. Where she hadn't pulled the curtains properly a pale light in the shape of a long finger crept across the ceiling, disappearing and appearing as clouds drifted in front of the silver moon in the winter sky.

Claire thought about Mitch. Wondered where he was. Wondered who he was with. Was he with Simone? Did he love her? Did she love him? She turned over and lay on her side, her back to her daughter and the eerie pattern of light. She loved her husband. She wanted him, needed him. It was then that she decided to go back to Oxford. She would leave Aimée at Foxden for the remainder of the Christmas holiday and she would go and find her husband. She would take Esther's advice and return to Canada if she had to.

Christmas morning the Dudley family attended Mysterton Church. It had been a tradition for as long as Claire could remember. They walked the short distance back to the Foxden Hotel chatting and laughing. The family had grown, so the venue for opening the presents that Father Christmas had left during the night had been moved from the old nursery to the library. There were squeals of excitement from the children as they found their parcels and opened them, and oohs and aahs from the adults who had also been given token gifts; the Dudley women, scent, soap and talcum powder, the men, handkerchiefs, ties and socks.

Frank and Bess, having gone downstairs to make sure everything was running smoothly in the kitchen, returned with glasses of eggnog and brandy and a tray of snacks. As always, the family would have their Christmas lunch with the staff when the paying guests had finished eating and vacated the dining room.

At three o'clock, the flamboyant Chef swept into the library and announced lunch was being served. To cheers and thanks, Alfredo bowed to Lily Dudley and offered her his arm. Together they swanned down the wide staircase, across the marble hall and into the dining room.

Claire's mother sat at the head of the table, on her right her son Tom and his family. Like her sisters, she was proud of her older brother. In the army, he had saved the lives of a dozen soldiers when he repaired the engine of a motorboat and, under fire, drove it from the pier at Dunkirk harbour out to sea to a waiting British warship. He now bred horses and managed an estate owned by his in-laws, Lord and Lady Hadleigh, in Kent. His wife Annabel had worked with Bess in the war. She may have been a lady, but Annabel was as much a land girl as any of the women who lived and worked on the Foxden Estate.

Claire turned her attention to the other end of the table and caught Bess's eye. Are you all right, Bess mouthed. Claire nodded and swallowed the mountain of emotions that threatened to erupt from her.

Bess and Frank sat at the far end of the table. Frank, Claire's ever-practical brother-in-law sat nearest the door, ready to leap into action if he was needed. Claire pulled out chairs for Aimée and Nancy. Once they were seated she took her place between them, next to Ena and her husband Henry. Margot, her husband Bill and their daughter Natalie sat opposite.

Claire put on a smile. For the first time in several years, her family were gathered around one table. Only Mitch was missing.

NINE

Claire set off for Oxford on her own the day after Boxing Day. She had promised Aimée that she would come back and fetch her as soon as her daddy returned from Canada. Claire forced herself to smile when she left her daughter with Bess and Frank for the remainder of the Christmas holiday. Aimée had always loved spending time up at Foxden with Claire's family. She enjoyed it even more now she had a cousin of her own age to play with. Aimée and Nancy got on from the minute they met and had become the best of friends.

Claire hadn't told her mother she was going back to Oxford today, there hadn't been time. Driving down the lane from the hotel her mother's cottage, which had once been part of the Foxden Estate, came into view. For no reason that she could think of her WAAF documents came into her mind. They could come in handy, she supposed, but for what? She couldn't get the documents out of her mind so she pulled up outside the cottage and jumped out.

She walked up the path to the back of the house and knocked the door.

'Come in, love,' Lily Dudley said, opening the back door. 'I've just put the kettle on. Have you got time for a cuppa?'

'No, thanks. I've only popped in to say cheerio.'

'You're going back early, aren't you? I had it in my mind you were staying for the New Year's Eve party,' her mother said. She looked to Claire's left and right. 'Our Aimée not with you?'

'No, she's staying with Bess and Frank. It's nice for her to have Nancy to pal up with – nice for Nancy too. I'll come up and get her the weekend before she goes back to school.'

Lily Dudley picked up the kettle, filled it and put it on the gas stove.

'Mam?'

'Yes, love?'

'Is it okay if I have a rummage around in the attic?'

'Of course,' Claire's mother said, 'but there isn't much up there. And it'll be dusty. I haven't been in there for years. No one has. I think our Bess was the last one up there when she helped me clear out your father's stuff. He was a hoarder, bless him. What is it you're looking for?'

'Nothing important. I just want to have a look at my WAAF papers. They're in an old case. I put it in your attic for safekeeping after I was demobbed. I'm being sentimental, but—' Claire's mother shot Claire a glance as if to say *You, sentimental? Never.* Claire laughed. 'I know it's unlike me, but I've got a feeling there's something I need in the bag. And I think there might be a photograph of Mitch and me at WAAF Headquarters in Morecambe in it.'

'Well you'll need the ladder,' Lily Dudley said, making for the door.

'I'll get it. You stay here and have your tea.'

Claire went outside to the wooden shed at the top of the garden. Her father had kept chickens in it during the war. Now, except for old paint tins and empty beer bottles, kept by her mother out of habit, the shed housed her bicycle and the ladder.

'I will have a cup of tea with you, Mam,' Claire said, carrying the ladder through the kitchen. 'I won't be long.'

Unable to see anything in the attic because it was so dark, Claire crawled on her hands and knees to the far wall. She ran the flat of her hand along the brickwork until she came to eaves on the left. A few inches further along she found a pile of old curtains, and behind them, her WAAF case. She opened it and took out a leather shoulder bag. She undid the buckle at the front of the bag and pulled open the middle section. She found what she was looking for and put it in her pocket. After buckling the bag, she returned it to the case, pushed it against the wall and covered it with the old curtains.

'Good God!' Lily Dudley said, when Claire returned to the kitchen. 'You look as if you've been up the chimney.'

Claire leant to the left and caught sight of herself in the small mirror that her mother kept on the kitchen windowsill. 'I do, don't I?' she laughed.

'I hope you found what you were looking for, girl.'

'I didn't actually. My old military bag was in the suitcase, but there wasn't a photograph in it. There were a few papers, but nothing of importance. Never mind, I expect the photo will turn up at home. I'll have put it somewhere safe...'

'Too safe,' her mother said, adding boiling water to the teapot.

'I expect so,' Claire said, laughing. 'I'll put this back,' she said, dragging the ladder out of the kitchen door into the yard.

'I'll pour your tea,' Claire's mother called after her, 'and I'll put a pan of water on the stove. You'd better have a wash before you go.'

As she turned into the short drive at the front of her house, Mitch's grandmother pulled up behind her in her car. The old lady wound down the window and beckoned Claire. 'Don't leave your car outside the house. Put it in the garage, dear. I'll park around the corner, so mine's out of sight,' she whispered, put her foot on the accelerator and sped off.

Claire did as Esther said. By the time she had unlocked the garage door, put her car inside, taken her case out of the boot and locked the garage, Esther was waiting for her at the front door. 'What's going on, Esther?'

'I'll tell you when we're inside. Quickly, unlock the door, dear,' Esther said. She looked up and down the road. 'Best if no one knows you've come home.'

Claire opened the front door and Esther jostled her into the hall. 'Is this cloak and dagger stuff really necessary, Esther?' Claire asked, doing her best not to laugh.

'Yes, it is!' Esther said. 'I'll tell you why when we're inside.' Esther glanced over her shoulder before closing the door. 'We don't want Commander Landry and his bully-boys to know you're back yet, so we'll go through to the kitchen. If they come knocking, they won't see us in there.'

Claire took off her coat and kicked off her boots, replacing them with a thick cardigan and her old slippers. 'How did you know I was back? Are you psychic?' she asked, following Esther into the kitchen.

'Nothing as exotic as that, I'm afraid. I called round to see you this morning, on the off chance you'd be here, but you weren't, so I telephoned the Foxden Hotel and spoke to Bess. She told me you had just left and estimated the time you'd be arriving home,' Esther said, out of breath.

Claire felt a sudden surge of panic rise from her stomach to her throat. 'What is it, Esther? Is it Mitch? Have you heard from him?'

'Yes.'

'Is he all right? Where is he?'

'No. I mean, yes. I have heard from Alain but I don't know how he is, or where he is. The reason I needed to see you as soon as you got home was because – well it's two things really, but the first is, I had a visit from Alain's commanding officer.' Esther shook her head. She looked flustered.

'Sit down. I'll make us a drink.' Claire pulled out a chair from under the kitchen table and Esther dropped onto it. 'Now, start at the beginning and tell me what happened.'

'Commander Landry said he came to see you yesterday, but you weren't here, so he came to my house,' Esther said, wringing her hands.

Claire filled the kettle, put it on the stove and took a bottle of milk from her shopping bag. 'And?' she said, looking over her shoulder at Esther.

'And the commander said RCAF intelligence has received information that Alain is in France.'

'France? Why would he go—?' Claire stopped speaking mid-sentence. Simone!

'The commander had received Alain's medical file. He told me that the doctor who treated Alain in Canada said that under hypnosis, Alain had talked about a woman in the French Resistance who he became... close to.' Esther paused, took a handkerchief from her handbag and dabbed her nose. She cleared her throat. 'Apparently, this French woman was in the prison with Alain and—'

'Go on!'

'She worked for the Germans. She was a double agent, a plant, according to Alain's doctor. He said she supplied the Germans with information that she got out of Alain about the Resistance movement. He said Alain told this woman when and how he and the other prisoners were going to escape, and she passed the information on to the Germans. It was because of this woman that Alain was shot in the leg,' Esther hissed.

'Simone!'

'Yes!' Esther said, clearly shocked. 'How did you know her name was Simone? Did Alain tell you about her?'

'No. Not directly.' Claire's heart began to pound. She swallowed hard and blinked back her tears. 'It's Simone who Mitch – Alain – talks about in his sleep.' The whistle of the kettle made her heart skip a beat. She jumped up as if she was on autopilot and made the tea. 'How do you know all this?' she asked, handing Esther a cup. 'Did the commander tell you?'

'No! All he said was Captain Mitchell is in France and the Canadian and British Military Police want to question him about a German agent named Simone who they believe he consorted with during the war.'

Claire nodded thoughtfully. 'You said there were two things you needed to tell me?'

'Two things? Oh, yes! Just a minute, dear.' Esther took off her coat, unbuttoned her cardigan and blouse and pulled a brown envelope from between her vest and brassiere. 'This came – from Alain.' She handed Claire the envelope. 'I think it's a copy of what the professor in Canada sent to Commander Landry. The envelope looks like the one I saw on the commander's desk yesterday.' Esther forced a smile. 'I put it here for safekeeping.' She tapped the small roll of flesh beneath her bosom. 'Not even a commander in the Royal Canadian Air Force would dare to have a lady of my age strip-searched. Not in peacetime anyway.'

If the situation hadn't been so serious Claire would have laughed. She took several pages of thin tissue-like white paper from the envelope and, while she drank her tea, read her husband's medical notes and a letter that Professor Puel had written to his commanding officer. She shook her head. 'These notes are transcripts of the private sessions between Mitch and Professor Puel. As his doctor, Puel should not have sent them to anyone. It's a blatant disregard of doctor-patient confidentiality.

'I read similar transcripts when I was with the SOE in the war. They were mostly interrogations.' Claire laid the letter that Professor Puel had written next to Mitch's medical notes, sat forward in her chair and scrutinised both. 'Did you read these thoroughly, Esther?'

'Yes, of course.'

'Then you know the two accounts are different. Nowhere does Mitch say that Simone is a double agent feeding the Germans information. Puel has assumed that. He must have known of a double agent called Simone, put two and two together, and decided that Simone the German agent and Simone in the Gestapo prison were the same woman.' Claire looked at the transcript again. 'There's nothing in this document that even hints that Mitch is in cahoots with a German agent who was in the French Resistance; not when he was in the Gestapo prison nor at any other time.'

'Look!' Esther said, pointing to the second page of the letter, 'it says here, *Captain Alain Mitchell spent an unnecessary amount of time while in the Gestapo prison with a German spy known as Simone who, in my professional opinion, turned him.* He doesn't say he knows Simone turned him, he only says in his *opinion* she turned him.'

'That's right. We already know from the transcript that Mitch was in the prison with a woman named Simone.' Claire picked up the transcript. 'If this is an exact record of what Mitch said in the meetings he had with the professor, it's more likely that he had an affair with Simone.' Out of the corner of her eye, Claire saw Esther flinch. 'He talks about her in a very loving and caring way,' Claire said, almost to herself.

'This letter is rubbish. There is nothing in the transcript, which was taken down verbatim, about Simone being a German agent. And nowhere is the phrase *turned him* recorded.'

'So how can the professor know this Simone *turned him?*'

'He can't know,' Claire said. A smile crept across her face.

'What is it?'

'That's why Mitch missed the plane home. He went back to the hospital to copy this. He would have known when he read

it, as I did, that it was rubbish.' Claire flicked her hand at the
documents in front of her. 'He would also know the professor
would have to send a copy of his findings to Commander
Landry, which is why he posted his copy to you.'

'My grandson, a spy? It's laughable. This professor chap
might be an eminent doctor, but he doesn't know anything
about people.'

'He doesn't know Mitch that's for sure.' Claire looked
through the report again, then shook her head. 'There's something here I'm not seeing. Something Mitch remembered
perhaps.' Folding the letter, Claire returned it to its envelope
and gave it back to Mitch's grandmother. 'Keep it safe, Esther,
Mitch will need it when he comes back.'

'I think you should have a good look around, Claire, make
sure there's nothing missing,' Esther said, returning the envelope to its place of safety between the layers of her underwear.
'The commander telephoned me and asked me to go to the base.
He sent a car for me, so I didn't have much choice. When I got
there, he and another officer gave me a good grilling. His driver
brought me home and within half an hour two military officers
arrived. They searched my house. They took all sorts of things
away with them; Mitch's notepads and sketchpads. They even
took the books he read at university. Some of them, as you know,
were written by social and political idealists.'

Claire shook her head. 'I hope they don't use his old books
to back up what Professor Puel said. All students are idealists
and most have strong political views – it goes with being a
student. Come on,' Claire said, getting to her feet, 'there's
nothing out of place in here, let's look round the rest of the
house while it's still light.'

It was obvious to Claire as soon as she went into the sitting
room that someone had been in there. A thread of cotton hung
from her sewing basket and when she pulled on the top of
Mitch's bureau it was locked. The key was always left in the

lock, so it didn't get lost, but Mitch never locked it, there was no need. She checked inside. It was tidier than she remembered but she wouldn't have a clue as to whether any of her husband's papers were missing. She closed the lid and followed Esther to the door. Before leaving she turned, looked back into the room, and shivered. She was cold and needed to build a fire. She was worried, too.

Nothing looked as if it had been disturbed in her bedroom. She opened Mitch's wardrobe. His shirts and jumpers were folded and stacked on the shelves. Too tidy, Claire thought. And his lightweight sports coat and jackets in the hanging section of the wardrobe were lined up too neatly.

'I'm not sure I'd have noticed anything was amiss if you hadn't suggested we check, Esther,' Claire said. 'I wouldn't have looked, but now.' Claire shivered again. 'Come on, let's go down, it's cold up here. I'll make a fire in the sitting room, while you— Shush!' Claire put her arm out to stop Esther from leaving the bedroom. 'Did you hear that?' Esther shook her head. 'It sounded like metal clinking.'

As the women approached the top of the stairs a knock on the front door halted their step. Esther took a sharp and very loud breath. 'Shush...' Claire put her forefinger to her lips. Whoever was at the door knocked again. This time louder.

Before they began their descent, Claire heard the jangling sound again. Whoever was outside had keys, and they were about to let themselves into her house. She looked at the older woman, questioningly. 'Alain?'

Esther shook her head. 'It's more likely to be Air Force intelligence,' she hissed.

'Go back to the bedroom and ruffle your hair. I'm going to say you came to see me, didn't feel well and went up for a lie-down.' Esther nodded. 'Come down in a couple of minutes and follow my lead.'

'Just a minute!' Claire shouted, running down the stairs.

'I'm coming!' She flicked on the hall light and opened the door. 'Where's the fire?' she asked the two uniformed men standing on her doorstep. She looked at the taller of the two officers. 'My keys, I think,' she said, snatching them out of his hand. 'Would you like to explain why you were about to let yourselves into my house with a duplicate set of keys when you thought I wasn't at home?' Neither officer spoke. 'Perhaps you'd rather I telephoned Commander Landry and asked him?'

'What's going on, Claire?' Esther croaked from the top of the stairs.

'My husband's grandmother wasn't feeling well. She went upstairs to have a rest.' Claire almost burst into laughter when she saw Esther. Her hair looked more like a bird's nest than it looked ruffled because she'd been lying on it. And to say her clothes looked dishevelled was an understatement. Claire hoped Mitch's letter hadn't been dislodged when Esther pulled one side of her blouse out of the waistband of her skirt.

'Can't you give this family a bit of peace,' she said, hanging on to the handrail swaying and yawning. 'What do you want now?'

Esther was being so dramatic she was on the verge of giving the game away. 'Come on, dear,' Claire said, helping her down the last couple of stairs then physically turning her in the direction of the kitchen. 'Light the oven. The room will soon warm up. I'll be in in a minute to make you a hot drink.'

As Esther toddled off to the kitchen, Claire showed the Canadian Air Force officers into the sitting room. 'It's rather cold in here. I've been away. But then you know that, don't you?' She glared at the tall miserable looking officer. 'So,' she sighed, 'what do you want from me?'

The shorter officer stepped forward and gave her a warm smile. 'We'd like to know if you've had any contact with your husband, Mrs Mitchell?'

Claire straightened and looked him in the eye. She knew

the game, good officer-bad officer. When she was with the SOE she had been in worse situations and been grilled by harder and more experienced interrogators. Even so, she must be careful. These men would know Mitch had worked undercover in occupied France during the war. They may not, however, know that she had been an agent too – and she didn't want them to know. To them, she was only the wife of a suspected traitor. Even so, Claire was not about to let either of them intimidate her. 'I have not.'

'He hasn't telephoned, or written to you?'

'I've just told you. My husband has not contacted me!' Claire checked herself. 'I know you have your job to do, but I'm worried about him,' she said, her eyes moist with tears. 'I'm sorry.' She pretended to pull herself together. 'Mitch has not telephoned me or written to me.'

'Thank you, Mrs Mitchell.' Good Officer turned and motioned for Bad Officer to leave. At the door, Good Officer turned to Claire. 'Commander Landry would like you to come to the base tomorrow.'

'What? I spent hours being interrogated when I got back from Canada. Nothing has changed. I don't know any more now than I knew then, so why does he want to see me again?'

'I don't know, Mrs Mitchell. The commander said to tell you he'll send a car.'

'All right!' Claire put up her hands as if she was giving in. 'Do you know what time?' she asked, as calmly as she was able.

'I'm afraid I don't.' He saluted and left.

Claire waited until she heard their car drive off, then locked and bolted the door.

TEN

The alarm clock rang at six o'clock. Claire, having hardly slept, had been up for two hours. She had relegated the clothes she wore at Christmas to the laundry basket and added clean underwear, socks, jumpers and a pair of corduroy slacks to the clothes that remained in her suitcase. She checked that she had the relevant documents in her handbag, dropped it next to her case and sat on the bed.

In the stillness of dawn, she heard the sound of an approaching car. Its engine grew louder, stopped, and idled for a second, before it cut out altogether. She went to the window and drew back the curtain enough to see the street immediately in front of her house. Mitch's grandmother was getting out of her car. Letting go of the curtain, Claire ran downstairs and opened the front door. 'Good morning, Esther.'

'Good morning, dear. Right!' she said, looking around. 'What can I do?'

'Nothing. I'm pretty near ready to go,' Claire said, returning to the bedroom with Esther hard on her heels. She looked through the drawers, grabbed a couple of pairs of Mitch's socks and threw them on top of the clothes in her case. 'New Year is always colder than November and December,' she said, 'best to be on the safe side.' Claire took a woollen scarf that Édith Belland had sent Mitch one year for his birthday. She held it up to her face and breathed in his scent before tying it around her neck. 'For luck,' she said.

'Did you telephone Foxden and speak to Aimée?' Esther asked, her voice cracking with emotion.

'Yes, last night. I told her I was going to bring her daddy home.'

'You didn't tell her where you were going, did you?'

'Good Lord, no! The fewer people who know the safer it will be for me, and for Mitch. I asked her if she'd stay at Foxden with her aunt and uncle and, *if* we're not back before the school term starts, go to school with Nancy.'

'And?'

'And she said yes. She made me promise I'd fetch her as soon as we get back.' Claire's throat tightened and she swallowed. 'I could tell she wasn't happy about it, and who could blame her? First she was dragged out of school and taken to Canada and now, just when she was looking forward to going back to her old school in Oxford and seeing all her friends, she's having to get used to the idea of going to a school where she won't know anyone except her cousin.' Tears blurred Claire's vision and she sat on the end of the bed and sobbed.

Esther sat next to her and held her in her arms. 'Claire, your daughter is intelligent and resilient. She will come to terms with the change and she will cope with it.'

'She shouldn't have to come to terms with anything at her age,' Claire said. 'Nor should she have to *cope*. She's eight years old for goodness' sake. It isn't right.'

'What's happening to her father isn't right either. Whether she understands now or not, she will when she's older. When you tell her why her father had to go away, and why you had to go after him, I promise you she *will* understand. Right!' Esther stood up. 'It's time we left,' she said, 'I'll wait for you in the car.'

Claire jumped at the sound of the front door slamming. She looked in the dressing table mirror. She looked a fright. Her face was pale and blotchy and her eyes were red-rimmed. The way she looked now she would attract the wrong kind of attention, and she didn't want to do that.

She set about repairing her make-up. By the time she had calmed down, so had her puffy eyes. Dropping her make-up into her handbag, Claire picked up her suitcase, put out the light and went downstairs.

She looked in each room, checking nothing was out of place or looked suspicious. She put on her coat and hat, tightened Mitch's scarf around her neck and pulled on her gloves. With her handbag under her arm and her suitcase in her hand, Claire left the house, quite possibly for the last time.

Neither women spoke on the way to the railway station. When they arrived, Esther parked the car, joined Claire at the ticket office, and walked with her to the platform. 'Thank you,' Claire said.

'For what?' Esther asked.

'Making me see sense,' Claire said. Esther's brow creased. 'About Aimée.'

Esther waved the compliment away. 'You don't need me to tell you what a remarkable child your daughter is. Come here,' she said, hugging Claire. 'She takes after her mother.'

'Stop it!' Claire said, carefully wiping the skin beneath her eyes with her finger. 'I haven't time to repair my make-up, again.'

'You look lovely,' Esther said. Claire rolled her eyes and gave the old lady a wry smile. 'When you see my grandson, give him my love, will you?'

'Yes. *If* I see him.'

Esther tucked Alain's scarf under the collar of Claire's coat.

'And don't be too hard on him,' she said, 'I'm sure he had a very good reason for going to France.'

Claire heard the train's breaks hiss and engage as the train pulled into the station. 'I'd better go. I don't want to miss the train.'

'Of course not. Let me know you've arrived safely if you can.'

'I will.' Claire kissed Esther and hurried across the platform to the train bound for Paddington. The station attendant helped her to board, passed her suitcase to her, and slammed the door shut. Claire pulled down the window and thanked him. A second later he blew his whistle. She raised her arm to wave goodbye to Esther, but she had gone.

On the occasions she had travelled by train during the war, it had been standing room only. She'd had to fight her way through crowded corridors, sometimes changing carriages until she found a seat. And when she did it was like sitting in a fog, there was so much tobacco smoke in the air. Now, because passenger trains were no longer used to transport troops and freight, they were cleaner, less crowded, and there were always vacant seats.

She took a few steps along the corridor to the first compartment, opened the door, and put her handbag and gloves on the nearest seat. She hauled her suitcase onto the overhead rack, closed the door and sat down. She felt sick with anticipation. The feeling of not knowing what lay ahead had once excited her. But that was in wartime, when she was with the Special Operations Executive. She had been young and idealistic, determined to beat the Germans into submission and send their army back to Germany defeated.

Claire inhaled and let out a long calming breath. It wasn't a decade ago, but it felt like a lifetime. She was a different person then, with only herself to worry about. Now she was a mother and a wife – and she was separated from both her child and her husband. Claire bit her lip. She had a long journey ahead of her. She must call on her training, be detached and committed to the job she had to do. If she let sentimentality get in the way, she wouldn't get beyond the next town along the railway track.

When the train pulled into Didcot station the woman sitting next to the window on the opposite side of the aisle to Claire gathered her belongings and left the compartment. Claire glanced at her fellow travellers. One man was asleep, one was engrossed in the financial pages of *The Times*, and the other passenger, a woman, was frowning as she pondered an official-looking document that she had been reading since Claire entered the compartment. No one attempted to move to the seat next to the window, so Claire jumped up, grabbed her handbag and gloves and claimed it.

She relaxed back in the seat, took a French dictionary from her handbag and began to flick through it. She had been teaching French to new recruits at Brize Norton for three years. It had kept her fluent in the language, but she needed to remind herself of the regional accents. She needed to be confident if she was going to pass herself off as French. Eight years ago she had not only been fluent in French but she spoke and understood German. She could also get by in Polish. Not that she needed Polish when she worked and lived with the French Resistance in France. French was vital – a matter of life and death – and understanding German came in very handy, especially as German officers spent their days sitting in cafés bragging about their army, toasting its successes and plans. Not in a million years did they think Claire, an ordinary young French girl, could understand what they were saying – and often said things in front of her that were helpful to the Resistance.

Claire's cover story at the time was that she was born and brought up on the French coast and her parents had sent her to stay with her aunt in Gisoir. Claire had lived in France and worked with the French Resistance for several years. One mistake, however small, could have been fatal. That care she needed to apply now if she was going to find Mitch.

She looked out of the window at the English countryside blanketed in snow. The train pulled into stations and people boarded laughing and joking, looking forward to a day out in London. The war seemed like a very long time ago.

Standing in a queue at Calais, Claire looked at her watch. By now Commander Landry would have sent a car to collect her, as she'd been told he would, and he'd have been informed she wasn't at home. He'd have deployed a number of intelligence officers to search the house again. The commander was an intelligent man who would assume she had gone to France to look for Mitch. Claire smiled to herself. He'd be dumbfounded when his officers found her passport beneath a loose floorboard behind the tallboy in her bedroom. She hadn't made it easy for them to find, but she knew they would. Landry's men were thorough.

Claire opened her handbag and took out the French passport and identity papers that she had retrieved from the attic of her mother's house at Foxden and handed them with her ticket to the port official in Calais. The official glanced at the passport thanked her and handed it back. He was on to the next passenger before Claire had returned her papers to her handbag.

No matter which mode of transport Commander Landry's men checked, they wouldn't find her name on the passenger list of any ferries or ships crossing the English Channel, nor on the passenger list of any aeroplanes flying out of Croydon to Paris. Claire smiled, said *Merci* to the port official and walked away, exhaling with relief.

FRANCE

JANUARY 1950

ELEVEN

The train from Calais slowed as it approached Gisoir station. Claire looked out of the window. The view was familiar. She gathered her belongings and left the compartment. Standing at the exit she pulled down the window, hung out and searched the sea of faces for her friend, Édith Belland. As the train juddered to a halt the passengers waiting to board surged forward and Claire saw her friend at the back of the crowd.

'Édith!' Claire shouted. The bright winter sun was shining directly into Édith's eyes. She may not be able to see me, but she has heard me, Claire thought, as Édith turned her head in her direction. 'Édith?' Claire shouted again. And shading her eyes with her left hand, Claire watched as Édith gripped the top of a walking stick with her right. Claire gasped. Her friend was bent over and leaning heavily on the stick. She looked older than the last time Claire was in France. But then she *was* older. It had been three years.

The platform attendant opened the carriage door and Claire waved at Édith. Édith returned the greeting, brandishing her stick in the air as she limped towards Claire. Édith's son André arrived at that moment. 'Here, let me.' He took Claire's suitcase and set it down so his hands were free to help her off the train.

'Claire, ma chère,' Édith Belland said, her eyes bright with tears. She held out her free hand.

'I am so pleased to see you, my friend,' Claire said, taking Édith's hand before wrapping her arms around her. 'And André,' she said. With one arm around Édith and one around André, she kissed them both in turn. 'It has been a long time.'

'Too long,' André said, taking a step back. 'Welcome home.' Claire had fought the emotion that had been building up inside her since leaving England, but she could hold her reserve no longer and gave into tears. Édith and André, their arms around her, cried with joy.

Gisoir station, but for a lick of paint, hadn't changed since Claire was last there. André, carrying her suitcase, walked on ahead to the car park, leaving Claire and Édith to follow at a slower pace.

'Are you well, Édith?' Claire asked.

'Yes, quite well. Except for arthritis in my knee and hip.'

'How long have you been using a stick?'

'A year, maybe a little longer. I don't need it in the house. I use it when I go out to the shops. It's for support more than anything. I fell on the cobbles when I was in the market last year and ever since André has insisted I use the stick.' She squeezed Claire's arm. 'He worries about me, says I'm not getting any younger. Who is, I ask him?' Édith laughed.

Claire looked out of the window as they drove from the station to the centre of Gisoir. The Town Hall, which had once been Gestapo Headquarters, where Mitch was held before he was taken to the prison in Périgueux had been reclaimed by Gisoir's town councillors when Germany surrendered. Any damage done by the allied forces had been repaired. From the outside, the building looked the same as it had done the last time Claire, Mitch and Aimée had visited Édith. Claire hadn't been inside, she hadn't wanted to.

A cold fist clutched Claire's heart and she turned her head away. They had plastered over the bullet holes and taken down the Nazi adornments, the red Swastikas and the portraits of Hitler. They had painted the walls and re-hung white shutters at the windows. But just looking at the building made Claire want to vomit. There was nothing that councillors, or painters and decorators could do to change the evil that had been done in that building and others like it all over France during the German occupation.

They drove past Café La Ronde. The striped awning was pulled down and a table and two chairs had been placed on either side of the door, but they were not occupied. It was too cold to sit outside.

André's wife, Therese, was at the window when Claire and Édith got out of André's car. By the time they had walked up the short path, Therese was at the front door. She welcomed Claire, hugging her and kissing her on both cheeks. Taking her by the hand Therese showed Claire into the kitchen. 'It is so good to see you,' she said.

While Édith put the kettle on to make coffee, Therese took cups and saucers from the cupboard. When she had laid the table, Therese sat down next to Claire. 'How was your journey?'

'The sea was rough. It was blowing a gale and there were particles of ice in the air, but it was more comfortable and a lot less frightening than the first time I crossed the English Channel to France.' Claire shuddered at the memory. 'Sitting on a cold metal floor in the belly of a Halifax, holding on to a safety line knowing I had to jump into the pitch of night through a hole in the bottom of the aeroplane, and then land goodness knew where.' Claire shook her head. 'All I could hear was the deafening roar of the aircraft's big engines. I was scared to death,' she laughed.

'And when you landed, there was no reception committee to meet you,' Édith said. 'I remember that night very well.'

'I was convinced we'd been betrayed, or the Resistance cell had been compromised and we had fallen into a trap, but Alain wasn't worried at all. He had every faith in the Resistance.'

'How is Alain?' André asked, entering the kitchen with Claire's suitcase.

Édith took the coffee pot from the stove and filled four cups of steaming black coffee. Claire added cream to hers, and took a sip, to give herself time to think how she was going to tell her friends that her husband, their comrade, was suspected of being a German agent. 'The truth is, I don't know,' she said, looking from one to the other of her friends. 'He has been ill you see, and—' She took another sip of her coffee. Her hands were shaking so much she spilt it. She put the cup back on its saucer.

Taking a dishcloth from the side of the sink Édith mopped up Claire's spillage. 'Drink your coffee, ma chère. Tell us about Alain when you are ready, *oui*?'

Claire nodded and smiled through her tears.

'In the meantime, let us get down to the serious business of photographs. I have an album of photographs of my grand-daughter, Lisette, to show you.' Édith looked at Claire pretending to frown. 'I hope you haven't forgotten to bring photographs of Aimée,' she said.

Claire got up, headed for her suitcase, then froze.

'What is it, ma chère?' Édith asked.

'Someone is at the door.'

André looked at his mother. 'Are you expecting anyone, Maman?'

'No.' Édith glanced at the clock on the dresser and shook her head. 'I never receive visitors this late.'

A sharp rap rang out, followed immediately by a second.

André shook his head. 'I had better see who it is. At this time of night, it must be important.'

André returned a few minutes later followed by two men in dark suits. He looked at the empty chair where Claire had been sitting and he physically relaxed. The first man, tall and thin with black hair and a pasty complexion, walked past André to the window and looked out. The shorter man, stocky build with sandy coloured hair and a ruddy complexion, stayed by the door.

'These gentlemen would like to ask you some questions, Maman.' André walked over to his mother and stood protectively behind her chair.

The shorter man bowed slightly. His tall colleague, with his back to the room, continued to look out of the window.

Édith eyed the men with suspicion. 'Good evening, gentlemen,' she said, looking from one to the other. 'Questions at this time of night? What sort of questions?' She stood up and began clearing the table of dirty cups. 'Would you like coffee, messieurs?' She smiled and nodded at the coffee pot that stood next to the half-empty cup which, until a couple of minutes ago, Claire had been drinking from. She casually moved the cup a few inches to the right so it was in front of Therese who smiled, picked it up, and drank from it. 'It has not been made long.' Édith put her hands around the pot. 'It is still hot.'

'No, thank you, madame,' the shorter man said.

The man at the window turned and observed the room. His eyes settled on Therese. 'We are trying to locate a woman about your age,' he said, in an intimidating manner. He then looked at Édith, 'An English woman named Claire Mitchell. You probably know her as Claire Le Blanc?'

'I know Claire very well.' Édith gave the man a broad smile. 'She is like a daughter to me.' She looked across the table at Therese who nodded in agreement. 'May I ask what you want with Claire?'

'She isn't in any trouble, is she?' Therese asked.

'No, madame, we just need to ask her a few questions.' Three pairs of eyes were focused on the tall man doing the talking. 'Her husband, Captain Alain Mitchell, is missing. We would like to help her find him.'

Édith gasped. 'Alain, missing?' she said, with genuine surprise. 'I don't understand. The last letter I received from Claire was— One moment please.' Édith crossed to the kitchen dresser. She stumbled and André turned to help her, but Édith waved him away. 'I am fine,' she said, opening the top drawer and taking an envelope with a Canadian postage stamp from it. Pulling out a thin page of paper, she began to read aloud. '"*Alain's parents are lovely people... Alain is responding to treatment... At last Aimée is enjoying her school lessons.*" And, what else?' Édith said, casting her eyes along each line until she reached the end of the page. 'Here we are. "*We shall be in England (at the Foxden Hotel) for Christmas, and in France with you, André, Therese, and your granddaughter late spring, early summer. Much love from the three of us, Claire.*"

'From what Claire wrote in this letter,' Édith said, waving it in the air before dropping it onto the table for the men to see, 'she is at Foxden, in England, with her family. I have the address of her sister and brother-in-law's hotel somewhere if you would like it,' she said, motioning to the door leading to the sitting room.

'Thank you, but we have the address.' The tall man turned to his colleague. 'If there is nothing else, we had better be going.'

'There is just one thing.' The shorter man smiled at Édith. 'Could I use your toilet, madame?' he asked, moving quickly to the back door.

'We have an indoor lavatory, monsieur,' Édith said, proudly. 'It is the door directly opposite the top of the stairs. We keep wood and coal in the old outdoor lavatory, monsieur. You're welcome to look. The keys are on the window ledge.'

The man took his hand from the doorknob on the back door and turned to her. 'Thank you, madame, that won't be necessary. 'Upstairs, you said?'

'Yes. André, show our visitor where the lavatory is.'

André opened the kitchen door, flicked on the hall light, and the man put up his hand. 'There is no need for you to show me, monsieur.' He looked over his shoulder at Édith. 'Top of the stairs?' Édith nodded and the man began his ascent. André closed the door and sat down next to Therese. He looked at his mother and raised his eyebrows.

'Monsieur?' Édith said, joining the man who did most of the talking at the window. 'Are you sure I can't get you a cup of coffee?'

His body tensed. He shook his head, but his eyes stayed glued to what was on the other side of the glass. 'No, madame. It is very hospitable of you, but when my colleague returns we will be leaving.'

'Then if you'll excuse me?' Édith said, leaning on the sink and peering out of the window. 'It has begun to snow and my bicycle is in the yard. I must put it in the shed. The temperature drops to below zero in these parts, and if the tyres freeze and the rubber hardens—' Édith clicked her tongue, 'they puncture.'

'I'll put your bike away,' André said, jumping up. He grabbed the keys from the window ledge and his coat from the hook on the back of the door. Putting on his coat he left, closing the door behind him.

Freezing air gusted into the room and Édith shivered. From the window, she and the man watched André take her bicycle from the far wall and wheel it across the yard. He held the bike with one hand, while he unlocked and opened the shed door with the other. Then, taking hold of the handlebar and saddle, he lifted the front of the bike and rolled it into the shed on its back wheel.

For a moment it appeared that André had disappeared into

the small wooden structure with the bike. Out of the corner of her eye, Édith saw the man's body stiffen. He leant forward and squinted. A second later André came out of the shed, closed the door and turned the key in the lock. Édith watched her son go back to where she had left the bike and lock the door in the wall. She turned on the tap and filled the kettle.

'It is already freezing,' André said, blustering into the kitchen and blowing hot breath into his cupped hands. He closed the back door as the man who had been upstairs using the toilet opened the door opposite. 'All locked up,' André said, turning the key and smiling at his mother.

'Thank you, son. You can't be too careful these days,' Édith explained, looking first at one of the men and then the other. 'It wasn't so long ago that you could leave the gate to your yard open. You could even leave the door to your house open. My mother never locked her back door. No one did in those days. But,' she said, throwing her arms up in the air before taking the coffee pot from the table, tipping out the used coffee and rinsing it out under the tap, 'times have changed. I can remember—'

The kettle whistled and the man looking out of the window jumped. 'They have,' he cut in. He looked at his associate. 'It is time we were on our way.'

'André? Show the gentlemen out, please,' Édith said.

'Goodbye, madame.' The man standing next to her offered Édith his hand and she shook it.

'Monsieur.' Édith looked across the room to the man standing in the doorway and nodded. After wishing them a safe journey to wherever they were going, she set about making another pot of coffee.

TWELVE

'Where is Claire?' André asked, flustered.

'She left,' Therese said, 'when you went to answer the front door she went out the back door. Did you not see her in the yard?' she asked. 'Or in the shed?'

'No!'

Therese joined Édith at the sink and stared out of the window. 'She must be out there somewhere.'

'Unless she went out of the door in the wall. If she did, she won't be able to get back in because André locked it.' Édith made for the kitchen door, but André put out his arm and barred her way. 'I must unlock it, André. The girl will freeze to death if she stays out there much longer.'

'It isn't locked, Maman.'

Édith looked up at her son. 'But I saw you lock it.'

He shook his head. 'No. You saw what I wanted you to see, or rather, what I wanted the intelligence guy to see. I put the key in the lock, but I did not turn it. I loosened my grip and turned my hand. I made it look as if I was locking it, but when I realised Claire was not in the yard or the shed, I guessed she had left by the door in the wall so I pretended to lock it.'

Worry was etched on Édith's face. 'She'll catch her death out there in this weather. Could you not take a look along the avenue, see if you can see her?'

'No. We don't know who those men are, or the real reason they want to speak to Claire. We must be cautious. They might still be outside, so let us go through to the front room as we would on any other night. I shall go in first and switch on the light. You and Therese come in a couple of minutes after me. If they are watching the front of the house, we need them to see there are only three of us here. I shall add coal to the fire while you turn on the wireless, Maman, and Therese closes the curtains.'

André switched off the kitchen light and escorted his mother and wife into the hall. 'If the men are watching the back of the house, I want them to think we have retired to the sitting room for the evening.'

'And Claire?' Édith said. 'The child—'

'She is not a child, Maman! Claire worked with us in the Resistance for years, or have you forgotten?' Édith lifted her shoulders and nodded. André put his arm around his mother. 'Do not worry. Claire will be fine. She will stay out of sight until she is sure the men who are looking for her have gone.'

André gave his mother's shoulder a squeeze, went into the sitting room and flicked on the light. The women followed two minutes later. When Therese had drawn the curtains, André went back to the kitchen. He stood in the dark, stared out of the window, and scanned the yard for movement. There was none.

An hour passed before he heard a faint tap on the back door. He opened it without putting on the light and Claire stumbled in. 'I thought they would never leave,' she hissed, from between chattering teeth. André closed the door, turned the key in the lock and slid the bolts at the top and bottom of the door into place. 'God, I'm freezing,' Claire said, her voice hoarse, and her throat sore from being outside in the freezing air for so long.

André took her suitcase out of her hand and put it in the scullery, before guiding her out of the dark kitchen and into the sitting room.

'Good Lord, child,' Édith exclaimed when she saw Claire. 'Your clothes are soaked, you'll catch pneumonia. Come here and warm yourself.'

Shaking from being so cold, Claire fell to her knees in front of the fire. She put out her hands, but quickly pulled them back. 'They're too cold,' she croaked, 'I must warm them slowly.'

'I'll get Claire a blanket, then make her a hot drink,' Therese said. 'Maman?'

Édith shook her head. 'Not for me, but Claire must have something.' Therese looked at André.

'Yes, but first I need to take a look around outside. And I must lock the back gate. I won't be long.' Therese followed her husband out of the room.

Claire fell sideways against the settee where Édith was sitting and Édith put her arm around her. When Therese returned, it was with a winter skirt, a blouse and a thick woollen cardigan. The two women helped Claire out of her wet clothes, replacing them with the dry ones – and Therese wrapped a knitted blanket around Claire's shoulders.

When André came back he was smiling. 'No sign of them,' he said, 'and this time I *have* locked the gate.'

'Then I shall make coffee and we shall all relax.' Therese jumped up. 'And we should eat. If someone is watching the house, and we don't eat, they'll think it abnormal.'

'You are right. I made soup this morning. It's in the larder. I shall heat it through,' Édith said, pushing herself up from the low settee. 'We won't be long, my dear,' Édith called over her shoulder to Claire as she and Therese left.

Claire smiled her thanks. She crossed her arms, put her hands under her armpits, and scrunched up her shoulders. 'Argh! The pain,' she said. 'In England, when our hands are so cold that they hurt when they get warm, we call it the hot-aches.'

'In France we say, hot-throbs,' André said. 'Not heartthrobs, but hot-throbs.' Unable to help herself, Claire chuckled.

'Coffee?' Therese called, carrying in a tray with a pot of coffee and cups and saucers. 'Pour Claire a coffee, darling. I'll fetch the cream.' Therese was back a second later with a small jug which she placed next to her husband, before returning to Édith in the kitchen.

'Mm...' Claire held the coffee cup with both hands and sipped. 'This is good,' she said, and closing her eyes breathed in the coffee's rich earthy aroma. The two old friends drank their coffee in silence.

'Maman is bringing in the soup,' Therese said, nudging the sitting room door open with her knee. She carried a tray with soup dishes, spoons, and a basket of bread rolls, over to the table.

Édith followed her daughter-in-law into the room carrying a tureen of soup. 'Come now,' she said to André and Claire, as she spooned soup into the four bowls that Therese had placed on the table, 'eat it while it's hot.'

Claire pulled herself up, stumbled, and held on to the arm of the sofa. 'I'm all right,' she said, as André spun round to help her. 'I'm just a bit stiff after sitting in one position for too long.' She shook out her shoulders and bent her ankles and knees. 'That's better.'

'Have you thawed?' Therese asked.

'Just about. Oh?' Claire said with surprise. 'I've got my voice back.'

'And here was I thinking we were going to have some peace and quiet while we ate,' André said.

Édith looked up at the ceiling and rolled her eyes, Therese wagged her finger at her husband and Claire laughed. 'It is good to be back,' she said, looking around the table at her friends.

'It's good to have you back, Claire,' Édith said. And after

placing a bread roll on each side plate, Édith put her hands together, closed her eyes and thanked God for the food they were about to eat, and for bringing Claire safely back to them.

When they finished eating, Édith and Therese cleared the table and took the dirty dishes to the kitchen, returning with a refreshed pot of coffee and a galette. Édith poured the coffee while Therese cut the cake.

'Is that a king cake? A *galette des rois*?' Claire asked.

'She remembers,' Édith said, beaming a smile to the others at the table. 'You remembered, ma chère,' she said to Claire.

'Of course. But did you remember to put a bean in it?'

'Yes, child, I always put a bean in the galette – for luck.'

'What a good memory you have,' André said.

'I haven't really. It's just that in the war, when I lived here, king cake reminded me of English Christmas puddings. When I was a child my father used to drop a silver threepenny bit into the Christmas pudding while my mother was mixing it, in the same way that you put a bean in your galette.' Smiling at the memory, Claire picked up her coffee and took a sip. It was hot, but not so hot that she didn't enjoy it. She took another sip, relieved to feel warmth in the palms of her hands without the pain of hot-aches.

'I owe you an explanation,' she said, doing her best to swallow the emotion that threatened to erupt inside her. Édith put her hand on Claire's hand. 'I'm fine, Édith,' she said. Grateful for her friend's support, she inhaled deeply. 'I need to tell you why the men who were here earlier are looking for me, and why I need to find Alain before they do.

'The two men who came here today were either Canadian military or British government intelligence officers. Whoever they work for, they were intelligence. I was met by a similar pair when I returned from Canada and taken to RAF Brize Norton and interviewed. I took Aimée to my sister for Christmas and when I got home my house had been searched. They searched Alain's grandmother's house too and took Alain's university books away.

'It was Alain's grandmother who helped me to evade RCAF intelligence in England. I didn't fly to France, which I normally would have done, and which I'm sure they'd expect me to do. Instead, I took a ship across the Channel and several trains.' Claire looked from Édith to André. 'I wasn't followed here, of that I am certain.

'I am sorry they came here, but I couldn't risk using my English passport and papers. If I had they'd have stopped me before I left England. I had no choice but to use my French passport, and the name and travel permit that I used in the Resistance.' André lifted his shoulders and held up his hands as if to say it didn't matter. Claire was family. More importantly, she had been a member of the Gisoir Resistance cell during the war.

Claire knew she would always be loved and supported by the Belland family. Even so, she had brought the intelligence services to their door. Something she had not wanted to do. 'I knew it was only a matter of time before Alain's commander got in touch with the SOE, the organisation that sent me to France to work with the Resistance in forty-one, but I had hoped Mr Smith, the head of the organisation, would refuse to give the commander my Resistance name and address—'

'But the men who came here knew both, so he did,' André said.

'Yes.' Claire took a tired breath and let it out slowly. 'They might know I am in France, they might think I would come here at some point, but they can't be sure of anything.'

'Has your boss in the SOE betrayed you, ma chère?' Édith asked.

'He wouldn't have wanted to, but the intelligence services

would have made it clear to him that he had no choice, given the importance of the situation.'

'Which is?' André asked.

'Alain has been accused of spying for the Germans in the war.'

THIRTEEN

Silence hung in the air like a dead weight. It was Édith who broke it. 'Alain a spy? He is no more a spy than I am.'

André and Therese agreed. 'Is there any evidence to back up this accusation?' André asked.

'No, of course not,' Claire said, 'Alain has been ill. He has what the doctor at Brize Norton called shell shock.' She looked at Édith. 'We went to Canada so he could have specialist treatment.' Édith smiled sympathetically and nodded. 'Part of the treatment was hypnosis and the professor, Lucien Puel, an eminent Swiss psychiatrist, sent Alain's medical report and his findings to Alain's base commander.'

'Did you see the report?'

'I saw a copy of it. I also saw a copy of the letter he sent. The report was a transcript of the sessions Alain had with Professor Puel. The letter was something very different. It was the professor's personal opinion.'

'I don't understand how a doctor's opinion could differ from what is on a medical report, however eminent he is,' André said.

Claire blew out her cheeks and looked up at the ceiling. She'd have to tell them about Simone if she was going to tell them everything. She took a deep breath. 'Alain had bad dreams, which was part of the shell shock. In the dreams, he talked about a woman called Simone. Professor Puel told Alain that he had survivor's guilt. He said it was because when Alain escaped from the prison he left the woman behind.'

'That makes sense,' André said.

Claire didn't want to tell her friends that she suspected Alain of having an affair with Simone while he was in the prison, and feared they were still lovers. There was no point. They would hate him for it, and she didn't want that. Besides, she had come to France to prove Alain wasn't a German spy, not an unfaithful husband. She would find out about Simone later when she had cleared Alain's name.

'I agree,' Claire said, 'but in the letter to Alain's commander, Professor Puel said Simone was a German agent who had turned Alain while he was in prison.'

'No!' André slammed his fist down hard on the table. 'I have met men who have been turned, who have informed on their comrades.' His eyes flashed with anger as he spoke. 'These men wear the black shadow of guilt. They saved their own lives, but they live with the blood of their dead comrades on their consciences.' André shook his head vehemently. 'These traitors carry the souls of their dead comrades around with them. You can see it in their eyes. Alain Mitchell is not one of these men.'

The street at the front of Édith's house was deserted. There was not a car or a pedestrian in sight. Claire, dressed in Therese's boots, coat and hat, carried her handbag. 'Good night, *belle-mère*.' She kissed Édith and whispered, 'See you tomorrow.' André kissed his mother goodbye, then took Claire's arm, supporting her as they walked together along the slippery snow-covered path to the car. Claire turned and waved to Édith while André opened the passenger door. 'Thank you, darling,' she said. Sitting in the passenger seat, she lifted her feet. Once they were clear of the door, André closed it.

Claire noticed André had looked in the rear-view mirror several times after they had turned out of the street onto the main road. She took her powder compact from Therese's handbag, held it a few inches wide of her right shoulder, but at the same height. She twisted her wrist to the left, and then to the right.

'We are not being followed,' André said.

'Sorry, I'm being paranoid.' She dropped the compact back into Therese's handbag.

'Old habits, eh?' André said.

'Yes.' Claire inhaled deeply and exhaled loudly.

'That was a loud sigh,' André said.

'I was thinking about Alain. Wondering where he is and what he's doing.'

'We'll find him and bring him back to you as we did in forty-four.'

'No, André, I am not putting you and the family in further danger. I shall find him. You have already done enough. You must stay here and look after Édith and Therese.' André opened his mouth to protest, but Claire didn't give him the chance. 'I have good friends in Paris who I can stay with. Canadian intelligence will be watching the stations so it won't be safe for me to travel by train, but if I can get someone to take me there by road, I'll stay with them for a while. I need to find the woman called Simone. They might have heard of her, they might even know her. If they don't, they'll know the Gestapo prison Alain was in because he was brought to Paris from a village close to it.'

Claire woke with a jolt. She had slept so soundly that for a moment she didn't know where she was. She swung her legs out of bed and left her friend's spare bedroom. Crossing the landing to the bathroom she heard men's voices. One was André the other – Claire stained to hear – was friendly but— She smiled to herself. The other was comrade Pierre Ruban, a fellow Resistance member, who had been part of the group when she had sabotaged a German troop train, and a dear friend, who had risked his life to bring Alain back to Gisoir after he'd escaped from the Gestapo prison.

Claire washed and dressed quickly and went downstairs to the kitchen where André and Pierre were sitting at the table drinking coffee. 'Pierre! It is good to see you,' she said, falling into her old comrade's arms.

'And you, ma chèrie,' Pierre said, patting and rubbing her back as if he were burping a baby.

'You have brought my suitcase from Édith's?' Claire said, seeing the case by the door. She cuffed a tear from her cheek. 'Thank you, Pierre.'

'My mother has told Pierre about Alain,' André said. 'When you're ready, he will drive you into Gisoir to meet her, and she will tell you when and where to meet the man who will take you to Orléans.'

'That's wonderful.' Claire looked at Pierre. 'What are we waiting for?'

'You! You are going nowhere without food in your stomach.' André took a large omelette from the oven where it had been keeping warm. 'It should not be dry. I made it only seconds before you came down.' He divided the omelette into three, sliding one portion onto Claire's plate and one onto Pierre's. The remainder he left on the tin oven dish for himself. He pressed the edge of his fork into the soft-cooked egg and lifted a sizable chunk to his mouth. Then, seeing that Claire wasn't eating her food, he said, 'Eat! That is an order.'

The three friends sat at the kitchen table eating and drinking, as they had done many times in the war. When Claire's plate was empty, Pierre drained his cup and stood up.

André made a performance of looking at her plate. 'Now you can go,' he said.

Claire laughed, saluted the man who had been the brave leader of the Gisoir Resistance cell and said, 'Comrade!'

'Those were the days,' André said. 'They called me a hero then. Now?' He raised his eyebrows, 'I wear a pinafore.' He lifted the sides of the tea towel that he had tucked into the waistband of his trousers and danced a jig.

Claire put on her coat and picked up her handbag. At the door, she turned back to André. 'Poor Cinderella left at home to wash the ugly sister's dishes,' she said, and pulling a hideous face, shouted, 'See you later.'

Claire and Pierre met Édith in Gisoir. She told them that a Resistance member who had been a courier in the war and was part of the group that brought Alain home to Gisoir ten years earlier was now a travelling salesman. 'He will take you to Orléans where you'll be met by another resistance veteran who will take you on to Paris.'

'Thank you,' Claire said, with a catch in her voice.

'What is it?' Édith asked.

'Three years ago, when Alain and I were here, we strolled happily hand in hand through the town with not a care in the world. I was so happy. I had my man and he was safe. I didn't think about the Germans, the SS, or the Gestapo. All that pain belonged in the past. This year,' she said, 'it is as if I have gone back a decade. I am looking for my man again.' Claire gave in to her tears and broke down.

'Come,' Édith said, leading her to a bench in the square. 'Sit for a while and then we will go to Café La Ronde, ask the proprietor if he has seen Alain. If he is retracing his steps he may have been to the café.'

Claire looked around the small square. The statue of Napoleon that the Germans had ripped from its plinth when they marched into the town had been replaced. Claire could see the market stalls. Beneath colourful canopies, wooden tables were stacked with produce. Further along the street, the patisserie's window, no longer empty, displayed a variety of cakes and bread.

'It's good to see the town so busy,' Claire said. Bringing her gaze back to Café La Ronde her eyes settled on the section of street where the Gestapo officer had arrested and had Mitch beaten, before he was dragged off to Gestapo Headquarters.

Emotion very nearly getting the better of her, Claire took Édith's hand in hers and gave it a gentle squeeze. She was only alive today because of Édith's youngest son, Frédéric. He had stopped her from going to Mitch's aid. And thank God he had. She was pushing her way through the crowd when a black Mercedes pulled up. She turned as an SS Waffen Captain wearing a green field uniform, with a highly polished death mask on his peaked hat, stepped from the car and strode across to the pack of grey uniforms. Claire recognised the officer. She had seen him several times in the Café La Ronde. He once asked her if Alain was her lover. When she laughed, wrinkled her nose, and said no, he had asked her out to dinner.

She was at the edge of the gathering when Frédéric appeared at her side and dragged her back into the crowd. He put his arms around her and told the men who had left their beers and coffees in the nearby cafés and bars to see what the commotion was about that Claire was his woman. He joked with them saying she was a tiger, and he wished she was as passionate in bed as she was about a stranger being arrested by the Germans. The men had laughed and made lewd comments. Frédéric had held her so tightly she could hardly breathe, and all the time he was talking her down. Claire looked at Édith. Her youngest son had saved her life that day. Not long afterwards he had lost his own.

The Café La Ronde, like all the other cafés and bars around the square, had been packed with Germans, mostly officers, during France's occupation. Claire greeted the proprietor with a smile when she and Édith entered. He lifted up his arms and tilted his head in a welcoming gesture before walking from behind the counter and shaking her hand.

'What a pleasure it is to see you again, madame,' he said, to Claire. 'Édith?' He kissed Édith Belland's hand. He showed them to a table at the back of the café. While he was taking his notebook and pen from his top pocket, Claire sidestepped into the booth where she and Mitch used to sit. 'Ah... You remember, madame,' he said to Claire beaming her a smile.

'Coffee and a slice of almond cake,' Édith said.

'And for Madame Mitchell?'

'The same.' Claire started to ask him if he had seen Alain recently, then stopped. Instead, she nodded her thanks and watched as he moved deftly between the blue-and-white checked tablecloths on the small tables back to the counter.

The café's door opened and Claire half expected to see Jacques the Resistance wireless operator come in. He wouldn't of course. Jacques had been killed when his house was singled out by a German surveillance van with radio search equipment on the roof. The Germans had smashed down Jacques' door, seized the wireless, and Jacques was never seen again.

That night, while she slept, Claire saw the face of the SS officer who had asked her out. She had often wondered whether it was because she had turned him down that he had Mitch arrested. She woke up in a panic, breathing heavily with her hair soaked in sweat, stuck to her head. She looked around the familiar room, the room where she and Mitch had slept when they last visited Édith. She put on her dressing gown, went to the window, and sat on the sill looking out. A ribbon of light on the horizon to the east told her it would soon be dawn. She leaned into the recess between window and wall and lifted up her feet.

The first time she and Mitch stayed with Édith Belland they had a dangerous mission to perform with the local Resistance movement. Before the end of their work in France Aimée was born, and later they were married. Claire's thoughts were interrupted by a knock at the door.

'Claire, are you awake?'

'Yes, Édith. Come in.'

'André called. He has gone to pick up your new passport and identity papers.'

Claire felt butterflies stirring in her stomach. She inhaled and let her breath out slowly. She felt no calmer. 'Did he arrange for me to travel by motorcar?'

'Yes. He is seeing one of the men who brought Alain on the last leg of the journey after he had escaped from prison. Bernard is his name. You may remember him? He was a member of a cell in Orléans.'

Claire shook her head. She might remember his face when she saw him, but she had known several men named Bernard and it was a long time ago. 'It was Eddie and Antoinette Marron who brought Alain to Orléans from Paris,' she said, as much to herself as to Édith.

'It was,' Édith said. 'Those dear brave women brought Alain all the way by ambulance.'

There wasn't a day went by that Claire didn't think about her friend Eddie and how saving Mitch's life got her killed. 'I know the leader of Paris Centre, the Paris Maquis, Thomas Durand,' she said, changing the subject. 'I know it was a rogue cell, but he was highly respected, all the members of the cell were. Monsieur Durand might know where Alain was taken after he was shot.'

'Someone must know,' Édith said, thoughtfully. 'Someone somewhere took the bullets out of Alain's leg and nursed him until his leg had healed. Monsieur Durand might know people who can help,' Édith said. 'Anyway, Bernard will take you wherever you need to go tomorrow. But before that, André will be here with your papers.'

'I wish there was time to visit Therese and your granddaughter,' Claire said.

'There will be plenty of time when this nonsense about Alain being a traitor is cleared up.'

'Then we will visit as we had planned, with Aimée.' Claire had every intention of jumping down from the window. Instead, she slumped back. 'You must think I am a terrible mother to leave my child in England with my sister while I travel halfway across Europe looking for Alain.'

Édith went to her and, holding Claire's face in her hands, said, 'I think no such thing. You must do what you have to do, child.' Claire hung her head. 'Look at me,' Édith said. And when Claire looked up at her old friend, she said, 'You will find Alain. You found him once before – and that was in the middle of a war – you will find him again.

'Come now,' she said, helping Claire down from the windowsill. 'Get washed and dressed and come down for breakfast. André will soon be here with your passport and papers. I should like us to have eaten and cleared away before he arrives.'

FOURTEEN

Wearing Édith's brown walking shoes, a dark brown and gold flecked two-piece beneath a bottle-green belted coat, and sandy coloured scarf and beret – a mismatch of colours that Claire would never wear – she climbed into Pierre and André's friend Bernard's Renault pickup truck. She was grateful for the old coat. Unlike Pierre's warm motorcar there was no heater in the truck.

The journey from Orléans to Paris was less comfortable than the drive from Gisoir to Orléans had been. Not only because Pierre's car was new, warm, and had soft seats, but because Pierre thought it best that Bernard stuck to the country roads that he normally took when he delivered produce to the market towns. Many of the narrow roads were in disrepair and Claire felt every bump and pothole the truck drove over.

Bernard was a man of few words. Claire tried to engage him in conversation several times, but a grunt and a nod, or a tobacco-stained toothy grin were as much as she got out of him.

'Smoke?' he said, taking a roll-up of brown paper from an old dented tobacco tin.

'No, thank you.' Claire was about to say *I don't mind if you smoke* when he put the torpedo-shaped cigarette in his mouth and flicked open the lid of a battered old American lighter.

'GI gave to me this lighter.' Bernard lit his cigarette and inhaled deeply. 'Very good,' he said, loudly, enunciating every syllable. Suddenly he began to cough. 'Argh!' he shouted, took his hand off the steering wheel, made a ball of his fist and beat his chest.

As the truck weaved its way along the road, bumping the grass verge several times. Claire looked at the handbrake, ready to pull it on if necessary. 'Yes,' he gasped, when he had finished coughing, 'it is *very* good.'

Within seconds the cab was filled with smoke, so when Bernard said he was hungry and suggested they stopped for lunch at a small café he knew, Claire agreed. She had smelled some strong French cigarettes in the war – Mitch had occasionally smoked Gitanes and Gauloises – but never in all the years she had lived in France had she smelled anything as pungent as the cigarette Bernard smoked.

He swung the truck off the road onto a patch of waste ground, bringing it to a halt in front of a small roadside café. 'Very good,' he said, miming putting food in his mouth.

She smiled. To Bernard everything he said to her he said loudly and finished with *Very good*. Perhaps it was because he knew she was English. 'I am feeling peckish, but not hungry,' Claire said, in perfect French.

Bernard replied, 'Very good,' and led the way along a narrow path of loose gravel to the shabby café with grey threadbare curtains at its two filthy windows. As he opened the door and stood aside to let Claire enter, a combination of cigarette smoke and burnt cooking oil filled her nostrils. She had swapped one smoke-filled space for another.

Bernard swaggered into the small café to jokes and leg-pulling because he had a female passenger with him. He put up his hands, 'Gentlemen,' he said, puffing out his chest. He was secretly enjoying the attention, Claire thought. 'This is my good friend André Belland's cousin, so mind your manners.'

'Then welcome,' said one man. 'A good man, André Belland,' said another. 'The best! Give my regards to Madame Édith when you next see her,' another said, pulling out a chair for Claire to sit down.

Bernard nodded that he would sit in the chair opposite her. 'But first I shall order lunch.' Claire glanced along the table: there was no menu. She looked at the other tables in the prefabricated cabin. No menus on them either. But above the gas stove where the cook was frying steak was a blackboard. She read down the list of dishes. Soup of the day, some sort of steak, which Claire thought must be a local dish, pork chop and fillet of fish. She was just about to tell Bernard that she would like soup when he returned and sat down.

'It will not be long,' he said, grinning. 'The steak here is...' He put his fingers to his mouth and blew a kiss into the air, making a smacking noise with his lips, 'very good.'

'Steak?' Claire said. 'Delicious. Thank you, Bernard.'

The steak was indeed delicious. And, thank goodness, not too filling.

During the last part of the journey Bernard smiled at her every now and then but he was no conversationalist. 'How are we doing?' Claire asked. 'Have we made the halfway mark yet?'

'Yes,' he said, 'and twenty kilometres.'

'That's good. We're over halfway to Paris.' Claire looked out of the side window. They had left the country lanes behind and the road they were now travelling on was straight and wide. She supposed it was a new road that had been built since she and Alain were last there. Her stomach churned at the thought of her husband with another woman. She tried to concentrate on the landscape but at this time of year there was nothing much to see. She closed her eyes and was soon asleep.

Claire woke to Bernard shaking her by the shoulder. 'If you

would like to change your clothes now, the toilet is round the back of the café. I shall fill up with petrol for the return journey while you are getting changed, yes?'

'Yes, thank you, Bernard.' Claire opened the door and jumped down from the cab of the truck. Walking in the direction of the toilet, she noticed a road sign. It was old and some of the letters were worn, but she could make out the words: *Paris Centre: 20 kilometres.*

She wondered if the vehicle taking her to Paris was already in the parking area. She screwed up her eyes and searched the windscreens of several parked cars. None had a driver at the wheel. They probably hadn't arrived yet. She entered the lavatory, which was used by both men and women. Trying to ignore the stench coming from the holes in the wall, she went into a narrow cubicle and closed the thin wooden door. There was hardly room to turn round, let alone change from one set of clothes to another, but at least there was a window ledge to put her bag on.

She turned to lock the door, but there was no lock. Avoiding the hole in the floor, Claire held her breath and quickly took off the thick clothes she had worn as a disguise and put on a smart grey costume. Kicking off the brown brogues and thick socks one at a time, she slipped her feet into a pair of classic black court shoes. Changing from socks over stockings to only stockings took Claire's breath away. The difference in warmth was unbelievable. After checking her hair in the broken mirror, she wrapped the shoes and socks in the clothes she had taken off and took them outside.

There was no one on the road but she and Bernard had passed a dozen, probably more, men and women trudging through mounds of snow that had built up on the verge along the side of the main road leading into Paris. They looked half frozen as they trailed along one behind the other. December had been recorded as one of the coldest in France for a decade. It felt to Claire as if January would soon be taking the record.

She left the clothes on the top of a stack of crates in full view of the road. Hopefully, one of the women she'd seen earlier on the road would pass by, see them, and change from their wet clothes to dry ones. She looked up. Snow clouds hung heavily in what was otherwise a bright blue sky. She hoped the clothes were found before the next snowfall.

'It is bitter out there, Bernard,' Claire said, climbing into the cab of the truck and slamming the door. 'What time did you say the person taking me to Paris would be here?'

'Anytime now,' he said, consulting his watch.

'And how will we know him, or her?'

'We won't, he or she will know us.'

The situation reminded Claire of her time with the Resistance in the war. Except it wasn't nearly as dangerous. A black Citroën pulled up on the driver's side of the truck and Bernard said, 'A man,' as he wound down his window.

Claire slid down in the seat. 'Is it him?'

'I don't know. If it is he will know my name.'

The driver of the Citroën, muffled up with the brim of his trilby pulled down against the biting wind, got out of the car. He stretched his legs, then took a pack of cigarettes from his coat pocket. 'Do you have a light, monsieur?' he asked, looking up at Bernard's open window.

'I do, monsieur. I was just about to have a cigarette, myself.' Bernard closed the window and opened the truck's door. Jumping down he shook the man's hand before flicking the lid on his American lighter. He cupped his hands against the wind, lit the stranger's cigarette and then his own.

'Thank you, Bernard,' the man said.

'You are welcome,' Bernard replied. Exhaling a long stream of smoke into the freezing air, he banged on the driver's door. A signal to Claire that her ride into Paris was here. 'Madame wishes to go to the 8th Arrondissement,' he said, turning back to the driver of the Citroën. 'From there she will take the Metro.' The man gave one sharp nod.

Claire arrived at Bernard's side from the back of the truck. She put out her hand. 'Hello, monsieur, I am—'

'Madame Belland! How do you do?' A lopsided smile crept across the man's face, as he took Claire's suitcase and put it in the boot of his car.

'Thank you for bringing me all this way, Bernard.' Claire put her arms around the burly lorry driver and kissed him good-bye. 'I am grateful to you for all you have done.'

'You just find Alain. And when you do, bring him to Gisoir and we will celebrate.'

The driver of the Citroën opened the car's passenger door and Claire got in. She couldn't see Bernard from the passenger side of the car, but she would put money on him standing beside his truck waving her off. And he was. When the car pulled away, she looked out of the back window and waved until Bernard faded into the distance.

'So,' the driver of the Citroën said, 'you have lost your Canadian again.'

FIFTEEN

'Thomas Durand?' The driver of the car that was going to take her to Paris had been the leader of the Paris Centre, Maquis Resistance cell, during the war. 'Oh my God,' Claire said, 'it is you.'

'Yes, it is me,' he said with a twinkle in his eye. 'And you must be Madame Belland?'

'For the time being.' Thomas Durand laughed. 'It is not funny,' Claire said.

'No, it is not,' Thomas Durand agreed.

Neither spoke for a while, and then Thomas said, 'I know something of the Canadian and, for what it is worth, I do not think he is a traitor. A womaniser?' he said, laughing. 'That is another thing. He is a man after all.' Claire began to protest, but Thomas cut in, 'I joke.'

'Again, not funny,' Claire said, as casually as her aching heart would allow.

As they drove through Paris's southern suburbs the two ex-Resistance members talked about the war; the successful missions to stop the trains transporting German troops to

Normandy, the friends they had worked with, and the brave Resistance fighters that they had lost.

'I know Antoinette Marron,' Thomas Durand said, 'from the University. Through her, I met your friend Eddie.'

'Eddie,' Claire said, tears welling up in her eyes, 'was the best friend anyone could have. We were young WAAFs together. We learned French together, trained together, the SOE put us through our paces at the same time,' Claire said, sniffing back her tears. She shook her head. 'Eddie was killed in Paris after she and Antoinette had smuggled Mitch out of the city in an ambulance. Those two brave women drove him all the way to Orléans.

'When they got back to Paris, Eddie insisted she took the ambulance back to the hospital on her own and dropped Antoinette off at the house where she lived with her parents.'

'Why did she risk driving the ambulance back to the hospital? She could have left it in a street nearby.'

'Antoinette told me Eddie was worried that if there was an emergency during the night the depot would be an ambulance short, which could cost lives.'

'So she took it back to the depot on her own?'

'Yes. Apparently, everything had gone to plan. The ambulance was back in its bay when a side door leading into the hospital opened and one of the medics, who Eddie knew really well, came out wielding a gun. He shot Eddie at point blank range. After saving Mitch's life, Eddie was murdered by someone she thought was a friend.' Claire didn't try to stop her tears, she let them flow. 'That murdering— was a Frenchman who was born and brought up in Paris.'

'But paid by the Germans,' Thomas added.

Claire nodded and wiped the tears from her face with the back of her hand. 'Poor Eddie. She was so full of life.'

Thomas put his arm out of the window to indicate he was turning left and brought the car to a halt in a side street. He pulled on the handbrake but left the engine ticking over. 'There's a café,' he said, pointing to the opposite side of the road. 'I think you could do with a drink. I suggest brandy?' he said, grinning.

'But I need to get to the Metro or I won't be at Antoinette and Auguste Marron's house on time. They're expecting me for dinner and I don't want to be late.'

'I'll drive you to their house. Then you'll be there in plenty of time. Come on,' Thomas said, 'what do you say?'

Claire reached behind her and grabbed her handbag from the back seat of the car. 'Okay, you win. It's been a long day, I could do with a drink.'

Weaving in and out of the slow moving traffic, Claire and Thomas ran across the street. 'Mm...' Claire said, entering the café, 'smell that coffee.'

Thomas ordered two coffees and two brandies and led Claire to a table next to the fire. 'Are you hungry?'

'Yes, ravenous, but I'm not sure I could eat anything. My stomach feels like a coiled spring. Besides, Antoinette will have made dinner. I think I should wait but thank you.' Thomas nodded, took a sip of his coffee, and began to laugh. 'What now?' Claire asked.

'I was thinking about the first time we met. Do you remember?'

'Of course, I do. I don't remember the exact date, but it was outside Le Park Café on the Champs Élysées.'

'You had an old map of the Metro underground and I had to ask you if you were a visitor to Paris.'

'And my reply was something like, "Not exactly, I am visiting my grandmother, but I want to see the sights." Then I asked you if you were a visitor and you said—'

'"No, I'm waiting for a friend, but she has not arrived."'

Claire hooted with laughter. 'And that was my cue to leave. But before I could, I had to take the money for my coffee from my purse and leave it on the table. Then I had to put my wallet on the table, under the newspaper, without drawing attention to myself. It was the first time I'd delivered money to a Resistance cell and I was petrified I'd get it wrong.'

'Is that why you waited on the other side of the avenue for such a long time?'

Claire's mouth fell open. 'You knew I was there? You knew I was watching you?'

'Well... yes.'

'And there's me thinking I was blending in with the crowd, that I was invisible. You must have thought I was stupid.'

'Not at all!' Thomas sat back in his seat pretending to be shocked. 'Nor do I think you would blend in with a crowd,' he said. Claire rolled her eyes. 'No,' Thomas said, 'I assumed you had your reasons, though I couldn't think what they were.'

'Fear and doubt that I had got it wrong, that's what my reasons were.' Claire laughed. 'There was a fortune in that wallet. I had never seen so much money. Carrying it from Gisoir to Paris was a huge responsibility, never mind about meeting up with the right person and handing it over,' she said. 'It wasn't until you picked up the newspaper and I saw the wallet had gone, that I dared leave.'

'The *Paris-Soir*.'

'That's right!' Claire laughed. 'What a memory.'

'Some occasions and some people are hard to forget,' Thomas said.

Claire felt the blush of embarrassment creep up her neck to her cheeks. She took a drink of her brandy. Was this handsome Frenchman with curly, slightly-too-long hair, rugged complexion and smiling eyes flirting with her? Or, was he still joking?

By the time they had finished their drinks it was dark outside. And when they left the café it was snowing. Shielding Claire from the snow, Thomas draped the left side of his long coat around her shoulders and huddled together they ran across the road. He unlocked the passenger door and Claire dropped onto the seat. When she was safely in the car, Thomas closed her door, and ran round the front of the car to the driver's side.

'Next stop 65 Avenue St Julien,' he said, jumping into the car and slamming the door. The engine popped and spluttered a couple of times, then fired on the third press of the ignition. Feeling even colder after the warm café, Claire pulled up the collar of her coat and hugged her handbag. Only a short time passed before Thomas turned on the heater. Tepid air at first, and then warmer air blew onto Claire's legs. She relaxed back in the passenger seat and looked out of the window.

They drove alongside the River Seine for some time, crossing by the Austerlitz Bridge. The last time she was in the area it was summer and the sun was shining. She strained to see out of the window but the snow made everywhere look the same. The streetlights came on, but it was still too dark to see what was written on the street signs.

'Rue de Lesseps,' Claire said, as they cruised along the familiar wide tree-lined street. 'We must have been in the 8th Arrondissement for ages, surely we are almost there.' Thomas turned the steering wheel to the left and Claire whooped with excitement. 'Look. Three-storey townhouses. And look,' she said again, 'that one has a tall arched window. We are here.'

Claire stepped out of the car and caught her breath. From the street, she hardly recognised the Marron house. New white shutters adorned the windows where during the German occupation the old shutters had been pulled off their hinges to make the house look as if it had been abandoned, and so deter looters. And the lower balconies, which had been purposely ripped out of the wall so thieves couldn't climb into the house through the downstairs windows, had been replaced to match those at the upper windows, giving the house symmetry and balance.

When Claire had last been inside number 65 Avenue St

Julien, it had appeared derelict. If anyone had broken in through the front door and had ventured beyond the leaking entrance with rotting floorboards to the main hall, which was bare but for a smashed mirror and several empty boxes, they would have assumed the house had already been stripped of its valuables.

She stood frozen to the spot. The white stone townhouse, with its tall upstairs windows and black wrought-iron balconies, was nothing like the house Claire remembered. She turned at the sound of Thomas slamming the boot of his car.

'After you,' he said, arriving at her side with her suitcase. Unable to quiet her heart Claire climbed the steps and stood at the front door. 'It's green,' she said, beaming a smile at Thomas who frowned and shook his head. 'The door,' she said, 'in the war it was green. The paint was chipped and flaking off when I was last here but it was green. And it is still green,' she laughed.

Thomas reached past her and rang the bell. The door opened immediately.

SIXTEEN

'My darling Claire.' Antoinette put her hand up to her mouth. 'I have longed for this day.' Antoinette threw her arms around Claire and rocked her. 'Come, it is cold out here. Hello, Thomas.' Taking one of Claire's hands, Antoinette held out the other to Thomas. 'Come in, my dears, come in.'

Claire looked around, amazed at what she was seeing. The hall was no longer rundown. Where previously there had been bare dull floorboards, there was now a beautiful red Turkish carpet. And around the edge, eight or nine inches of highly polished wood between the fringes of the carpet and the wall.

'Auguste?' Antoinette shouted. 'Auguste, look who is here,' she cried when her husband, Claire's old mentor, Professor Auguste Marron came ambling into the foyer.

'Claire!' he said, taking Claire in his arms. 'It has been a long time.'

'Too long,' Antoinette added, as she and Thomas followed Auguste and Claire past the main salon and along the passage to the living rooms at the back of the house.

Instinctively Claire looked across the room, expecting to see Antoinette's mother and father in their armchairs on either side of the fire. She wasn't surprised the old couple weren't there. They had been elderly when Claire knew them in the war. They had probably moved to a smaller house, or an apartment, somewhere on one level that was easier for them to manage. Even so, she felt a strange sadness at their absence.

'Mother passed away in the autumn,' Antoinette said to Claire.

'I am sorry.'

'Without her, father-in-law doesn't want to go on,' Auguste said.

'We'll see about that!' Antoinette looked sternly at Auguste. 'He had the flu in December, which wouldn't clear up. We were worried that it would turn into pneumonia. Our doctor agreed with us and we had father admitted to hospital. He is better now. He is recuperating in a residential home for elderly people.'

'The residents are mostly ex-military men from the 1914-18 war – and a good percentage of them are Jewish.' Auguste laughed. 'He's having such a good time with all the other old boys, he doesn't want to come back here.'

'I do not think it is that, at all,' Antoinette said to Claire. 'It's more that he doesn't want to be here without my mother.'

'I can understand that,' Claire said.

'Yes,' Antoinette said, wistfully. 'I can too.' She gazed at the empty chairs by the fire.

'This room, well the whole house, looks very different to the last time I was here,' Claire said. 'The room is hardly recognisable. The light in the centre of the ceiling is on and the curtains are still open. Something that would not have been possible during the war.'

'And not a dust sheet in sight,' Antoinette said. 'I shall show you the rest of the house later. You won't recognise it.'

'If it hadn't been for the tall arched window that Eric told me to look for before I came to Paris the first time, which has stayed in my mind, I wouldn't have recognised the outside of the building with the new shutters and balconies at street level.'

'And not one broken window,' Antoinette added.

Their reminiscing was interrupted by a young woman carrying a tray with coffee, cups and saucers, and a cake. Antoinette introduced her as Gabrielle, the daughter of a friend from Marcheroux in the Loire Valley. 'Gabrielle is staying with us while she is at the Sorbonne.'

Gabrielle laid the refreshments on the table, said how do you do, and shook Claire's hand. Turning to shake Thomas's hand, she blushed scarlet.

'She insists she must help Antoinette in the house when she isn't studying,' Auguste said.

'To earn her keep,' Antoinette added, 'as if she needed to.' She smiled at the pretty girl.

'We have lost our daughter to the Université de Genevveat. Mélanie will be there for another two years, but we have gained Gabrielle.'

'And thank goodness we have. With Éric working every hour God sends at a hospital in the city, and Auguste lecturing at the university, I would become a lonely old spinster.' Gabrielle smiled. 'And,' Antoinette said, 'with the study-work she brings home, she keeps me on my academic toes.'

Gabrielle looked at Thomas and blushed again.

'So, Éric works at the hospital?' Claire said. 'I should love to see him. Will he or Mélanie be home while I'm here.'

'Mélanie doesn't travel back from Geneva often, but Éric occasionally comes home at weekends.'

Over dinner Claire told her friends how erratic Alain had been, how he was eventually diagnosed with shell shock, and how the doctor on the aerodrome in England suggested he went to

Canada to a hospital that specialises in nervous disorders. 'Apparently,' Claire said, 'shell shock is not uncommon.'

'It is a mystery why some otherwise strong men are affected, others not at all.' Auguste shook his head. 'What Alain must have suffered...'

'And seen,' Claire said. 'He didn't talk about the Gestapo prison much, but... Anyway, the base doctor referred him to a Swiss psychiatrist named Professor Lucien Puel.

'At first Alain seemed to be getting better. He responded well to Professor Puel's treatment, but then he began to go backwards.' Claire told them about his nightmares, and how he often called out for Simone in his sleep. 'It is Simone I'm here to find,' she told them. 'Find her and I might find Alain.'

'Simone is a popular name in France,' Thomas said. 'Finding this woman will be virtually impossible.'

'What if I told you she had been a member of the Resistance?'

Thomas raised his eyebrows. 'That would make it easier. Do you know which cell?'

'No. And it gets worse.' Claire looked from Thomas to Antoinette and then to Auguste. 'In the letter Professor Puel wrote to Alain's commander he said there was a German agent in the prison, a woman, and her name was Simone. The professor said it was his professional opinion that the German agent known as Simone had turned Alain during the time they were together.' Claire took a faltering breath. 'He said Alain was suffering from guilt, not because he had to leave the woman behind, but because he had betrayed his fellow prisoners by divulging details of their escape plan to the Germans.'

Neither Antoinette nor Auguste believed Alain would work for the Germans. But it was Thomas who made the best argument in her husband's defence. 'Captain Mitchell was shot. He could have been killed—' Thomas stopped speaking mid-sentence, put his forefinger to his lips, and deep in thought looked into the middle-distance.

'What is it, Thomas?' Claire asked.

'There was a woman, a German spy whose code name was Simone. But she was not in the prison at Saint-Gaudens when Captain Mitchell was there.'

'How do you know?' Claire asked.

'We had intelligence confirming she was in Périgueux prison.'

'So was Alain at first, then they moved him. They could have moved her as well.'

'They didn't.'

'How can you be sure?' Antoinette asked.

'Because she never came out of Périgueux.' Thomas looked across the table at Claire. 'The Germans kept it quiet to save face, but she died in Périgueux. An accident, they said.'

'An accident?'

Thomas shrugged. 'The official line was she fell down a flight of concrete steps and broke her neck.'

The four friends sat in shock. Then Antoinette put her hand on Claire's arm. 'It is obvious,' she said, 'Professor Puel has made a mistake.'

A huge mistake. One that will cost Mitch his job with the military, and probably his life, Claire thought. 'So who is this Simone that he knew when he was in the prison at Saint-Gaudens?'

'Maybe she wasn't in the prison. She could be someone Alain met after he had escaped, after he'd been shot. She might have helped to nurse him, or she could have been one of the drivers who brought him to Paris.'

Thomas picked up his napkin, dabbed at the corners of his mouth and laid it on the table. 'Thank you for the meal,' he said to Antoinette and Auguste. He then looked at Claire. 'I have a friend who was in the Paris Maquis with me. He now lives in the north. I will arrange for him to take you to the prison. From there it will be easier to trace Alain's steps and hopefully find the woman called Simone.'

And find Alain with her, Claire thought. Her heart plummeted.

'Claire?'

'Yes? I'm sorry. I—'

'Begin with the doctor who saved his leg, and then talk to the Resistance guys who brought him to Paris. Someone must know who this woman is.'

'Thank you, Thomas.'

'I'll be in touch,' he said, getting up. 'It might take a day or two to organise things, so use the time to relax. Go and see the sights.' Claire nodded, though sight-seeing was the last thing she wanted to do.

Claire and Antoinette walked Thomas to the front door. With Antoinette's arm around her shoulders, Claire watched the muscular Maquis leader open the driver's door of his car and, holding on to the doorframe, swing himself onto the seat. It was snowing heavily but after a slippery start, the sporty Citroën was soon down the road and out of sight.

Claire and Antoinette quickly stepped inside out of the wind. Antoinette closed and locked the door and arm in arm the two friends returned to the dining room. 'Let's take a brandy through to the sitting room. Sit by the fire for ten minutes before we clear the table.'

Auguste took the decanter and a glass from the sideboard, indicating with a nod to Gabrielle that she should take the rest of the glasses and join them.

'I had better not drink brandy,' the young woman said, 'I have a paper to write.' She picked up two bell-shaped brandy glasses. 'I'll take these through, then clear the table and wash the dishes before I go up to study.'

'No, you will not!' Antoinette said, taking the glasses out of

Gabrielle's hands. 'Take a glass of brandy upstairs, for when you've finished your paper, with pleasure.' Gabrielle wrinkled her nose. 'Then make yourself a mug of hot chocolate but go up and do your work. I am grateful for the help you give around the house, but you are here to study not to skivvy!'

'Thank you,' Gabrielle said, and poking her head around the sitting room door, called goodnight to Auguste.

A log fire blazed in the hearth warming Claire on the outside while the brandy warmed her on the inside. The three friends talked and laughed, discussed the changes that had taken place in both their countries since the autumn of 1945 when what the government and the newspapers were calling the Second World War ended. Claire didn't like the phrase, it implied there might be a third, or even fourth, war. She hoped there wouldn't be and shuddered.

'Are you cold, Claire?' Auguste asked.

'No, not at all. I was thinking about the war, and the future.'

Paris was as exciting as Claire remembered – but much safer. There seemed to be little austerity, even though some things were still rationed. Shop windows advertised fashionable coats and shoes, couture gowns were displayed on slender-waisted mannequins and there were chic hats of every style and colour.

On the left bank of the Seine street artists attracted crowds as they painted buildings on the far side of the river or boats sailing on it. The two friends walked down to the Latin Quarter in the fifth arrondissement where they met Auguste for lunch.

The airy modern restaurant overlooked a cobbled square where every few yards there was a bench beneath an elm tree. A smart but casually dressed waiter in a white open neck shirt and grey slacks, instead of the traditional buttoned to the neck white shirt, black tie and black trousers – showed the trio to a table that was near enough to the window for Claire to watch the students in the square. Some were laughing, some were serious, some were simply eating their lunch, but they all had one thing in common – they were free.

'How different life is today,' Claire mused, watching dozens of young people from Paris's universities larking about.

Auguste laughed. 'Now they can speak without fear of being arrested, most of them don't know when to stop. It seems everyone has an opinion,' he said, shaking his head and laughing again.

'A good thing too,' Antoinette gently chided, 'they were denied a voice for far too long.'

SEVENTEEN

Instead of carrying food around all day, Claire and Antoinette left the tram a couple of stops before Avenue St Julien to buy bread and meat. Like England, some food was still rationed – and again like England, it was mostly food that was imported from abroad.

Arm in arm, Claire and Antoinette walked along Boulevard Victor Hugo. They passed the statue of the Duke of Orléans on his horse, a familiar landmark from the time Claire had spent with Antoinette and her parents in the war. Claire had many bittersweet memories from those days, but now was not the time to remember them.

She was surprised to see that the large apartment block en route to Antoinette's house, which had been damaged by both enemy and allied bombs, had been pulled down. As she walked on she saw to her delight that the dwellings being built in its place were houses.

'I met up with some of my comrades who fought with me in the Maquis,' Thomas said that evening. 'I asked them if they had heard of a woman in any of the other resistance cells called Simone who was captured by the Gestapo and imprisoned at Saint-Gaudens. One of the guys said he knew of a Resistance woman called Simone, but he didn't know how we would find her because Simone was her code name, not her real name. He didn't know the surname she used, so we'll have to go the long route,' he said, 'via Mauzac.'

'We?' Claire said.

'Yes. The guy who brought Alain to Paris in forty-four was going to take you to Saint-Gaudens, but he is about to become a father, again, and his wife threatened to leave him if he didn't stay at home and look after their other children.'

'I don't blame her,' Claire said. 'But what about your work, Thomas? Isn't the university term about to start? Won't it be difficult to get time off?'

'Yes, the new term begins next week. But I don't have any one-to-one tutorials for a while and my lectures are being covered by my assistant. He's younger and better looking than me, so the female students will be happy.' Claire looked at Thomas in the soft light of the Marron's sitting room and thought his assistant must be very special to look at if he was better looking than Thomas Durand. 'So, the sooner we go the sooner we'll be back. We'll set off early tomorrow morning. Claire?'

'Sorry?' She felt her cheeks colour. She had been thinking about silly things instead of listening.

'Tomorrow. Saint-Gaudens is near Mauzac, we'll leave tomorrow.'

When they had finished eating and the dishes had been cleared, Thomas and Auguste spread a map of France across the table. 'Saint-Gaudens, where the Gestapo prison was, looks big enough to have at least one hotel where we can stay,' Thomas said.

Auguste leaned over the table and studied the map. 'The

other places around are no more than hamlets.' He gave a short sharp whistle. 'It is a nine-hour drive to Mauzac, maybe longer, and then another half an hour along country roads to Saint-Gaudens.'

'It's a heck of a drive. Are you sure it wouldn't be better if we went by train?' Claire asked, when she and Antoinette brought in the coffee. She put the tray down on a side table and looked over Thomas's shoulder. 'Look! Périgueux,' she said, scrutinising the map, 'that's where Mitch was taken first. Would it be possible to go to Périgueux and then to Mauzac by train?'

'Anything is possible. But I thought we were hoping to follow the route Alain took when he escaped from the prison at Saint-Gaudens. What would we do if one of the small towns, or a village at the foot of the Pyrenees, didn't have a railway station?'

Claire frowned. She hadn't thought the travel arrangements through properly. 'Mm... In that case, we'll drive down to south-western France. We'll take it in turn to drive.' Thomas raised his eyebrows in surprise. 'I drive every day in England. I've driven in Canada, too,' she said, which was true. She had driven in Canada once.

'It was on a busy three-lane freeway.' She waited for Thomas to show signs of being impressed. He didn't, so she carried on. 'We will take regular breaks. Vierzon, or Châteauroux, and again at Limoges, Montaurban, or Cahors,' she said, pointing to towns on the map that they would be driving through.

'To get to the prison at Périgueux it will take six hours, maybe longer, then it will take another four hours at least to get to Mauzac,' Thomas said, with doubt in his voice.

'We won't go to Périgueux, then,' Claire said. 'He wasn't there long before they moved him to the prison at Saint-Gaudens. It's who he knew while he was there and what happened after he escaped that we're interested in.'

While they drank their coffee they discussed the journey. Thomas and Auguste found the quickest route to Mauzac, and because Auguste and Antoinette had been to the Pyrenees on holiday they were able to recommend good cafés and restaurants where Claire and Thomas could stop and eat to break their journey. They also knew a couple of hotels where they could stay overnight if necessary.

Thomas needed to fill up the car with petrol and left the Marron house promising to be back the following morning at six o'clock. Claire walked him to the door. Before he left she took twenty francs from her pocket. 'For the petrol,' she said. But Thomas refused to take her money.

'Keep your money,' Thomas said, 'we don't know how much this jaunt will cost altogether.' Before Claire had time to protest Thomas was out the door and halfway down the steps. Waving him goodbye, Claire returned the money to her purse.

'Thomas wouldn't let me pay for the petrol, or even make a contribution towards it. I can't let him spend his money on me,' Claire confided to Antoinette.

'He was being chivalrous. Give it to him when the two of you are on the road. He'll take it then.'

Refusing a nightcap, Claire asked her friends to excuse her. She felt tired and wanted an early night. She also wanted to pack her suitcase for the morning. She took a plate of sandwiches up to her room, put it on the bedside table, and looked through the wardrobe. The weather forecast on the wireless earlier said France should prepare for a big freeze. So, as she had no idea how long she'd be away, or how many changes of clothes she'd need, she packed everything she had brought with her from England.

When she had finished she sat on the bed and contemplated the coming days. The nerves on the top of her stomach tightened every time she considered what might lie ahead. And when she thought about Mitch with another woman her heart hammered in her chest. She nibbled the corner of a sandwich she didn't want and put it back on the plate.

Taking off her clothes Claire put on her nightgown and crawled into bed. She lay on her side and closed her eyes but couldn't sleep. She turned over and lay on her back. She stared at the ceiling, terrified of what the next days or weeks might bring.

After being on the road for three hours, Claire and Thomas stopped for refreshments. Claire used the lavatory and tidied her hair before joining Thomas in the small restaurant. 'I was surprised when Antoinette told me you were a lecturer at the university,' Claire said.

Thomas lifted his head from reading the menu and a curl of unruly hair fell onto his forehead. He pushed the offending lock back into place. 'Why?'

'I had you down to become a politician after the war.'

Thomas sat back in his seat; a look of astonishment on his face. 'I am far too honest to be a politician,' he said. 'Besides, I can do more good teaching fresh young minds that are eager to learn than I can trying to influence old men and women to change their outdated ideas. And, don't forget, my field is *history* and politics. My students are fascinated with the Seventeenth Century, the history and the difference in the parliamentary set-up then, compared to today. Most of the politicians I've met don't remember half of the political history they learned when they were young, and they don't want to remember the recent stuff.'

The conversation was interrupted by the waiter who put a dish of olives and one of bread on the table. 'Would you like wine, monsieur?'

'Do you have a decent wine of the region?'

'Yes, a very good red wine.' The waiter beckoned to a

younger version of himself who arrived with an unlabelled bottle, poured a thumb measure into a wine glass and gave it to Thomas to try. He inhaled its bouquet, took a sip, and nodded his approval.

The waiter motioned to his junior to fill both glasses. 'Are you ready to order, monsieur?' the waiter asked.

Thomas looked at Claire. 'I'd like sausage,' she said, looking down the list of sausage meals. '*Boudin Blanc*, please, with mashed potatoes.'

The waiter nodded and turned to Thomas. '*Carbonnade*. And bring more bread, will you? The best part of beef stew and onions is mopping up the ale-gravy with newly baked bread.'

Claire ate some bread and potato, but her stomach was home to an army of sleeping butterflies that woke up every time she swallowed, making her feel nauseous. Putting down her knife and fork, she watched the handsome ex-Maquis fighter with long hair mop up the beer-gravy he loved so much. When he had cleaned the plate the waiter arrived, topped up their wine glasses and cleared the dirty crockery.

Thomas raised his glass, 'To you,' he said, looking into Claire's eyes.

Claire lifted her glass. 'Thank you, Thomas.' She felt her cheeks colour. It was warm in the small restaurant. She'd also had too much wine. 'I appreciate everything you have done, are doing, for me.'

Thomas waved the compliment away, swished the last of his wine around in the glass and drank it down. 'We should go,' he said, 'we have a long journey ahead of us.'

'What is the matter, Thomas?' He didn't answer. 'Something is bothering you,' Claire said, 'please, tell me what it is?'

'You will not find what you are looking for in the prison.'

'I know. But I need to see the place. I need to see where Mitch, Alain, was. And if he did have... get close to Simone in there, I want to try to understand.'

'And if Simone is a woman in the village who Alain had an affair with while he was laid up and unable to travel?'

'I shall try to understand that too. But we won't know until we find the doctor who took the bullets out of his leg, and the only way to find him is to go to the prison and follow the escape route.'

'*If* we can find the prison,' Thomas said, with sensitivity. 'Many of the prisons the Germans commandeered were in remote areas.' He put up his hand and beckoned the waiter who brought the bill on a small tray. Thomas replaced the bill with ten francs and put his hand up again to say he didn't want change. Claire made a mental note to add half the cost of the meal to that of the petrol and the other food and drink that Thomas had already paid for.

EIGHTEEN

A fierce wind drove spikes of ice and rain into the faces of Claire and Thomas as they stood at the barbed wire fence and stared with horror at what was left of the prison. Rusting railway tracks that had transported trainloads of prisoners, some of whom would never return home, were distorted and twisted, and the lookout towers, half covered with blackened snow, lay bent and broken where they had fallen when they were pulled down. The only buildings still standing were brick-built: the hospital and a round windowless building with a chimney on the top.

Most of the huts that had housed the prisoners – part corrugated metal and part wood – were without roofs. Claire gasped in horror. Neither the wavy metal or the flimsy wood that remained was thicker than hardboard. The walls were so thin that they wouldn't have given any shelter. With her gloved fingers like claws, forced between the rectangular shapes of wire, Claire seized the fence and shook it as she wept at the sight before her.

Physically and emotionally exhausted, her knees buckled

and she slid to the ground, her fingers still hooked in the woven steel and her face pressed against the rusting wire. Thomas crouched down beside her. 'It is time we left,' he shouted, his voice drowned out by the howling wind. He pointed to the gunpowder grey sky. 'It will soon be dark.' He took the scarf from his neck and wrapped it around the lower part of Claire's face before pulling her to her feet.

Overcome by the horror of what she had seen, Claire stumbled. Thomas caught her and with his arms wrapped around her, he walked her back to the car. Before getting in, she looked back. Out of an angry and malevolent sky a curtain of sleet and hail thrashed down, pounding and battering what remained of the horrific Gestapo prison.

Thomas opened the passenger door and pushed Claire into the car. The wind buffeted the car and hail hammered noisily on the roof and windscreen, making it impossible to hear what each other was saying or to see anything other than balls of ice building up in the corners of the windows.

Claire stared open-mouthed as a white shroud of hail covered the windscreen, blocking out what was left of the daylight. The car's interior became eerily dark and Claire began to panic. She turned to open the door, but Thomas grabbed her and pulled her to him.

'The noise!' Claire shouted, through chattering teeth. In a fit of anxiety, she forced her hands free of Thomas's hold, pressed them against her ears and buried her face between the lapels of his coat.

When the storm ended, sleet and rain melted the hail leaving the windscreen relatively clear. Straining to see through the rivulets of icy rain running down the windows, Claire watched the sky brighten.

Taking his arm from around her, Thomas lifted Claire's chin and looked into her eyes. For a moment she thought he was going to kiss her. Instead, he whispered, 'Breathe...' Claire looked at him and nodded. She suddenly realised she'd been holding her breath. After inhaling and exhaling several times, slowly, she felt calmer.

Thomas started the car. 'What are you doing?' Claire asked. Ignoring her, Thomas put his foot on the accelerator and the engine roared into life. 'We can't go,' Claire said, 'not while it's still daylight. We haven't found the escape route. Thomas, please,' she begged, 'we can't go yet.'

'We can go and we will!' He put the car in reverse gear, spun the steering wheel and turned to look out of the back window. 'You are soaked to the skin,' he said angrily, 'we both are!' Claire wiped the cuff of her coat across her face, transferring mud to her cheek. 'You'll catch your death of pneumonia,' he shouted, 'and then you won't be any good to your husband, or to anyone else!'

Claire slumped down in her seat, dejected. She looked out of the passenger window and watched the leafless trees around the desolate prison fade into the distance.

Hôtel Garonne, on the outskirts of Saint-Gaudens on the Garonne River, was once a private chateau, which had turned into a hotel between the wars. Thomas carried in the suitcases and asked for two single rooms.

From the outside the hotel had the red-brick charm of buildings in Toulouse. On the inside the décor was tired and the woman behind the reception desk looked as if she had something unpleasant stuck to her top lip. She clicked her fingers at a lad dressed in an ill-fitting bellboy's uniform standing like a statue at the bottom of the sweep of stairs. He jumped and ran over to the desk. The woman behind it glared at him. 'How long will you be staying, monsieur?' she asked, looking at Thomas from beneath hooded eyelids.

Thomas raised his eyebrows in question at Claire. Still

annoyed with him for insisting they left the prison without looking for the escape route that Alain had told her about, Claire shrugged her shoulders. 'One, possibly two nights, madame. We are not sure how long we will be staying in Saint-Gaudens.'

'In that case, I will need a deposit to hold your rooms after tonight. It will be fifteen francs monsieur,' she said, leaning over the reception desk and looking with distaste at the floor where Claire dripped water on the cheap carpet. 'Each!'

'It is raining, madame!' Claire said, her voice clipped with sarcasm.

'Then it is a good job there is a fire in your room so you can dry your coat,' the receptionist countered. Turning her attention back to Thomas, the woman reeled off a list of hotel rules: 'Dinner is at seven. Do not be late. The kitchen stops serving at eight. The dining room closes at nine. The bar, which is for residents only, closes at eleven.' The sour-faced receptionist handed Thomas the keys to both rooms and turned to the bellboy. 'Rooms seven and eight.'

Claire and Thomas followed the boy up the thinly carpeted stairs to the first floor. Outside room seven the boy put down Claire's case. 'Do you want to look at the other room?' Thomas asked. 'It might be—'

'This one will be fine.' Claire shivered. 'As long as there is a fire?' She directed the question to the bellboy who nodded. Taking the key from Thomas, Claire unlocked the door.

'If you feel like a drink, I shall be in the bar from...' he looked at his watch, 'six thirty.'

'I might join you; I'll see how I feel. If I don't, I'll see you in the dining room at seven.' The bellboy followed her into the room and set her suitcase down by the wardrobe. 'If you need anything, madame, anything at all,' he said, with a glint in his eye, 'ring down to reception. Madame la propriétaire will be happy to help you.' He pointed to a telephone on the dressing table. 'Pick up the receiver, there is no number to dial, and you will get through to reception and Madame's cheerful voice.'

'Thank you,' Claire said. Taking a couple of coins from her purse she gave them to the lad. 'I'll make sure I need something while I'm staying here,' she said and laughed. The bellboy laughed with her, touched his cap and left, closing the door.

The room was small. Besides a single bed, there was a narrow wardrobe, small window, and a desk-cum-dressing table on one side of the room. On the other side was the fire and a wash basin, with a towel hanging from it. Claire was tempted to hide the towel and ring down to reception and ask the miserable woman to bring a towel up, but the woman would probably keep her waiting, and she needed it to dry herself now.

Claire took off her wet clothes and hung them on the picture rail at the side of the fire to dry. After towelling her arms and legs, she put on her dressing gown and knelt in front of the fire to dry her hair. Feeling warm at last, Claire sat back on her heels and gazed into the flames. She watched as they licked the underside of each lump of coal turning one after the other red as each caught alight. She leaned back, rested her head on the foot of the bed, and closed her eyes.

A knock on the door woke her from a light sleep. Her stomach lurched as she got to her feet. She held her breath and without making a sound, crept to the door. Damn! It wasn't locked. She pulled her dressing gown tightly around her waist, knotted the belt and put her ear against the wood. There was a second knock followed by, 'Room service, madame.'

Claire recognised the bellboy's voice and exhaled with relief. Quickly returning to the side of the fire she shouted, 'Come in.'

'Monsieur Durand thought you would like coffee, madame,' the bellboy said, treating Claire to a cheeky grin. A Jack of all trades as far as the hotel was concerned, Claire thought, and smiled back at him. 'Monsieur Durand took my advice and telephoned reception for it.' He grinned again. 'Madame la propriétaire had dropped off in her chair in the office and when the telephone rang, almost jumped out of her skin.' The lad giggled. 'She was not happy,' he said, crossing the room and putting the tray on the dressing table.

Claire laughed. 'Is Monsieur Durand having coffee?'

'Yes, madame, I'm about to take it in.'

'Thank him for me, will you? And tell him I'll see him downstairs in the bar at six thirty.'

When the boy left, Claire turned the key in the lock. She didn't think military intelligence would have had time to catch up with her. All the same, it was careless of her to leave the door unlocked, especially as she had fallen asleep. She took her diary and a pen from her handbag and sat cross-legged on the floor in front of the fire with her coffee. She recalled the events of the day, jotting down the places they had stopped to put fuel in the car, writing down the cost next to the name of each petrol station. The last entry was the hotel. Two rooms for one night, possibly two nights if they didn't find the doctor who had looked after Mitch tomorrow.

Replacing the diary in her handbag, Claire got up and closed the curtains. She took off her dressing gown. Turning to throw it on the bed she caught sight of herself in the mirror. She looked thin. She had lost weight while she was in Canada, which she hadn't minded because she had been a few pounds overweight when she went out there. She hadn't eaten as much as she would normally have done at Christmas either. She'd had hardly any treats, she had been too worried about Mitch to bother with candied fruit or chocolate.

Thinking about it, Claire had hardly eaten since she got back to Oxford. She stared at herself in the mirror and

grimaced. Loose flesh at the top of her arms and legs made her
look skinny. Antoinette had noticed she'd lost weight, she had
said as much. Claire laughed. 'That's why she fed me up while I
was in Paris,' she said aloud.

She put the plug in the basin and filled it with hot water. As
she washed, she decided she needed to eat to keep up her
strength. She would start eating properly tonight – if she could
get the image of the prison out of her mind.

Claire felt the coat and the hem of the skirt she'd worn in
the afternoon's downpour. Neither were dry. Give them a few
hours more, she thought. The clothes were relatively clean, they
were just wet. Tomorrow she would ask the delightful Madame
la propriétaire if she could borrow an iron.

Claire crossed the room and opened her suitcase. The
outside of the case was damp, but the clothes inside were dry,
they just felt cold. Tonight she would put on something smart to
go down to dinner. Apart from a blue silk dress, which she had
brought in case she went anywhere where she needed to dress
up, she had packed mostly thick, serviceable clothes; skirts and
jumpers to keep her warm, which she laid on the bed.

She took out a navy-blue tailored skirt and a pale blue twin-
set and hung them on the outside of the wardrobe. The only
other outfit suitable for dinner in a hotel that wasn't creased
from being in the suitcase all day was a tailored suit in a tweedy
mix of green, blue and mauve. She wore the jacket in the
daytime, and a fine mauve cardigan in the evening. She hung up
the dress, skirts and the jacket, folded her underwear, cardigan
and jumpers and placed them on the shelves in the wardrobe,
leaving the door open so the heat from the fire, that had already
taken the chill off the small room would drift across to the
wardrobe and air them.

She quickly dressed and combed her hair. Pushing a few
stray curls into place she trapped them beneath a Kirby grip.

Slipping her feet into her shoes, Claire picked up her handbag and looked over her shoulder, taking a last look in the mirror. Her face was pale with dark rings under her eyes. She looked as if she hadn't slept for a month. She blew out her cheeks and took her make-up out of her bag. After applying powder, rouge and lipstick she looked better – and she felt better.

NINETEEN

The bar was busy when she arrived at six thirty. Thomas was hunched over a newspaper in the corner of the room. As she approached him he jumped up, folded the paper and dropped it onto the table. 'What would you like to drink?'

She was about to ask him what he was drinking but saw a glass of beer on the table. She didn't feel like beer. It was too cold. 'Wine,' she said, 'red, please.'

Thomas strolled over to the bar. After a short conversation with the bartender, which Claire wasn't able to hear, he came back with a glass of wine. 'The barman said this is a good local wine. He told me that it is medium bodied and a little fruity – and then he winked at me.' Thomas put Claire's wine on the table and sat down. 'Make of that what you will,' he said, laughing.

Claire took a sip of the wine. 'Mm, it is fruity,' she said, and laughed too.

When Claire and Thomas were sure they would not be overheard by any of the hotel's guests, they made plans for the following day.

'So,' Claire said with a shiver, 'we go back to that horrific prison.'

'No, we don't.'

'But we must! How else will we find out how Mitch escaped and which village he was taken to?'

Thomas put his hand on Claire's hand. She flinched and he withdrew it immediately. 'I'm sorry, I didn't mean to– '

'No. It's me who should be sorry. I'm a bit on edge. Go on?'

'We do not have to go back to the prison,' Thomas said. Taking a map of the area from his pocket, he spread it out on the table as any tourist visiting the town might do. 'The escape route must be on the south or southeast boundary of the prison grounds. Somewhere around here there is a wood,' he said, pointing to an area on the map that was green. 'They couldn't have escaped to the north or west. If I remember correctly the two main lookout towers were on the northern perimeter and la Garonne runs along the western fence.' Thomas pointed to the blue meandering line of the river.

'I can see that,' Claire said. 'They would have been target practice; picked off one by one if they had tried to cross the river.' Thomas moved his finger north. 'Why risk trying to get past two watchtowers without being seen, and then have to climb a mountain when you could hide in undergrowth in a forest of fir trees a little further south, which is on an incline?'

'But they were seen,' Claire said. 'Mitch was shot. So, they might have gone north to the mountain,' she reasoned.

Thomas shook his head. 'No. I spent a year training with a Maquis group in the mountains. Not in this region, in the Alps at Chamonix. You have to be fit to climb a rock face like the one near the prison. They couldn't have done it, they would have been too weak. Besides, if they were hoping to cross the Pyrenees to Spain...' Thomas pointed to the Spanish border on the other side of the mountains, 'they would have to end up around here.' He drew his finger back across the map to France. 'That would be the shortest and the quickest route.'

'But not the safest,' Claire said. Her heart was beating fast. 'And this area,' she said, indicating with her finger to a clearing on the far side of the wood, 'would be a perfect place for a sniper to wait and shoot the escapees.'

'Yes, it would.' Thomas folded the map and slipped it into the inside pocket of his jacket. 'The good news is, there are a couple of villages within walking distance, so we could start at the edge of the wood, at the clearing, and from there go to the first village.'

Before Claire could respond a crowd of youths crashed through the door. The last one let the door slam behind him. Claire jumped and spun round. With the horrors of the prison still in her thoughts her nerves were on edge.

'Time for dinner,' Thomas said, getting to his feet. He stood behind Claire and when she stood up, pulled her chair away to give her space to step away from the table. He gestured to her to walk in front of him. Instead, she offered him her arm. When he drew level with her, Claire linked her arm through his and together the two friends strolled into the dining room.

There was a choice of three main dishes, beef, chicken and fish with seasonal vegetables – and apple cake for dessert. Thomas chose beef and Claire chicken; they both said yes to apple cake. The food was tasty and there was plenty of it. Neither of them had eaten for several hours and they both cleared their plates. After dessert, they sat for a while and drank coffee. Refusing a refill, they left the dining room and went back to the bar.

A roaring log fire in a large red-brick fireplace attracted Claire and she headed for the nearest table to it, while Thomas ordered their drinks.

'I'm sorry,' Claire said, when Thomas returned with two glasses of brandy, putting one in front of Claire and taking a drink from the other. 'You were right. The weather was too bad today, and it was too late to start looking for the escape route.'

'I understand why you wanted to go on,' Thomas said, smiling. He lifted his glass. 'Here's to a good night's sleep and finding the route out of the prison tomorrow!'

'Tomorrow,' she said, and took a drink.

Fingers of ice seized Claire's heart as the memory of the prison came into her mind. Like the pull of a magnet, the feeling that she must return there was luring her. She craned her neck and looked out of the window to get a glimpse of the prison, which lay beyond the trees to the right. Thomas turned the car in the opposite direction. He steered it off the road, down a narrow lane that ended on the south side of the wood and turned off the engine. 'We have to go on foot from here.' He pointed to a clump of small spruces. 'We'll enter by those saplings and walk straight ahead until we find the path. Then we'll follow it down to the clearing.'

'Listen?' Claire said, getting out of the car. 'Can you hear that?'

'No,' Thomas whispered, 'what is it?'

'Nothing. There is no sound at all. Yesterday at the prison, the noise the storm made was so loud we couldn't hear ourselves speak. But now?' Claire fell silent and strained her ears. 'Not even birdsong. This place is as quiet as the grave. There is not even the sound of the breeze in the trees.'

In the eerie stillness, Claire followed Thomas into the wood. The saplings on the edge allowed daylight to filter through for a few yards, but further in, the fully-grown firs were so tall that, with the winter sun low in the sky, only the tops of the tallest trees would see daylight.

Claire stumbled. Thomas stopped and turned round. 'Are you all right?'

'Yes. My eyes haven't fully adjusted to the darkness but go on, I'll be fine.'

'Take this.' Thomas took a torch from his rucksack, switched it on and gave it to Claire. They had only taken a further half a dozen steps when Thomas stopped and took the torch back. 'I think this is it,' he said, shining the beam of light across a patch of barren earth in a small clearing. 'Come,' he said, taking Claire's hand. 'Stand here. Can you feel the ground is hard?'

'Yes.' Claire scraped the sole of her shoe from side to side, disturbing a thin layer of moss. Excited, she took a couple of steps and stopped. 'The ground here is slightly raised and is soft under my feet.' Taking smaller steps, she followed Thomas along a sloping path and within a short distance she saw rays of light flickering through the trees. They were near the edge of the wood.

With fewer trees there was more light. They could see where they were going but with every step the gradient of the path became steeper. Putting out her hands and holding on to the trunk of each tree as she came to it, Claire was able to defy gravity and stay upright. Thomas was not so careful and when the path suddenly dipped his strides turned into short staggering steps. The momentum of the downward slant pulled him forward, he lost his balance, and went hurtling down the mossy path on his backside.

'Stay where you are!' Thomas shouted when Claire reached the edge of the wood. 'Can you see me?'

'Yes.'

'If you were a sniper, you wouldn't have to find any higher ground than where you are standing now, would you?'

'No.' Claire raised an imaginary rifle, her left arm and hand the barrel, the butt against her right shoulder and her right elbow crooked. She curled her right forefinger loosely around the imaginary trigger, and with Thomas in her sights, she tightened it. 'Click!'

With no trees to hang on to, Claire slipped and stumbled and, on her hands and knees, slid down the path stopping only when she reached level ground. 'Thomas?' she looked around. There was no sign of him. 'Thomas?' she shouted. 'Where are you?'

'Here,' he said, scrambling out of a ditch. 'That's what Alain did, didn't he? He rolled into a ditch and stayed there until the Germans stopped looking for him?'

Claire nodded. She looked up at the trees. 'The sniper wasn't lying in wait after all. He followed them from the prison.'

'That's what it looks like. Alain took a bullet because he was the last man down the hill from the wood. A few seconds later and he would have been away.'

The clearing was littered with chunks of the mountain that had broken off or been worn away over the years by the weather. Claire hobbled over to a large rock and sat down.

'Have you hurt your ankle?'

'No. It's mud.' She lifted her foot. 'It's so caked on it's difficult to walk properly that's all.' She picked up a stick and began digging out clods of mud from between the ridges of tread on the soles of her boots. 'Ouch!' She threw the stick away and lifted her hands. The ends of the fingers and the palms of her gloves were ripped to shreds, and her hands were bleeding.

'What about you?' Claire looked up at the steep bank that they'd slid down, and then back at Thomas. 'Did you hurt your bottom?' she asked, trying not to laugh.

'What?'

'You said you had trained in the Alps, and...' Claire began to laugh. 'You looked so funny flying down the bank on your rear end.'

Thomas stood up and put both hands on his backside. 'It is muddy. Other than that, my bottom is fine, thank you. So unless you wish to be left here, I advise you to stop laughing.'

'I'm sorry,' Claire said, putting on a serious face. She

couldn't keep it up and burst into laughter. 'Come on, you have to admit it was funny. The way you—' She couldn't get the words out for laughing.

Thomas strode over to her and pretending to be angry, grabbed the lapels of her coat and pulled her up until her face was level with his. Looking into his eyes, Claire saw the feigned look of anger change to a caring smile. She could feel his warm breath on her cheeks and her heart began to pound. 'I'm sorry,' he said, letting her go.

'It's all right.'

'I didn't mean to...'

'No. Of course not.' Claire backed away. With her heart still pounding she looked around. 'So,' she said, 'where do we go from here?'

'Not back up that damn mud bank,' Thomas said, 'and not that way.' He pointed in the direction of the car. He took the map from his pocket. 'If we went south we would eventually come across the trail to Spain, over the Pyrenees.'

'Which we know Alain didn't take.'

'Right! So, it must be east,' Thomas said. He rummaged around in his overcoat pockets and then pushed his hand into the inside of his coat. 'Got it.' With a stub of pencil, he drew a circle on the map. 'There are two villages nearby. One,' he said, leaning towards Claire so she could see the map, 'is just over that hill.' She closed her eyes and pressed her lips together making them a thin line, to stop herself from laughing again. Thomas sighed and nudged her, taking her by surprise, and she almost lost her balance. Ignoring her, he continued. 'The only other village within *carrying a body distance* is on this road.' He pointed to a wide straight line leading to a jumble of smaller lines that represented country roads leading to clusters of dwellings.

'I think we should try the nearest village first. Alain didn't remember much about it when he got home, but he said it was more like a village than a town.'

Thomas turned the map sideways and squinted. 'St. Emile it is then. Ready?'

Claire took a deep breath. 'Ready!'

TWENTY

It was a church that first came into view, and then the building next to it, which Claire assumed was the vicarage. There were probably two dozen houses altogether, built in a semi-circle around a pond. On the walk up to the church they passed a school on the left and a grocery shop and doctor's surgery on the right. Claire nudged Thomas and nodded towards the surgery. 'Do you think it could be that doctor who helped Alain?'

'Possibly. They wouldn't have two doctors in a village this size, would they?' Claire lifted her shoulders as if to say she didn't know. 'You are sure Alain didn't tell you the name of the doctor?'

'Positive. You know yourself names were never exchanged. It was safer not to know someone's name, then you couldn't tell the Bosch if you were arrested. What you didn't know, they couldn't beat out of you.'

'I know. I just wondered if he met the woman—'

'Simone!' Claire said. 'You can say her name.'

'If she was in the Resistance, or the daughter of the doctor – and not in the prison with Alain – she might still be around.'

'Well we'll soon find out,' Claire said. 'There's a woman coming out of the church. I'll ask her.'

Thomas took hold of Claire's arm. 'Wait!' he said, stopping her abruptly. 'What exactly are you going to ask her?'

'If she knows of a doctor in the village who helped an injured Canadian airman after he'd escaped from the Gestapo prison who might, or might not, have a daughter named Simone.'

Thomas shook his head. 'Leave Simone out of it. If she is the daughter of the doctor and she was working for the Germans, chances are the doctor was working for them too.'

'If that was the case, the doctor wouldn't have saved Alain's life. Think about it.'

'Doctors take an oath to save lives, whatever the nationality,' Thomas argued. 'But never mind about that. I just don't think we should say anything about Alain, the prison or Simone until we've met the doctor and got the measure of him.'

'And how are we going to do that?'

'Your hands are cut, aren't they?'

'Scratched.' Claire took off her gloves and turned her hands palms up.

'Good God! They are more than scratched,' Thomas said, surprised to see the skin on Claire's hands torn and bleeding. 'You really should see a doctor. You need to get them cleaned and dressed or they'll become infected.'

'They look worse than they are, but you're right, they do need cleaning, and they will get us into the surgery.'

Thomas rang the bell and stepped back so he was standing next to Claire. The door opened after a few minutes and a young woman in a white nurse's uniform invited them into the surgery's waiting room.

'As this is your first visit to Doctor D'Aramitz I need to take down a few details. We'll start with your name?' the nurse said, her pen poised above a large notepad.

'Therese Belland, Mrs.'

'And your address?'

Claire had been trained by the SOE to give an address, any address, as long as it wasn't her own. But that was in the war. It was peacetime now. A dozen reasons why she still shouldn't tell this girl the truth crowded into her mind. She could hardly say Oxford, England. Should she give Édith or André and Therese's address? Perhaps it would be better to give a false address ...?

'We are staying in Saint-Gaudens,' Thomas said. 'We are only visiting the area, so it might be best to give you our address in Paris?' The nurse nodded and Thomas gave her his address, but with the wrong house number and saying road instead of avenue.

'Thank you. If you would like to take a seat I will see if Doctor D'Aramitz can see you,' she said, leaving the waiting room.

Claire sat down and exhaled loudly. 'She made me feel uncomfortable, nervous.'

'She was just being efficient. I don't suppose they see many new patients, especially visitors from Paris.'

'Doctor D'Aramitz will see you now.' The nurse stood at the doctor's door like a soldier on sentry duty.

Claire smiled her thanks as she passed her and entered the surgery. Thomas followed Claire and the nurse followed him. Closing the door, the nurse took up her position at the doctor's side. It was obvious the moment Claire saw the doctor that it could not have been him who took the bullets out Mitch's leg in 1944. He would have been too young.

He lifted up his head after reading the few lines of information about his new patient. 'Good afternoon, Madame Belland. What can I do for you?' Claire showed him her hands. 'Goodness, those cuts look nasty,' he said, taking her hands in his and inspecting them. 'We'll need to wash them first, so we can see to remove any splinters or grit.' He turned to the nurse. 'Would you prepare a sterile bowl, please, Nurse? Three parts warm water to one-part antiseptic solution.'

The nurse nodded, walked briskly to a small cupboard labelled Poisons, took out a bottle with skull and crossbones on it and a measuring jug. She took both to the sink, turned on the taps and, after carefully measuring water and solution into the bowl, she placed it on the table.

'Thank you, Nurse.'

'Doctor!' she said and left.

Taking Claire's hands, the doctor lowered them into the warm water. 'Ouch! That stings.'

'Yes, the antiseptic solution is strong. But it needs to be. The soil up at the old prison is polluted with toxins. Except for the entrance the Germans used, the guards regularly sprayed the camp's boundary with an extremely toxic unknown poison. At least,' he corrected, 'it was unknown to us. They must have been tipped off that the allies were about to liberate the camp because before they arrived the Germans buried barrels of it in the woods. As they rusted they began to leak. The filthy stuff was stored behind the camp's hospital and laboratory, too. It will take decades before the ground up there is safe.'

'Were you not able to have samples analysed?' Thomas asked.

'Yes, and some of the substances we found up there were known to us. Many others we had never heard of and most of the stuff we knew was illegal; banned by the French medical profession in this part of the world. Some of the substances we identified are so toxic that if they get into your bloodstream they will kill you.'

A wave of nausea swept over Claire. 'There couldn't be enough poison in my bloodstream to kill me from this number of shallow scratches could there, Doctor D'Aramitz?' Claire's heart was thumping against her breastbone.

'No, but don't go up there again,' the doctor warned.

Claire shot Thomas a look of panic. He had hardly contributed to the conversation. She knew what he was doing. He was watching and listening, to get the measure of the doctor. But it was now time to join in the conversation. She raised her eyebrows.

Thomas took the cue. 'How did you know we had been to the prison, Doctor?'

'This is a small community, monsieur. When strangers come into the area, neighbour tells neighbour until everyone knows.' The doctor lifted Claire's right hand out of the bowl, dried it on a soft cloth and took a pair of tweezers from a black leather case. 'Did you know someone who was in the prison?' the doctor asked as he took splinters of wood and chips of stone from Claire's palms.

Thomas nodded to Claire that she should answer. 'Yes, my husband,' she said.

'Was he killed in the prison?'

'No, he and several other prisoners escaped. My husband was shot in the leg and was found by some local people. They might have been Resistance members. My husband didn't know. He was unconscious at the time and later, in case he was captured again by the Gestapo, he wasn't told. Anyway, the men took him to a village where an elderly doctor operated on him and saved his leg. The doctor hid my husband until he was fit enough to travel, by which time the Gestapo had stopped looking for him. Via a network of local people, he was taken to Paris, and then brought home to me.'

'The Canadian.'

'Yes. Did you know him?'

'I knew of him. I was in Switzerland training to be a doctor at the time. I wasn't allowed to come home for the holidays. Grandfather said it was too dangerous. Much later I learned that my grandfather had treated a Canadian officer who had escaped from the prison.'

Claire's pulse quickened with excitement. 'Could we meet your grandfather?' she asked.

'There!' Doctor D'Aramitz said, dabbing iodine on the cuts that remained on Claire's palms. 'All clean. The grit and splinters are gone.'

'Doctor?'

'My grandfather is old,' he said, looking up into Claire's face. 'He lost many loved ones in the war, more than most people around here, as I did,' the doctor said, as much to himself as to Claire and Thomas. 'And he is not in good health. He hasn't been for some time. I fear to drag up the past and the pain it holds would be too much for him.

'Keep your hands dry. Don't wash them more than you have to for a day or two, and the cuts will heal.'

'Thank you,' Claire said, 'how much do I owe you?'

'Nothing. Just promise me that you will not go to the prison again.'

'I won't. I have no need to return there.'

The doctor picked up the wet cloth, swabs, and bowl and took them over to the sink. He poured the solution away, dropped the towel in one basket, the bloodstained swabs in another, turned on the hot water tap, and began scrubbing his hands.

Claire looked at Thomas and putting her hands together, as if in prayer, she mouthed *Say something, please.*

'Madame Belland was hoping to find information about a woman who might have been in the prison at the same time as her husband. But the only buildings still standing have been gutted and by the look of them set on fire. I guess personnel records, if there were any left after the prison was liberated, perished when the buildings were burned,' Thomas said. The doctor continued washing his hands and didn't reply.

'My husband has been accused of being a traitor, Doctor, of spying on his fellow officers and reporting to a woman who it is thought was also in the prison, and who his superiors believe worked for the Germans. He is now missing. There are men looking for him. Your grandfather saved my husband's life once,' Claire cried, 'he may know something that could save his life again.'

The doctor called the nurse, who straight away bustled into the room. 'I have to go out, Annette. Anything urgent, telephone me, I shall be at home. Otherwise, ask patients to come back this evening or tomorrow morning.' He turned to Claire and Thomas. 'Come with me.'

Thomas picked up his rucksack from the floor, and Claire grabbed her filthy gloves and threw them into the medical waste basket before following the doctor out of the building and into the street.

'Where are you taking us?' Claire asked, catching up with the doctor.

'To see my grandfather,' he said, without slowing down.

TWENTY-ONE

'Grandfather, these people would like to speak to you,' Doctor D'Aramitz said.

Hauling himself out of his armchair, the old man stood up. With the aid of a walking stick he hobbled across the room to meet them.

'Thomas Durand, sir.' Thomas offered his hand.

'I am pleased to meet you,' the old gentleman said, shaking Thomas's hand. He turned to Claire.

'Therese— Belland—' Claire faltered. She had lied to the man who saved her husband's life. She looked into his rheumy eyes. There was a deep sadness there. He smiled kindly and put out his hand. 'How do you do, Doctor?'

'How do you do, my dear.' He took Claire's hand. 'I am retired now,' he said, looking at his grandson with pride. 'Let us dispense with the title. My name is Lucien, Lucien Puel. What can I do for you?'

Claire snatched her hand away from the old man. The ground shifted beneath her feet. She raised her hand to ward Lucien Puel off, but he smiled and took hold of her hand again. She quickly withdrew it for the second time. 'I— we must go,' she stuttered. 'I— Thomas,' she said, 'need to get out—'

Thomas took Claire's arm and walked her to the door. 'Thank you for your time, sir,' he said to Lucien Puel.

Doctor D'Aramitz opened the door, but before Thomas and Claire could pass through it, Claire collapsed.

Between them, the two younger men picked Claire up, carried her across the room, and lowered her onto a chaise longue. 'Give her air,' Doctor D'Aramitz said. Thomas stepped aside and the doctor took Claire's pulse. 'She'll be fine. She has only fainted. I'll get her a glass of water.'

'When was the last time she ate?' Lucien Puel asked Thomas.

He thought for a moment. 'We haven't eaten since break-fast.' He looked at his wristwatch and grimaced. 'Eight hours ago.'

'That's why she fainted. Keep an eye on her, I'll be back shortly,' Puel said, leaving the room.

'Claire?' Thomas whispered, kneeling down beside her. He shook her gently by the shoulders and said again, 'Claire?'

She opened her eyes and looked around the room. 'We need to get out of here before he comes back.' She pushed herself up into a sitting position but feeling disorientated slumped back against the headrest of the chaise longue. 'Where is he?' she hissed. 'Where's Puel?'

'I think he might have gone to get you something to eat. His grandson went for water.' Thomas looked over his shoulder at the door. 'They're taking their time,' he said, as an afterthought. Focusing his attention on Claire, he said, 'What was that all about? You looked as if you'd seen a ghost when the old guy told you his name. Who is he?'

'I don't know who he is, but he is *not* Doctor Lucien Puel. Lucien Puel is the Swiss psychiatrist at the Louis Bertrand hospital in Canada who treated Mitch. I don't believe in coincidences, Thomas. There cannot be two doctors called Lucien Puel, can there?'

'Yes, Madame Belland, there can, but there is not.' Claire turned to see Lucien Puel hobbling across the room. He offered Claire a glass of water, which she took without thinking. Then she remembered what Doctor D'Aramitz had said about poisons and didn't drink. 'There was once another Lucien Puel—' A loving smile softened the old man's features and tears filled his eyes.

'Grandfather!' Doctor D'Aramitz had followed his grandfather into the room and now stood next to him. 'You do not owe these people an explanation,' he said. 'You saved Madame Belland's husband's life.' He gave Claire a cold hard stare. 'Is that not enough for you, madame?'

Before Claire could answer, the old man said, 'No my dear, Matthieu, it is not enough.' Leaning heavily on his walking stick, he walked back to the door and tugged on a maroon bell-rope. 'If you trust that my housekeeper will not try to poison you, madame, I would like to invite you and Monsieur Durand to join my grandson and me for refreshments. Then I shall tell you about the other Lucien Puel. What is more, we cannot have you fainting again, can we?'

Claire felt her cheeks colour. Her mouth was dry. She took a drink of water and felt better for it. 'Thank you,' she said, looking at Thomas to make sure he agreed.

'We should both like that, sir,' Thomas said.

Lucien Puel acknowledged their acceptance with a nod. He motioned to the fire and offered Claire his arm. Getting to her feet, she accepted the old man's help and he guided her to a large comfortable looking sofa. When she was seated, he sat in the armchair on the left of the fire, Thomas sat next to Claire and Doctor D'Aramitz took the armchair on the right.

'There are things you wish to know about a woman in the Resistance?' Doctor Puel said. 'And there are things I wish to know about the man in Canada who has my name.' Claire's eyes widened. Did she hear what the old man said correctly? Did he know Simone?

'But first—' He stopped speaking when a plump, rosy-faced middle-aged woman who Claire assumed was the housekeeper and a teenage girl, probably the housekeeper's daughter, entered the room carrying trays with coffee, sandwiches and cakes, which they placed on a long table in front of Claire and Thomas.

When the housekeeper and the girl had left, Doctor D'Aramitz poured coffee for them all and handed round the sandwiches. Claire's stomach was a tangle of nervous knots, but she was ravenous and took two sandwiches. They ate in silence. When Doctor D'Aramitz had finished eating he refilled their coffee cups.

'So, where to begin?' Lucien Puel said, when he had finished. 'Perhaps I should start by telling you that it was my other grandson, also Lucien Puel, who found your husband after he had been shot. And it was Lucien, with two young men from the village, who carried him to this house.'

Claire's eyes brimmed with tears. She rubbed them quickly with the back of her hand. 'Forgive me, Doctor Puel, I am confused. You said there was not another man with your name.'

'And there is not.'

Claire frowned suspiciously. The old doctor was not making sense. He put up his hand. 'Bear with me, madame, and I will explain.' He took a shaky breath. 'I was blessed with two wonderful grandchildren.' He looked at Doctor D'Aramitz with watery eyes.

'Grandfather, you don't have to—'

'Oh, but I do, Matthieu.'

Claire sat back on the sofa and listened to what the old doctor had to say. 'By the time your husband was brought to me he had lost a great deal of blood from gunshot wounds to his legs. I operated and took out two bullets. I did all I could, but I had no way of telling whether it was enough to save your husband's leg, or, more importantly, his life. We had no blood you see, and— Well, you know your husband survived.'

Claire leaned forward, tears falling onto her cheeks, and whispered, 'Thank you.'

A wan smile brushed the old man's face. Closing his eyes, he nodded. 'Eventually, Lucien returned to his education and the Resistance arranged for your husband to be taken to Paris.' Turning to his grandson, he said, 'I think we could all do with a brandy, Matthieu. Would you?'

Doctor D'Aramitz jumped up, fetched a decanter and four glasses from a side cabinet, and poured each of them a generous measure. Fortified by the drink, the old doctor continued. 'When the war ended, the prison you visited yesterday was one of the first the Allies liberated. Our small village being so close to the camp was a dangerous place to be at that time. I had told Matthieu and his cousin Lucien not to return to St Emile, but Lucien... He was young and high-spirited – and he disobeyed me.

'He wrote to his mother saying he was coming home. He said he was excited that he had become a doctor, like his grandfather.' Looking into the mid-distance with sad eyes, the old doctor lifted his glass and drained it. 'On the day he was due to come home, the Allies liberated the camp and somehow Heinrich Beckman, the camp's doctor, escaped.

'When Lucien hadn't arrived by suppertime my neighbours and I went out to look for him.' The old man took a large handkerchief from his trousers pocket and wiped his eyes. 'He was lying in the road, naked but for his vest and pants. He had been beaten so badly he was hardly recognisable. I took off my coat and covered him, and he smiled at me. *He smiled at me!*' the old man roared.

Matthieu jumped up, but his grandfather put up his hand

and he sat down. 'I knelt on the road beside him and cradled him in my arms. "I am a doctor, grandfather," he said. "I am Doctor Lucien Puel." I told him I was proud of him but he should save his strength. He gave me a knowing smile and whispered something. I didn't hear what he said, so I leaned in close, my face next to his, his lips touching my cheek. "Gestapo—Doctor." They were the last words my grandson said.

'We carried him home and laid his broken body on his bed.' The old doctor picked up his glass. 'Would you, Matthieu?' When his grandson had replenished his drink, he carried on. 'There were no papers on him; no identity papers, travel permit, nor the doctor's certificate that he was so proud of. How could there be?

'The next day members of the local Resistance cell searched the woods. They found a half-burned Gestapo uniform and the identity papers of Doctor Heinrich Beckman!' With tears in his eyes, the old doctor looked at Claire. 'And that I am sure is how your doctor in Canada got his name, madame.'

TWENTY-TWO

Shocked by what the old doctor had told her, Claire was unable to speak. She needed to digest what he had said, understand the implications. If what he'd told her was true, and she had no reason to think the old man was lying, the Swiss professor Lucien Puel who had been her husband's psychiatrist was a German Nazi called Heinrich Beckman. She caught her breath. If Mitch had recognised him from the Gestapo prison at Saint-Gaudens it would have been reason enough for Beckman to write to his commander and concoct the story about him being a traitor, in order to discredit him.

The old man had been heartbreakingly honest with her, now it was Claire's turn to be honest with him. 'Doctor Puel, forgive me, but I have not been truthful. My name is not Therese Belland. That is the name I am travelling under.'

The old gentleman smiled. 'It was your *nom de guerre*, your Resistance name, no?'

'No, sir.' Surprised that he'd guessed that she had been in the Resistance, she said, 'My Resistance name was Claire LeBlanc, my code name China Blue. If I may, I would like to explain.' Claire told Doctor Puel and his grandson, Matthieu, the little she knew about the treatment Mitch had received in Canada. She told them that the doctor, who she now knew was Heinrich Beckman, demanded complete secrecy. 'He said under no circumstances should I question my husband about his treatment, so I didn't.' She told them about Mitch's nightmares, how in his sleep he would call out for a woman who Claire suspected her husband was having an affair with. 'His eyes would open and he would talk to her as if he could see her. Afterwards, he had no recollection of the dream or of what he had said. On the few occasions that he had talked about the hypnotherapy sessions he'd had with the doctor, he didn't remember anything about them either.

'I knew something was wrong when, not long before his treatment ended, Mitch, Alain, was kept in hospital overnight. He was put in an empty psychiatric ward with restraints on the beds and bars at the windows. When he woke he was confused, he didn't know what he was saying. He called me by my undercover code name, China. Fortunately, Beckman wasn't there and the nurse thought he was talking about the country.'

'And is your husband still being treated by this man in Canada?' Doctor Puel asked.

'No, sir. The treatment finished and Alain was told he had been cured of shell shock. But he is now missing. At the airport, while my little girl and I were waiting for my husband to join us to fly back to England, an official told me that he had been informed by Canadian military intelligence that my husband had gone AWOL. He said we were to leave without him. That information led me again to think that Alain was having an affair with the woman he talked about in his sleep and he had stayed in Canada to be with her. But,' Claire said, looking at the old man and then his grandson, 'whether he was having an affair or not, I knew something sinister was going on. And I was right.

'When I got back to England, to our home, Alain's grandmother showed me a letter and a copy of my husband's medical report. The originals were sent to Alain's commander at the aerodrome and signed, of course, Professor Lucien Puel.'

'How did you see a copy of such a report? Surely it would have been classified?'

'It was classified. It had classified stamped all over it. But I assure you it was the real thing, as was "the private and confidential" letter written by "Beckman." I now believe my husband missed the plane home because he returned to the hospital. I think he somehow got hold of his medical records, the report and the letter, copied them and posted them to his grandmother for safekeeping. If this professor is the doctor from the prison and Alain had recognised him, Alain would know he couldn't stay in Canada, and because of the damning letter Beckman had written to his commander, he wouldn't be able to come back to England, either. At least not without being court marshalled and sent back to Canada for trial.'

'What?' Doctor Puel and Doctor D'Aramitz exclaimed at the same time.

'The medical report, which included transcripts of one-to-one sessions between Alain and Doctor Lucien Puel— I'm so sorry...' Claire's cheeks flushed scarlet. She had called Heinrich Beckman by the name of the old man's beloved grandson, again. He shook his head and lifted his hand as if to say, it's all right, carry on. Claire took a breath and began again. 'The medical report said pretty much what I expected it to say – that my husband had been suffering from severe shell shock, which had been getting progressively worse over the years. And that the treatment he had received at the Louis Bertrand hospital under the specialist care of—' Claire shook her head and closed her eyes. She was loathed to say his name, 'the professor' had been successful and in the professor's opinion Captain Alain Mitchell was completely well and needed no further treatment.

'But it was the supposed eminent psychiatrist's accompanying letter that did the damage. He said, after talking to Captain Mitchell for many hours while the captain was under hypnosis, he believed the captain had worked for the Germans while detained in the prison at Saint-Gaudens.'

'And he said Captain Mitchell was recruited by a French woman,' Thomas added, 'also in the prison, who was a double agent.'

'It's all falling into place,' Claire said. 'From what Beckman wrote in the letter that Alain copied and sent to his grand-mother, and from what you have told us, I'm convinced that Alain did recognise Heinrich Beckman from the prison. It's the only explanation; the only thing that makes sense. Alain must have remembered being here with you – remembered your name was Lucien Puel and realised that the Lucien Puel who had been his doctor at the Louis Bertrand hospital in Canada was an imposter.'

'No!' Claire jumped at the sharp way in which Doctor Puel dismissed the idea. 'No!' he said again. 'We never told anyone our names, not even our first names. The fewer people that knew the names of the Resistance members, couriers, doctors like me who were willing to stitch a wound or take bullets out of a body, the less chance there was of anyone giving out that information if they were captured by the Germans.'

Claire knew the no-names, policy. The Gisoir Resistance Cell which she had been a member of had the same policy, all the Resistance cells did. She sipped her brandy. Doctor D'Aramitz added another log to the fire, and Claire sat back and relaxed. The house had a strange feel to it. Calm and peaceful yet with a profound sadness that made the atmosphere heavy.

She cast her eyes around. With maroon drapes at the windows, embroidered cream cotton antimacassars protecting the arms and backs of the chairs and settee, and delicate lace runners on the dining table and sideboard, the room was more feminine than masculine, even though two men lived there. She looked up at the mantelshelf. Photographs in silver frames stood in a row. She recognised Doctor Puel and Doctor D'Aramitz, though they both looked much younger. There was a photograph of Doctor Puel with a beautiful woman. He looked about forty and the woman early thirties. They were in summer clothes with cliffs and the sea in the background. It looked like a holiday snap that had been taken many years before. She guessed it was the beautiful woman who had made the soft furnishings, giving the house the feminine touch.

'My grandsons,' Doctor Puel said, getting up and standing by the fire. He held a photograph of two young men with bronzed arms and legs in shorts playing tennis.

Claire stood up and joined him. 'How long ago was this taken?' she asked.

'Some time in the late-thirties. Lucien and Matthieu were home from university for the summer.'

She held the photograph at arm's length, so she could see both the photograph and Doctor D'Aramitz. 'You haven't changed much,' she said. 'And this,' she held the photograph nearer and looked more closely at the other boy, 'must be Lucien.' Lifting her head, Claire glanced at Doctor Puel. With a warm smile, he nodded. Claire looked back at the image of the young Lucien Puel who, grinning cheekily, stood two inches shorter than his cousin. In an open-neck sports shirt, he looked handsome and relaxed.

The cousins were as different to look at as they could possibly be. Matthieu, well built with thick wavy black hair, dark eyes, high forehead, and a strong Norman nose, stood six-feet tall. Lucien, standing casually, hands in pockets, next to him looked about five-ten. He was slim with straight fair hair and boyish looks. On the photograph, Matthieu had a serious expression, Lucien a mischievous one. Claire tilted her head to the left and then right before passing the photograph to Thomas.

'I can see how Beckman got away using Lucien's papers,' Claire told him. 'Lucien has fair skin and his hair is blond or very light brown.'

'Matthieu's mother is my daughter. She has light brown hair and fair skin, like my late wife, but my son-in-law comes from just over the border in Spain and has an olive complexion. Lucien's father was my late son. His wife is Danish. So—' he said, opening his arms as if to say, that is why my grandsons look different.

Claire was desperate to find out anything she could about Simone, and although she had doubts as to whether this was the right time, she knew if she didn't ask now, she might not get the chance again. She inhaled deeply to steady her nerves and said, 'Doctor Puel, I told you that my husband spoke of a woman?' The old man nodded. 'Well, I believe he came to France from Canada to look for her. I was hoping that you might know her or know of her. I think my husband met her in the Gestapo prison, or later, while he was recuperating here in St Emile.'

Doctor Puel and his grandson looked at Claire with interest. 'What is her name?' the old man asked.

'Simone.'

TWENTY-THREE

Claire and Thomas sat and waited for Doctor D'Aramitz to return with news of Doctor Puel. The old man had left saying he needed to take his medication and would be back, but he looked exhausted and Claire wondered if saying he had to take medication was an excuse to leave and not return.

'He left pretty damn quick after I told him the woman we're looking for is called Simone,' Claire said. 'It's obvious he knows her.'

'That's what I thought,' Thomas said, going over to the window and pulling back the curtains. 'It's snowing, again.' He leant closer to the glass and peered out. 'Heavily!'

Claire heard a door open and voices in the hall.

Thomas turned back from the window as Doctor D'Aramitz came in. 'My grandfather has retired for the night.' He took a couple of steps into the room, but didn't return to his chair by the fire, which Claire took as a sign that she and Thomas should leave.

'Is your grandfather all right?' Claire asked. 'I hope we haven't worn him out.'

'Physically he is fine but emotionally he is drained.' Doctor

D'Aramitz took hold of the door handle. 'So, if there isn't anything else...?'

'Well—'

'No!' Thomas said, 'there is nothing. We must be going. It's only a few miles to the hotel, but the country roads around here are narrow and since it is snowing, we should try to get to town before it settles.'

At the front door the housekeeper brought Claire and Thomas their coats. They were dry and the mud had been brushed off them. 'Thank you,' Claire said, 'you needn't have dried and cleaned our coats—'

'It was no trouble, dear,' the housekeeper said. 'Besides, I didn't want mud dripping all over my clean floor, I'd not long scrubbed it.' She helped Claire into her coat and then picked up Thomas's rucksack. 'There was not much I could do with that.'

Doctor D'Aramitz opened the front door. A gust of wind took it out of his hands and it swung back on its hinges and crashed against the wall. He winced and looked up. Claire didn't want to delay him getting back to his grandfather but she had to try one last time to find out if Doctor D'Aramitz knew anything about Simone. 'Thank you for introducing us to your grandfather,' she said. 'What he told us about Heinrich Beckman will clear my husband's name. That is if we can find him.'

'I'm sure you will.'

The wind was so strong it drove the snow horizontally. 'I hope you're right. Thank you, again,' Claire said, 'and please thank Doctor Puel.' She put out her hand, but instead of shaking it, Doctor D'Aramitz gave her an envelope.

'My grandfather would like to see you again tomorrow – in Saint Gaudens.'

'When? Where?' Claire asked.

'It's in the letter. I'm sorry,' he said, 'but I really must attend to my grandfather. Good night.' Doctor D'Aramitz closed the door.

Claire looked at the cream envelope and bit her bottom lip. 'I wonder what it says?'

'We'll find out when we get to the hotel.' Thomas took the letter from her and put it in his rucksack. Buckling the bag, he gave it a tap. Then, putting his arm around her, he pulled her to him. Staying close they lowered their heads and struggled to the car through what threatened to become a blizzard.

Thomas put Claire's wine in front of her and drank the froth from the top of his beer before opening the rucksack and taking out the letter.

'He knows Simone. I know he does,' Claire said, ripping open the envelope excitedly and pulling the letter from it. 'I bet you ten francs Doctor Puel knows her.' While they thawed by the fire, Claire read the letter. 'Huh!' she said, 'He doesn't even mention Simone.' She turned the letter over in case he had written something on the back. He hadn't. Disappointed, she pushed the letter across the table to Thomas.

'He's going to the bank first, and then his solicitor, and he'll be here at twelve.'

'Here?'

'Not here, not in this bar. He says *I shall be finished with the bank and the solicitor by late morning. I should like to meet you at twelve o'clock in the restaurant next door to your hotel.*' Thomas read the letter again, to himself, then looked up at Claire. 'Well? Why are you frowning?'

'There *is* a restaurant next door to the hotel.'

'Which is why he said he would meet us there.'

'But how does he know we're staying in this hotel. I didn't tell him. Did you?'

'No but—' Thomas laughed.

'What?'

'It's the only hotel in town. Come on,' he said, 'let's go in for dinner. I don't want you fainting on me again,' he teased.

Doctors Puel and D'Aramitz were in the restaurant, seated at a table for four when Claire and Thomas arrived. 'I hope we're not late,' Claire said.

'You are not.' Doctor Puel held out his arm and stretched his hand to show a thin wrist beyond the sleeve of his jacket. He lifted his hand and squinted at his watch. 'You are right on time, madame. My grandson and I were early. Won't you sit down,' he said, indicating that Claire should sit in the chair nearest to him. 'Monsieur Durand?'

Thomas sat in the remaining chair, between Claire and Doctor D'Aramitz. Doctor Puel picked up the menu. 'This is one of my favourite restaurants in the Haute-Garonne area. The food is simple and wholesome. I would like steak tartare followed by rum baba, a liqueur to start, a bottle of red wine with my meal, several brandies afterwards, followed by a strong black coffee. Alas,' he said, laughing, 'my doctor would not allow that!' He looked at his grandson and pulled an unhappy but comical face. When the waiter came to take their order, both doctors asked for soup, followed by poached fish and green vegetables. Claire ordered the same but with potatoes, and Thomas ordered a medium rare steak and frites.

When they had finished eating, Doctor Puel ordered coffee. When it arrived, Claire poured each of them a cup while Doctor Puel took a large brown envelope from his briefcase. 'Now, to business,' he said, handing the envelope to Claire. 'This should clear your husband of treason. It contains everything you will need to prove that the so-called Swiss psychiatrist working under the name of Lucien Puel is the escaped criminal, Heinrich Beckman.'

Claire looked at the envelope with a mix of distaste and gratitude. 'You won't catch anything from it, my dear.' A mischievous smile crept across the old doctor's face. 'It has been in my safety deposit box, in the vaults of the Banque Populaire de France since the month after—'

He took a second, bulkier envelope from his briefcase. Before giving it to Claire, he held it against his chest. 'In here are the documents that will prove Heinrich Beckman killed my grandson Lucien and stole his identity. This envelope contains my grandson's birth certificate, a photograph taken when he was born, and one of him receiving his doctor's diploma a couple of weeks before he was murdered. It also contains the date the prison was liberated, the hospital report listing Lucien's injuries, Beckman's charred identity papers stating his name and rank, and a photograph which, although burned on one edge, clearly shows Beckman's face. And,' he took a shuddering breath, 'the death certificate of my grandson, the real Doctor Lucien Puel.'

Claire took the envelope, warm from being held against the old man's heart. 'I don't know what to say.'

'There is nothing to say, my dear.' With a shaking hand, he reached for his coffee. 'Oh,' the old doctor said, his eyes brightening, 'there is also a duplicate doctors diploma from the medical department of the Université Paris Descartes, dated and signed the same as the original certificate, which was stolen. They sent it to me after Lucien's death,' he said with pride. 'The documents are all dated and stamped by the various authorities.

'Take this to keep them in,' he said, giving Claire his briefcase. Claire nodded and sniffed back her tears. He lay his hand on the case. 'In here is a sworn statement from me, signed and witnessed by Matthieu and my solicitor.' He shook his head and lifted his hand as if to wave away the necessity of signatures. 'It gives you the authority to use the documents in whatever way you see fit.'

Claire looked for sadness in the old man's face. She only saw relief. 'I will look after them for you,' she promised.

'Do not look after them for me, I no longer have a use for them. Look after them for yourself, for your husband, and for my late grandson, Lucien.' Doctor Puel leaned forward and rested his elbows on the table. 'Can you trust your husband's commanding officer?'

Claire answered immediately. 'I can. Commander Robert J. Landry is one of the most decent and honourable men—'

'Then tell him what you have here. Clear your husband's name first, and then take the documents to the war crimes tribunal and get justice for my grandson.'

Overwhelmed by such a huge responsibility, Claire looked at Thomas. He smiled to let her know she had his support, then gave Doctor Puel a questioning look. 'Sir, I thought the war tribunals ended last year.'

The old doctor shook his head. 'Halted, temporarily, but not ended. They will never end.'

'Nor will the hunt for Nazis by the members of the Jewish Council.' Doctor D'Aramitz, like Thomas, had been silent until now. 'The aristocratic father of the Resistance woman you are looking for is one of the leaders of the organisation.'

Claire sat in silence, stunned by this latest revelation. Then she said, 'Simone is Jewish?'

'Half Jewish. Her father, Guillaume Cheval, married a Russian Jew. Like her daughter, she was something of an enigma, a mystery. They say she was a beauty. Tall and slender with raven black hair. She was Russian aristocracy. Her family escaped to France during the Russian Revolution.'

Doctor D'Aramitz sighed. 'She was one of the first Jews to be taken to Auschwitz. Her daughter, who fought with the Resistance under the name of Simone, and who was imprisoned with your husband at Saint-Gaudens, lives with her father at

Chateau Je Reviendrai, on the outskirts of a small village called
Vignes de la Seine, a couple of miles from Fontainebleau.'

'And is Simone her real name?'

'No. It is Eleanor. Eleanor Cheval.'

When they had finished their coffee Doctor Puel insisted on
paying the bill. Claire thanked him, and gently shook his hand.
Then holding both hands, reluctant to let him leave, she kissed
him. 'Thank you for entrusting me with the treasured belongings of your beloved grandson.' With tears in his eyes, he said
again that he didn't need them. 'What I have of Lucien that is
important is in here.' He put his hand on his heart. 'Goodbye,
my dear.'

While he was shaking Thomas's hand and wishing him
good luck, Claire turned to Doctor D'Aramitz. 'Thank you for
taking me to meet your grandfather. I can't tell you how grateful
I am for the help you have both given me.' She picked up the
briefcase containing the documents that would free Mitch and
put Heinrich Beckman behind bars, and said, 'I shall see you
both again, when this monster has been arrested and is locked
up where he belongs. Until then, look after your grandfather.'

Doctor D'Aramitz said he would. 'All this has been a strain
on Grandfather's health, but he was determined to do as much
as he could to help you clear your husband's name and know
that justice would, at last, be served on Heinrich Beckman.'

Doctor D'Aramitz said he was pleased that they could help
each other and looked forward to seeing Claire again. Then,
when Doctor Puel had finished speaking to Thomas, he turned
to his grandson, and together they left the restaurant arm
in arm.

TWENTY-FOUR

Claire sighed. There was so much going on in her mind; so much she needed to do, people to speak to, questions to ask, she couldn't think straight. So much had happened during the last three days it was impossible to take it all in. 'I can't do this on my own,' she said, looking down at the briefcase on her lap. She wanted Thomas to say *You don't have to, I'll be with you.* She looked up at him. He looked stunned, bewildered, which she suspected was how she looked.

'Brandy?'

Claire shot him a look of astonishment. 'Is alcohol your answer to every problem?'

'No, but it will help me, and *you*,' he said, 'to calm down and think. Yes or no?'

'Yes!' He called the waiter over and ordered two brandies. 'The problem is mine, not yours,' Claire said.

'That's where you are wrong,' Thomas said, 'it is also my problem.'

She wanted to shout for joy but was overcome by guilt. Thomas had a life in Paris, a job at the Sorbonne, how could she ask him to put it all on hold for any longer. 'What do you mean, it's also your problem? It's my husband who is accused of being a traitor, and if he is having an affair with Simone, or Eleanor, whatever her name is, that's my problem too.'

'I agree. Your husband's personal life is nothing to do with me,' Thomas said, 'but while you were saying goodbye to Doctor D'Aramitz, Doctor Puel asked me to help you and to keep you and the briefcase safe.' The waiter brought two glasses of brandy, put one in front of Claire and one in front of Thomas.

'He thinks because I'm a woman, I'm not capable,' Claire said, and drank her brandy down in one.

'I assure you he does not think anything of the kind. He *thinks* it could be dangerous getting the documents to Cheval, especially if Beckman has corresponded again with your husband's commander. He said if there are two of us we can watch each other's backs. He's an old Resistance man. He thinks we'll be safer as a couple, that's all. And I agree with him.' Claire tilted her head and shrugged. 'Anyway, I gave him my word, so you're stuck with me.'

Pleased she had someone she could trust to help her, Claire smiled with relief. 'So, what now?'

'I need to telephone my assistant at the University, get him to cover my lectures next week. Then I'll have to telephone the principal.' Thomas pulled a face.

'Could you lose your job?'

'No. I shouldn't think so.'

'I hope you don't.'

'I'll give Antoinette and Auguste a ring too. Fill them in with what's been happening.'

'And I'll make a couple of overseas calls,' Claire said. 'I ought to let Alain's grandmother know I'm all right. I also need to check she still has the documents he sent her.'

'Shouldn't you telephone your husband's commander first?'

'I suppose so. The sooner he calls off the military dogs the better. I'll ring him after I've talked to my daughter. It's been three days since we last spoke. She won't be happy with me.' Claire looked up at Thomas, her forehead lined with worry.

'She'll forgive you once she knows her father is safe.'

'But is he? We don't even know where he is.'

'No, but we soon will.' Thomas pushed his chair away from the table and stood up. 'Right, I'll pay for the drinks. You go up to your room and book the calls to England. It may take some time to get an overseas line.' He looked at his wristwatch, 'I'll see you in the hotel bar at six thirty.' Claire made no attempt to move. 'What is it?'

'I don't want to telephone England from my room. There aren't any outside lines. All calls go through reception and I don't want that nosy Madame to know I'm calling England, let alone listen in to the call, which you can bet your life she will. It wouldn't matter so much if she listened to what I say to Mitch's grandmother, but I'll need to tell Commander Landry about the documents Doctor Puel gave me if I'm going to convince him Mitch isn't the traitor.'

Thomas's brow creased in thought. 'Railway station! Every station has telephone booths. I've called all over Europe from my local station.'

That's in Paris, Claire thought, this is the back of beyond. Still, it was the better option. The call she needed to make to Mitch's commander was a matter of life and death – her husband's life or death.

The station at Saint-Gaudens was a commuter station, surprisingly big for such a small town – and it was rush hour. From the main concourse, Claire watched people in droves spilling out of city trains onto the platforms, running to other platforms, and jumping onto other trains. It was where city workers changed trains to go somewhere else by the look of the

swarms of people running from large locomotives to catch
smaller local trains.

Claire spotted a bank of five telephones along the east wall
by the ticket office. She stepped into the middle booth, Thomas
took the one next to her.

She thought she would never hear what the recipients of
her telephone calls said, but bedlam was happening on the platforms, not on the concourse. Inside the booth it was remarkably
quiet. She picked up the telephone and put two francs into the
metal coin box. A second later a voice asked her what number
she wanted. She asked for the international operator. It wasn't
long before an operator with a Parisian accent asked her which
country. Claire said England and a minute later a tired voice
with a London accent said, 'What number would you like to be
connected to, caller?'

Claire gave the operator the number of the Foxden Hotel.
From depositing two francs, to being connected to the English
operator, had taken five minutes. At this rate I'll be cut off
before I get through to Bess, she thought. Then she heard a faint
ringing in the background. The operator said, 'Putting you
through now, caller.'

The next voice Claire heard was that of her sister. 'Good
afternoon, Foxden Hotel.' Seconds later Bess had dispatched
her husband Frank off to find Aimée. When Aimée came on the
line she asked a dozen questions, hardly giving Claire time to
answer one before she asked another. Thomas was right,
believing her mother was close to finding her father and
bringing him home, Aimée forgave her for not telephoning for
three days.

Claire went through the same rigmarole with the French
and English operators before she was connected to Mitch's
grandmother. She didn't have to wait long for the telephone to
be answered. It rang only once before Esther picked up the
receiver.

As soon as she heard Esther's voice, Claire knew something was wrong. 'Hello? Hello?' Esther said, not giving Claire time to speak. 'Is anyone there?'

'It's Claire.'

'I can't hear you,' she said, 'it is a *bad* line.'

'Are you on your own?'

'*No!* I still can't hear anything. Now the confounded thing sounds as if it's in the middle of a storm,' Claire heard her say, her voice directed away from the telephone.

'I understand. I wanted to tell you that I think I've found what I was looking for, and I hope you are keeping yourself safe.'

'Perfect!' Esther spat, in an angry voice. Then, quieter, as if she had turned her head away from the telephone's mouthpiece. 'First, all I could hear was the sound of wind rushing down the line, now it's clicking like a pair of lovesick crickets.' The telephone went dead.

Claire left the booth after only making two calls. Deep in thought, she strolled across the ticket hall and sat on a wooden bench to wait for Thomas. An idea came to her and she took a pen and notebook from her handbag. By the time she had finished writing, Thomas had finished the call to his work colleague in Paris and had joined her. 'Where's the nearest post office?' she asked.

'No idea.' He looked around and shouted *Excuse me* to a porter who was pulling a wooden cart piled high with suitcases. The man stopped and Thomas ran over to him. 'The post office is on a street parallel with this one,' he said, on his return. 'Why?'

'Someone was with Mitch's grandmother when I telephoned and the phone was tapped. The clever old thing pretended she couldn't hear me and complained about clicking. I told her I thought I'd found what I was looking for. If someone was listening in, do you think that was too obvious?' Claire bit

her lip. 'I was more specific with Aimée.' Claire looked into
Thomas's face. 'We are close to finding Mitch, aren't we?'

'Yes, of course we are! But why do you want a post office?'

'I'm not going to telephone Commander Landry in case
they're listening in to his calls.'

'Why would he have his own telephone tapped?'

'It may not have been RCAF military intelligence tapping
Alain's grandmother's line. I thought it was at first, but now I'm
not so sure. After Canadian military intelligence searched
Esther's house, she was specific about which rooms they had
searched and what they had taken away, but she didn't say
anything about them going near the telephone. Someone
searched my house too, at Christmas, while I was at Foxden. I
assumed it was Commander Landry's people, but again, I'm not
sure. To be on the safe side, I'm going to send him a telegram.'
She ripped the page from the notebook and got to her feet.

'What if it's intercepted?'

Claire laughed. 'They won't understand it. The only thing
Commander Landry and I have in common is the love of
cryptic crosswords, I've made it difficult for anyone else to deci-
pher.' She laughed again, despite the seriousness of the situation. 'I'm not clever enough to make it difficult for the
commander. He'll know exactly what I'm saying.'

They arrived at the post office as the postmaster was turning
the open sign to closed. Claire gave him one of her most
endearing smiles, which he turned his back on. She knocked on
the glass in the upper half of the door. He ignored her. She
knocked again, louder, and he turned.

'Claire!' Thomas took her by the elbow. She lifted her arm
and snatched it away from his grip.

'Would you open the door, please? I'm begging you.'

'Claire? Stop now.'

'No, Thomas! I must send this telegram today.' She knocked
again. 'It is vitally important that I get a message to England,

sir.' The postmaster, eyes glazed as if he was bored and his mouth set in a downward arc, threw up his hands. 'Sir, I have written the message.' She held the piece of paper against the window. The postmaster didn't move. 'Thank you,' she shouted, and pushed the note through the letter box, followed by five francs. 'It needs to go to England tonight,' she shouted. 'It is very urgent.'

Turning his back on Claire again, the postmaster opened a door behind the counter marked private and flicked off the light. 'Bastard!' Claire shouted, kicking the door.

'No, no, no!' As she lifted her foot, Thomas grabbed her from behind and swung her round. 'He'll call the police as soon as he gets to his living quarters, I shouldn't wonder. Come on! We need to get out of here.' Thomas dragged Claire away from the post office door crying and complaining. 'We'll walk back to the hotel. Give you time to calm down.'

They walked along streets crowded with shoppers and office workers hurrying to get home, stopping only when they came to the restaurant next to the hotel. Seated with coffee and brandy, Thomas took the map of France from the inside pocket of his overcoat. He traced the road from Saint-Gaudens to Fontainebleau with his finger, pointing to various places where they could stop for refreshment. 'It will take the best part of a day to get there if the weather doesn't improve.'

Claire wasn't listening, she was racking her brain for ways to contact Commander Landry. There wasn't one, unless she went back to the station. She looked at her wristwatch, it was six thirty. He would have left his office by now and was probably at home. She didn't have his home telephone number. Even if she did, the number would probably be tapped. She took a long deep breath; there was no way of contacting him; not tonight anyway. Suddenly aware that Thomas had stopped speaking, she looked at him. 'Sorry, what were you saying?'

'It doesn't matter. Drink your coffee.'

Just before seven they left the small restaurant and went to the hotel for dinner. Again, being early meant they were served within minutes of sitting down and had finished eating before most of the hotel's other guests had ordered. Still annoyed with herself for not telephoning the commander from the railway station when she had the chance, Claire declined an after-dinner brandy, saying she was going to her room.

'I was hoping you'd have a drink with me in the bar.' She shrugged. 'Come on,' Thomas said, getting up from the table. 'There's something I need to tell you.' He waited at the door until Claire joined him.

'I'm sorry,' she said, 'I don't usually kick down doors and call tired civil servants bastards.' Thomas laughed and Claire laughed with him. 'Am I forgiven?'

Hardly able to speak for laughing Thomas said, 'I thought you were going to break the door down when the post guy put out the light.'

'I felt like it.' Claire ran in front of Thomas, stopped, and turned to face him. 'Thank you.'

'For what?'

'For dragging me away before the police got there.' She stood on tiptoe and kissed Thomas near his lips. She giggled. 'Now I've embarrassed you again.'

'Not at all,' Thomas said, pushing open the door to the hotel bar. 'What do you want to drink?'

'Wine!' Claire said. 'A gallon of it.'

Thomas went to the bar laughing and came back with a regular bottle of red wine and two glasses. 'They're all out of gallon bottles.'

'Well,' Claire sighed, 'this will have to do, won't it?'

Thomas poured wine into both their glasses, lifted his and when Claire did the same, he clinked his glass with hers.

'Do you forgive me for behaving like a hooligan and kicking the post office door?'

'Of course.' He took a drink. 'The guy was so smug, I felt like kicking the door myself.'

Claire was sure Thomas didn't feel anything of the sort but thanked him anyway. She took a drink of her wine. 'Mmmm... This is good. I shall know the difference between good and bad wine when I get back to England.' Anxiety took over, and she began to ramble. 'You see, where I come from it is beer or whisky, we never drink wine, except at my sister and brother-in-law's hotel, they—'

'Claire?' Thomas said.

'Sorry, I'm talking nonsense.'

'You are not talking nonsense.' Thomas leant his elbows on the table and looked at her, his face unsmiling, his mouth a straight line. 'There is something I need to tell you.'

The nerves on the top of Claire's stomach began to tighten. Thomas took another drink, put the glass on the table and holding the stem, turned it round between his fingers. 'Thomas, you look serious. You're worrying me. What is it?'

'I'm going back to Paris.'

'When?'

'Tomorrow.'

Claire felt as if a rug had been pulled from under her. 'Why? What has happened? Is it because of me?'

'No.'

'What then? The call you made to Paris?'

'Yes. There is a flu epidemic in the city and my assistant who has been lecturing for me has it pretty bad.'

'I'm sorry...'

'The principal said if I don't return to work on Monday, he would find someone to replace me.'

'Can he do that?' Claire asked, knowing full well the principal could, especially as Thomas had taken time off without giving him notice.

Thomas gave her a feeble smile and nodded. 'Yes, he can do

it. He has given me until Monday, so I shall drive you to Fontainebleau tomorrow, find you a safe place to stay, then drive on to Paris.' Claire cast her eyes down. 'You do understand, don't you?'

'Of course. You can't lose your job because of—' She was going to say *me*, but that wouldn't have been true. Yes, she needed to find Mitch, but what she had to give Guillaume Cheval from Lucien Puel was much more important. How was she going to do that without Thomas?

He poured the remainder of the wine into their glasses and lifted his to take a drink. 'Wait!' Claire said, 'I want to make a toast.' With her head tilted on one side as if she was getting the measure of her friend, she said, 'To the man who saved me from falling down a mountain, falling foul of the police and—' she was about to say *because you are leaving you have saved me from falling in love with you*. Instead, she said, 'Saved me from myself.'

The wine left her feeling mellow. She walked with Thomas through the hotel foyer and up the narrow staircase to their rooms. Outside her door, Thomas stopped and gave her a friendly hug. 'You'll be fine taking the documents to Guillaume Cheval,' he said, 'you know that, don't you?'

Claire nodded. 'I know. I'm just getting soft in my old age.' She laughed. 'I felt tonight like I felt the first time I came to Paris to deliver money to you. It was something I had never done before, I was scared to death every time a gendarme or SS officer checked my travel permit and identity papers.'

'And afterwards?' Thomas said, a knowing smile on his face.

'Afterwards, I could have done it the next day and the next.'

He laughed. 'I'll see you in the morning.' Claire watched the strong good-looking Resistance man amble along to his room and whispered, 'Good night, Thomas Durand, sleep well.'

. . .

Claire had planned an early night, but it was past eleven. She took off her clothes and put on her nightdress. She hung what she was going to wear the following day on the outside of the wardrobe and packed everything else, apart from her washbag which she needed in the morning.

She looked around the room. She'd left nothing out, so she put the fireguard in front of the dying embers in the grate and climbed into bed.

Unable to sleep, Claire tossed and turned for most of the night, falling into a fitful sleep around five o'clock and waking up again at six. Thomas knocked just before seven. 'I'm ready,' she called, and crossing the room opened the door.

'I'll put your suitcase with mine while we have breakfast,' he said, hauling Claire's case the short way along the corridor to his room. By the time he had put her case inside and locked the door, Claire was waiting for him on the landing, Doctor Puel's briefcase in her hand.

Claire and Thomas, first down for breakfast, were served quickly. When they had finished eating, Thomas asked the yawning bellboy to fetch his and Claire's cases from his room. With a cheeky smile and raised eyebrows, the boy ambled off. By the time they had paid the miserable proprietor the balance on three nights' accommodation plus the bar bill, the bellboy was back. He trailed behind them to the car where Claire thanked him and Thomas gave him a tip.

'Next stop, Fontainebleau,' Claire said, Doctor Puel's brief-case safely on her knee.

TWENTY-FIVE

The weather, while no warmer by any means, was not as bad as the wireless presenter had forecast on the morning news and they arrived at Fontainebleau earlier than expected. They turned off the main road at a junction that said City Centre left, Vignes de la Seine, right.

'We have twenty minutes before it will be dark. Do you want to take a look at Chateau Je Reviendrai?'

Claire closed her eyes and bit her lip. Her stomach churned at the thought of it, but without Thomas to take her there, she needed to know where she would be going and what she was to expect when she delivered Doctor Puel's documents to Guillaume Cheval. 'Yes,' she whispered.

Driving through a small industrial area on the outskirts of Vignes de la Seine, Claire saw several bombed-out factories. There was evidence along many of the streets that offices and houses in the southern suburbs had been damaged. Some so badly by incendiary bombs or shells that they had been demolished. A reminder to residents and visitors alike that less than a decade ago the German airforce had dropped bombs on the town's residential as well as industrial area.

Claire caught her breath when she saw the Chateau Je Reviendrai, an imposing eighteenth century charterhouse set back from the road in as much parkland as Foxden Hall before the war. Surrounded by manicured gardens, shrubs and flower beds, there was no evidence that Simone's family home had been touched by German or Allied bombs, let alone destroyed by them as some of the houses in Vignes de la Seine had been.

If she hadn't met Doctor Puel – and known better – Claire might have believed what Heinrich Beckman said about Simone and her family being German spies, sympathisers of Hitler's Reich. Claire shook her head to rid herself of the doubts Beckman's accusations had left her with.

A large black car passed them in the lane and swung onto the wide drive. Claire watched as a tall man in his mid-sixties, with greying hair, got out of the car and mounted the steps to the chateau's door. The man took a key from his coat pocket, unlocked the door and went inside.

They waited for half an hour, but there was no further sign of life. No one came to the chateau, no one left. 'It's getting late,' Claire said, 'I think I should find a hotel. Do you know any hotels in the town?'

'What kind of hotel do you want to stay in? Big and impersonal or small and friendly.'

'Big and impersonal. I want to be anonymous.'

'You'll be that in the Hotel Central,' Thomas said. 'It's huge. It's mostly used by business people whose head offices are in Fontainebleau. It was the first really big hotel to be built after the war. It calls itself an International Hotel,' he said, laughing.

'How do you know?'

'A friend of mine from the Resistance days is the manager of a small hotel here. I was going to suggest you stayed there, but I picked this up when we stopped for lunch.' He took a brochure listing hotels in the area from the pocket in the door and dropped it in Claire's lap.

It was too dark to read, so she put it in her handbag. They drove into the town and turned into Boulevard Principal. 'It is a big hotel for such a small town,' Claire said, looking up at four storeys of concrete and glass. I'll be anonymous enough in there, she thought, jumping out of the car. Thomas took her case from the car's boot and followed her into the hotel.

The foyer, a complete contrast to the hotel's stark exterior, looked welcoming and comfortable. Large ornate mirrors framed in gold hung on the walls above ruby red seating that ran from the reception area to— Claire stopped, and Thomas stopped immediately behind her. While taking in the hotel's ambience Claire spotted a man on the far side of the foyer reading a newspaper. Except he wasn't reading it. He was holding it in front of his face, but his eyes were fixed on the reception desk. On the opposite side of the room, a similarly dressed man was not smoking the cigarette he was holding.

'What is it?' Thomas asked.

Claire turned so her back was to the men, put her hand on his shoulder and stood on tiptoe looking dreamily into his face. 'The guy with the newspaper at ten o'clock,' she said, smiling, 'is more interested in who is booking a room at the reception desk than he is in reading the newspaper he is holding.'

'Uh-huh!' Thomas said, 'I see him.'

'And,' Claire swayed coquettishly, 'at three o'clock, there's a guy sitting with his back to the window holding a cigarette.'

'There are several men holding cigarettes.'

'Sharp features, small eyes, hooked nose. Holding a cigarette, but *not* smoking it. There's an ashtray on the table in front of him that is full of fag ends, but he isn't a smoker.'

Thomas looked over her shoulder. 'How can you tell?'

'He puts the cigarette in his mouth, takes a drag, then puffs out the smoke without inhaling.'

'I see him. He's looking around the room,' Thomas said.

'That's right,' Claire turned so she was side-on to the man

facing the door to observe him again. Beginning with the people on the left of him the beaky-nosed man began a slow sweep of the crowded foyer. From left to right he studied the face of every woman who had entered the hotel. Then, just as his eyes were about to reach her, someone shouted, 'Harlot!' The man's head whipped round and his attention was off the women in the foyer and focused in the direction of the shouting.

Claire and Thomas – and everyone else in the foyer – stopped what they were doing to see what was going on. A tall woman in her mid-forties, wearing a full-length black sable coat and a Cossack-style fur hat, sashayed into the reception area. At her side was a young man in a chauffeur's uniform, carrying bags and boxes displaying the names of some of the most prestigious Parisian designers.

Behind them, a short stocky man in his late fifties with a bald pate shouted, again, 'Harlot!'

The woman turned and gave the man a contemptuous look. 'Call me that once more,' she goaded, 'and I shall leave you. And this time it will be for good!'

The man ran ahead of her, turned, and opening his arms wide, blocked her way. 'Fine. Go! But you are not going out at this time of night with my chauffeur?'

'What? I am not *going out* with your chauffeur in the way you mean,' she said, smiling at the young man. 'He is taking me to visit my mother.'

'That old witch? She only wants to see you to get her hands on my money!' the man shouted. As the woman walked towards him the small man started to back off. 'Fine!' He put up his hands, but the woman didn't stop walking. 'Go and see your mother,' he said, 'but I forbid you to give her any of my money. And I forbid you to go in my car.'

'She-lives-miles-away...' the woman said, pronouncing each word deliberately. 'How do you propose I get there if I don't take the car? Walk?'

'Yes! The exercise will do your *grand derrière* good,' he shouted. Spurred on by the men in the foyer laughing, he continued. 'Take the Metro! Go on the tram! Fly on your broomstick! But you are not taking—'

'Er, hum!' Claire nudged Thomas, who like everyone else was transfixed on the pantomime argument between the tall woman and her short husband. 'We should leave while the two goons are being entertained.'

She turned, walked across the foyer to the revolving doors and stepped quickly into an empty section. Thomas followed but stopped at the door to let a young woman enter. She said thank you and he smiled. Still smiling he descended the hotel's steps and walked in the opposite direction to where he had parked his car. Claire stopped and opened her handbag. She took out her powder compact and powdered her nose. When Thomas passed her, she dropped the compact back into her handbag and walked a few paces behind him to the end of Boulevard Principal. At the corner, she stopped again and looked back at the hotel. There was no one standing around in the street or leaving the hotel. It was safe to assume they hadn't been seen.

Thomas tapped her on the shoulder. 'Did anyone follow us out?' Claire shook her head. 'Good. We'll wait here for ten minutes, to be sure, then I'll go and get the car. You hang on here.' Thomas handed Claire the suitcase. 'I'll drive around the block a couple of times and when I'm sure I'm not being followed, I'll pull over a few doors down,' he said, pointing along the street.

'I'll find a shop doorway.'

When the ten minutes were up, Claire watched Thomas walk casually back along Boulevard Principal. He passed the front of the hotel without looking in. She watched him arrive at his car, open the door, and slide in behind the steering wheel. When the car's lights came on, she made her way along the street. A quarter of the way down she found an entrance leading to a shop door. Looking over her shoulder, and then in front of her, to make sure she wasn't being followed, she stepped back and was soon out of sight in the shadows beneath the arch of the shop's doorway.

Cars came and went along the street until eventually she saw Thomas's Citroën pull up a few yards from where she was standing. She picked up her case and walked briskly to the car. She opened the back door, threw in her suitcase, and dropped onto the seat beside it. When Thomas pulled away from the kerb, the momentum slammed the door shut.

'Where too, madame?' he said, looking at Claire in the reverse mirror.

'The next anonymous hotel on your list,' Claire said.

Thomas laughed. 'I don't think there is another hotel that you could call anonymous.' Claire laughed with him, which she realised from the multitude of knots in her stomach was from nerves not amusement.

'How about my old Resistance comrade's hotel? I've only been there once, just after the war, but from what I remember it was a decent enough place. It's around here somewhere,' Thomas said, leaning forward and looking through the wind-screen trying to spot the hotel. 'There, look,' he said, 'Le Petit Château Hotel. I'll go in on my own first, and if he still works there I'll say hello, have a bit of a chat and see if he has any rooms.'

'If he remembers you, ask him if he's had anyone come into the hotel that just sat about? Anyone who looked as if they were waiting for someone who didn't show up.'

'Okay. Will you be all right out here on your own?' Thomas asked, steering the Citroën off the road and pulling into a narrow parking area in front of the hotel.

Claire tutted. 'Of course, I will. And, Thomas?' she called out of the window as he ran from the car. 'Be careful.' Thomas nodded and entered the Le Petit Château Hotel by a side door.

Claire wound up the window and blew into her hands. It was a bitterly cold evening. She hoped there would be a fire in her room – if there was a room available. It looked like a pretty small hotel from the outside. Not long after going into the side door, Claire saw Thomas coming out of the main entrance at the front of the hotel. As he neared the car he made an O with his forefinger and thumb.

'They've got a room then?' she said, when he jumped into the car.

'They have. And there hasn't been anyone hanging around that my old Resistance chum didn't know.'

'Then what are we waiting for? It's bloody freezing in here.' Thomas twisted round, leant his arm on the back of his seat, but didn't speak. 'For goodness' sake, what is it?'

'When I asked my friend if any strangers had been in, he *accidentally* left the hotel's register open in front of me when he went into the office to answer the telephone.'

'And? Thomas, if you don't tell me what the hell you're going on about, I swear I'll—'

'Alain is staying here!'

Claire gasped.

'I read his name; Alain Le Blanc, the undercover name your husband used when you and he were in the Resistance, is booked into this hotel.'

TWENTY-SIX

'How can I stay in the same hotel as my— estranged husband? I'm trying to find out if he's having an affair, for God's sake!' It took Claire a few minutes to recover from the bombshell Thomas had dropped. When she did, she said, 'Did the manager say anything about Alain?' Thomas lifted his shoulders then tilted his head to the left and right. 'You are the most frustrating, the most annoying man! The manager either said something about Alain or he didn't. Which is it?'

'He said Alain has a rich friend who he assumes lives nearby because he has visited Alain at the hotel several times.'

'Man or woman?'

'What? Oh, a man...'

Claire sighed with relief. 'And?'

'And... the man has a daughter.'

Claire's heart almost stopped beating. 'Did he tell you the name of the man and his daughter? Did he mention the name Cheval?'

Thomas shook his head. 'I wasn't able to ask him. A couple of guests came into reception to pick up the keys to their room.'

'Did he say whether she had been to the hotel?'

'Again, I didn't have time to ask. But I'm sure my friend would have said if he'd seen her. He has an eye for the ladies.'

Claire took a deep calming breath and shut her eyes. 'Right!' she said, opening them and exhaling. 'Plan B! We go to another hotel.'

'Not possible. I telephoned the two remaining hotels on the list and they are both full.'

'Then we'll have to go with plan C.'

'What is plan C?'

'The same as plan A,' Claire said, taking her powder compact and lipstick from her handbag. She frowned at her reflection in the compact's small mirror, before powdering her nose and applying a thick layer of red lipstick. She picked up a small round box of rouge, opened it, then dropped it back into her bag. 'Pale and mysterious, I think, like one of those Parisian models.' She poked her hair behind her ears, then reached across the back seat and opened her suitcase. She took out a felt hat. After giving it a shake, she held it with one hand and ran the thumb and forefinger of her other hand around its brim. She put it on, looked in the mirror again and tugged the right side of the hat until the brim was off-centre and angled over her right eye. Then, dropping the compact and lipstick back into her handbag, she gracefully stepped out of the car.

Standing as tall as she could, Claire pulled up the collar of her coat and tightened the belt, before putting on a pair of fashionable spectacles. 'Well?' she said to Thomas when he joined her on the pavement with her suitcase, 'How do I look?'

'If I thought you wouldn't slap me I'd whistle,' he said.

'I haven't overdone the lipstick, have I?'

'No, but I'm not sure about the glasses *and* the brim of the hat pulled down over your eye.'

Claire pushed gently on the front of the hat until it slipped back on her head an inch. 'Better?' Thomas nodded. 'Good God but it's cold out here. Come on, let's get inside.' She stopped.

'The receptionist will want to see my identity papers, so don't call me Claire. My name is Therese Belland.'

Le Petit Château Hotel was smaller inside than it looked from the outside – and it was a lot less impersonal. The manager, now on reception duty, and pretending not to know Thomas asked how many rooms. Claire said one, and signed the hotel register as *Madame Therese Belland.*

An elderly porter shuffled stiffly out of a doorway behind the reception desk, bent down, and picked up Claire's case. 'I shall take the suitcase to Madame's room,' Thomas said, taking the case from the porter. The old man raised his eyebrows and Claire, looking suitably embarrassed, made for the cage-elevator.

While the elevator juddered and rattled on heavy chains to the second floor, she held her breath. Once inside her room, she and Thomas collapsed into each other's arms in fits of laughter. 'I wish you didn't have to go,' Claire said, when she had recovered.

'Me too.' Thomas looked into her eyes, his arms still around her. 'But...' He clenched his teeth as if to stop himself from speaking and the muscles at the side of his face tightened and relaxed. Then he took a deep breath, exhaled, and smiled a sad smile. 'I think it's for the best.'

'Do you?' Claire said, holding his gaze. She could feel his breath on her cheek. Every rational part of her being told her to move away from him, but she was drawn to him, she wanted him. Her heart was beating so fast in her chest she thought it would explode. Thomas pulled her closer. He wanted her too, she could feel he did. She lifted her face to his and closed her eyes.

At that moment the shrill ring of the telephone burst into the room. Claire jumped, opened her eyes and lowered her head to Thomas's chest. He rocked her gently and kissed the top of her head. 'I'm sorry,' he said. Letting go of her he walked across the room to the dressing table and picked up the telephone. Claire dropped onto the bed.

'Yes?' He listened for some seconds. 'Did he say who he was going to meet? Was it Cheval? Thanks for letting me know.' Thomas put down the receiver and turned to Claire. 'That was my friend. Alain has just asked him to order a taxi to pick him up outside the hotel at 7.45 and take him to Le Restaurant du Parc.'

Sitting next to Claire, Thomas took her hand. 'He said Alain looked excited. He asked him if he was seeing a lady friend, and Alain said, yes, a very special lady friend.'

Claire leaned into Thomas, her head resting on his shoulder. 'Would you like me to drive you to the restaurant?'

'No. I'll get your friend to call me a taxi. If I get ready now,' she lifted her head and looked at her watch, 'I'll be there before him.'

'Are you sure you want to see Alain tonight?'

'Yes! I need to know for certain that he's having an affair. And there's that!' She pointed to Lucien Puel's briefcase. 'After tonight I shall know better how to get the information about Heinrich Beckman to Guillaume Cheval.'

Thomas stood up. 'Are you sure you don't want me to take you to the restaurant?'

'I am.'

'If you need me, ring me,' he said, walking to the door. 'Paris is only an hour away by car. I can come back at the weekend, if...' Claire nodded. 'Ring me anytime, whether you need me or not. You know my number in Paris.' Claire nodded again. 'Promise?'

'I promise. Thomas?' Claire said, as he opened the door. 'Will you telephone me tonight? When you get home? Let me know you've arrived safely.'

'It may be late,' he said, 'I need to call on Antoinette and Auguste, and then I have to pick up my tutorial notes from my sick assistant.'

'I don't care what time it is. Please say you'll phone. I feel as if we've been chasing ghosts for a lifetime. I—'

'I shall telephone.'

Claire sighed with relief.

'But now I must go, and you must get ready to dine at Le Restaurant du Parc. On my way out, I'll ask the manager to order a taxi to pick you up in,' he looked at his watch, 'half an hour?' Claire grimaced. 'It has to be that soon, if you want to be at the restaurant before Alain.'

'I know.'

Claire told Thomas to drive carefully and they said good-bye, kissing each other on both cheeks – as is the custom between *friends* in France. Claire opened the door and watched the man who had been her strength leave. 'I shall wait for your telephone call,' she said, as he walked away from her. At the end of the corridor, Thomas looked over his shoulder and gave her an encouraging wink. Claire blew him a kiss and waved. A second later he was gone. She returned to her room and closed the door. For the first time since she had been in France, she felt lonely.

Le Petit Château hotel was middle range, clean and comfortable, the type of hotel that catered for businessmen and women, managerial types who perhaps didn't want to stay in a large city hotel. She hadn't noticed a bar when she arrived. Without Thomas, she didn't want to socialise anyway.

She took off the clothes she'd travelled in, had a strip-wash in the small basin in her room, and put on a blue silk dress that was fitted on the bust and waist, had a high collar and a skirt that was cut on the cross so it swung fashionably around her knees when she walked.

After checking her make-up, which was a little thicker than she usually wore, she brushed her hair into soft waves and put on her hat. She again pulled it until it tilted over one eye, and after checking her stockings were not laddered and the seams were straight, she slipped her feet into a pair of smart high-heeled navy-blue court shoes.

Checking her appearance in the dressing table mirror, Claire was happy with what she saw and slipped her arms down the sleeves of a cream woollen coat that belonged to the real Therese Belland.

Satisfied that she looked more like someone else than herself, and therefore wouldn't be easily recognised, she wrapped a silk scarf the colour of her dress around her neck, picked up her handbag and left the room.

With her head held high, Claire strolled through reception. A few people, guests going into dinner she assumed, smiled and nodded good evening, but most of them didn't notice her.

She may not be anonymous in Le Petit Château, but she blended in.

The taxi pulled up as Claire left the hotel. She took the steps slowly and by the time she was on the pavement, the driver was out of the car and opening the back door for her.

TWENTY-SEVEN

The interior of Le Restaurant du Parc was dimly lit. It would have been bright and airy during the day because it faced south-south-west, but not at night. At night it was exactly the kind of place for a secret rendezvous, a clandestine meeting. And Claire should know, she'd had enough of them during her time with the Resistance in the war. She made for a booth at the back of the room and sat down. She looked around. She had a good view of the door. She watched a waiter lighting candles on the tables. Romantic, she thought, and tried to swallow the ache she felt in her throat.

'... Madame?'

'What? I'm sorry,' she said, 'I was miles away.' She glanced at the menu. It said at the top in bold letters *Evening Menu after seven o'clock*. Her stomach was churning. She didn't think she'd be able to eat anything, but it was gone seven, so she couldn't order a drink on its own, she had to order food too. 'I'm expecting a friend,' she lied, 'we'll order dinner when he arrives.'

'Would you like anything to drink while you wait? An aperitif perhaps?'

'Thank you. A dry martini.'

'Olives?'

'And a small selection of cheeses.'

'Bread with the cheese, madame?'

'A little,' she said. The waiter lit the candle in the middle of the table, bowed, and made his way around a cluster of neat tables-for-two to the bar.

Someone had left a copy of *Le Figaro* on the seat next to her. She picked it up and leaned back in her seat. The only news reported of any interest to Claire was the death of the former French president Albert Lebrun, who had died in Paris after a prolonged illness. When Nazi Germany invaded France in May 1940, and took Paris a month later, Prime Minister Paul Reynaud lost a cabinet vote and resigned, as did President Lebrun. He made the biggest mistake of his political career, Claire thought, appointing Marshal Pétain as his replacement.

She folded the newspaper, dropped it back onto the seat, and glanced around the room. Something had changed. She looked again, this time more slowly. A woman that she hadn't seen the last time she looked was sitting on her own at a table by the window. The waiter, all smiles, waltzed over to attend to her. Then, turning his back on the room and blocking Claire's view, he took the woman's coat. By the fuss the waiter was making the woman was a regular diner at Le Restaurant du Parc.

The waiter bowed again, and gaily zigzagged his way through the tables to coat hooks on the far wall. Claire turned her attention back to the woman. Her elbows were on the table, her hands were clasped in front of her, and she was gazing out of the window. Her pose was elegant. Seconds later she brought her focus back to the restaurant's interior. She was strikingly beautiful. Her dark hair framed her small face. She looked elfin-like with large brown eyes and full red lips. If this woman was

Eleanor Cheval, aka Simone, it was no wonder Alain had fallen in love with her.

From the little Claire could see of the woman's clothes she was sophisticated, stylish. She wore a light grey woollen jacket, edged in darker grey silk. The jacket had fashionably wide lapels and was cut low with a single button at the waist. Beneath it a high-necked silk blouse in a darker shade of grey and a double string of cream pearls, a flattering contrast to her smooth olive skin. The way the woman was sitting Claire could see the blouse fitted snugly over small breasts. She was what Parisians call, très chic.

Claire looked away from the woman when the restaurant's door opened. Her heart almost stopped. Mitch stood just inside the entrance. Claire slid down in her seat, lifted the menu up to cover her face and pretended to read. Out of the corner of her eye, she saw the waiter take Mitch's coat and show him to the table where the elegant woman was sitting. The waiter pulled out a chair, but Mitch didn't sit. Instead, he stood at the woman's side and looked at her for what seemed to Claire like an age. Then he leaned forward and kissed the woman on the cheek.

'Your aperitif, madame,' the waiter said, suddenly at her side. He took the glass of martini from a tray he was expertly balancing in one hand and set it down on the table in front of her.

'Merci.' Lifting the glass with shaking hands Claire took a sip. The chilled minty taste of vermouth and the bite of the gin slid down her throat. She took a second sip.

The waiter brought the olives, cheese and bread, placed them on the table and said, 'Bon appétit, madame.'

When the waiter left, Claire took enough money from her purse to cover the cost of the food and drink. Then, finishing the martini but leaving the food, she got up quietly and went to the toilet. Instead of using the facility she strolled past it. And, as

she had done many times during the war, she opened the back
door and walked out into the night.

The wind howled down the narrow passageway opposite the
restaurant, where Claire stood in the shadows. She stamped her
feet, tightened the belt of her coat and pulled up the collar. It
was freezing, but she was determined to wait until Mitch and
his mistress left the restaurant. A light came on in the restaurant's narrow porch and several more under the striped awning
above the restaurant's windows, making it difficult for Claire to
see Mitch and Simone.

The door opened and a man and woman came out. Claire
held her breath. The man walked out of the light, while the
woman stood under it and put on her gloves. Claire knew by the
way the man carried himself that he was not Mitch. She
watched the couple walk under the awning and stroll off down
the street arm in arm.

Shivering, Claire pushed up the sleeve of her coat and
squinted at her wristwatch. It was too dark to see the time. She
rubbed her gloved hands together, but it made no difference,
they were numb with cold. It must have been two hours since
she had left the restaurant – and she might have to wait another
two hours – a prospect that didn't please her. She leant against
the wall and closed her eyes. What could she learn about this
woman that she didn't already know, by watching Mitch leave
with her? Nothing. Her hands began to throb. She couldn't
afford a night in freezing conditions. She had been a civilian for
too long, she was soft now, her body wouldn't take it. She
pushed herself off the wall and was about to leave the alley
when the restaurant door opened. Mitch stood in the doorway.
Claire held her breath expecting to see Simone join him, but he
was alone.

As he walked into the light above the awning, Claire

watched her husband turn towards the restaurant's window. He lifted his arm in a half salute, half wave, before walking briskly on. So, Simone hadn't left with him. She had probably arranged with the taxi driver who took her to the restaurant to pick her up after she'd dined and take her home. Whatever the reason, it didn't matter, Claire had already lost her husband to a beautiful Parisian woman whose name was not Simone but Eleanor Cheval.

Keeping her distance, Claire followed Mitch back to the hotel. There were only two hotels in the town with vacancies. Even so, it was an extraordinary coincidence that she and Mitch were staying in the same one. She hung back in the shadows outside the door and waited until she saw him cross from reception to the lift. The doors opened and he disappeared inside. When the doors closed, and Claire could see the lift going up, she went into the hotel.

The night manager smiled as she approached the reception desk. 'Good evening, madame.' He took the key to her room from a pigeonhole on the back wall.

'Good evening.' Claire didn't move.

'Is there something I can do for you, madame?'

'No. Thank you.' She began to walk across reception to the stairs, then turned back. 'Yes,' she said, 'I'd like to...' She wanted to say *leave, go home to my daughter...* If she left now, or even first thing in the morning, she could be with Aimée in less than twenty-four hours. But she had promised Doctor Puel that she would take his grandson's papers and the other documents he had entrusted her with to Guillaume Cheval of the Jewish Council in order to arrest and put on trial the professor of psychiatry Lucien Puel – real name, Heinrich Beckman – for his crimes.

If she left now she couldn't keep her promise. She felt suddenly nauseous. The room began to spin. She lost focus and grabbed the reception desk. 'Are you all right, madame?' the night manager asked. 'You look quite unwell.' He came from behind the desk and took hold of Claire's arm. 'Perhaps you should sit down for a moment? I will get you a glass of water.'

Claire's heart was pounding. Her legs felt like jelly. Holding onto the desk and then the doorframe she let the young man guide her into a small office. It was sparsely furnished with only a filing cabinet, desk and chair – and a telephone fixed to the wall.

The night manager helped her across the room to the chair, then left her to fetch water. When he returned, Claire asked if she could make an important telephone call to Paris. 'I'm not supposed to... I would be dismissed if—' He tutted and exhaled loudly. 'Oh, all right,' he said, looking up to the heavens. 'As you are not well, we will call it an emergency. But please be quick, madame.' The young man went to the door and stood guard.

Claire dialled Thomas's number in Paris. It rang out for several minutes but there was no answer. Thomas probably hadn't arrived home. She thanked the night manager, told him if anyone telephoned for her, no matter what time of the night, even if it was in the early hours of the morning, he was to put the call straight through. The night manager looked bewildered, 'Very well, madame!'

Thanking the young man, Claire walked towards the lift. Halfway she stopped and returned to reception.

'Madame?'

'I will be leaving in the morning.'

The night manager looked shocked. 'I hope everything at Le Petit Château has been to your satisfaction, madame?'

'The hotel is fine, but I cannot stay here,' Claire said, near to tears. 'Please prepare my bill. Would you also arrange for a taxi to take me to the station in time to catch the nine o'clock train to Paris?'

'Certainly, madame. I shall do it now. And your bill will be waiting for you when you have had breakfast.'

'I'd like something light in my room, if that's possible?'

'Of course. Croissants and coffee at 7.45?' Claire nodded. 'I will send the porter for your luggage and arrange for a taxi to pick you up at 8.20. That will give you plenty of time to get to the station for nine.'

'Thank you.' Claire put two francs on the reception desk to cover the cost of the telephone calls the night manager would have to make. 'Good night.'

'Good night, Madame Belland.'

Claire undressed and got ready for bed. The few clothes she had taken out of her suitcase and hung up in the wardrobe when she arrived at the hotel she took down, folded, and put back in the case. Then she washed and dried her face, sat on the stool in front of the dressing table mirror and dabbed Nivea cream on her cheeks, neck and forehead. She rubbed the face cream in with the tips of her fingers, washed her hands and brushed her hair.

She looked around the room. With nothing left to do until morning, she sat on the bed and set the small travelling alarm clock for seven. She slumped back against the bed's headboard and closed her eyes but couldn't sleep. She sat up and stared at the telephone. Like a watched kettle, the phone didn't ring.

With frustration more than anything, she laid down and curled up in a ball. Her eyes were tired and she closed them. A minute later, or so it seemed, she was woken by the ring of the telephone echoing around the room. She leapt out of bed, stumbled across the room to the dressing table and picked up the receiver. 'Hello.'

'Hello, Claire? It's Thomas.'

'I thought you'd forgotten to ring.'

'I'm sorry it's late, but I've only just got home. There was an accident on the road into Paris. Then, because it was late,

Antoinette and Auguste insisted I stayed and had something to eat. By the time I got to my colleague's apartment it had gone midnight. How was your evening?' Claire daren't speak. She didn't want Thomas to know she was upset. She fought back her tears and took a calming breath. 'Claire, are you still there?'

'Yes, I'm here,' she whispered, 'but I am leaving first thing tomorrow. I cannot stay here. I'm going to get the nine o'clock train to Paris. From there I shall go to the airport at Orléans and catch a flight home. I shall ask your friend, the manager, to put the documents Doctor Puel gave me in the hotel safe. You said you were only an hour away, and you would come back at the weekend if I needed you, well, I do. I need you to take the documents to Guillaume Cheval.'

'I will do as you ask, of course, but why are you leaving so suddenly? Is it Alain? Was he with Eleanor Cheval?'

'Yes, very much with her. The way he looked at her tonight in the restaurant was how he used to look at me. He loves her, Thomas. I know he does. It's over between us. I shall return to England, tell Alain's commander what Doctor Puel told me, and that will be the end of it as far as I am concerned. Then I shall go to Foxden, to my daughter.'

'Won't you put off leaving until after the weekend? We can take the documents to Guillaume Cheval together. Afterwards, we can talk.'

'No. I couldn't bear to see Alain with her. And, Thomas—?'
'Yes?'
'I'm sorry.'

TWENTY-EIGHT

'Come in,' Claire called. She glanced at her watch, it was 7.30. She dragged her suitcase into the middle of the room and turned to take her coat from the wardrobe.

'Is it just the one case, Madame Belland?'

She spun round. 'Mitch? How...?'

'Did I know you were here?' Claire felt her cheeks flush scarlet. 'I had a telephone call in the middle of the night from someone saying he was a friend, and if I didn't want to lose you forever, I was to ask at reception for the room number of Madame Therese Belland.'

'Thomas,' Claire whispered. Overwhelmed by the kindness and generosity of her friend, she blinked back her tears.

'Not a very original cover name.'

'It was the best I could come up with at short notice.'

There was a second knock on the door. Mitch raised his eyebrows questioningly and Claire nodded for him to open it. 'Your breakfast, madame,' the waiter said, looking from Mitch to Claire before crossing the room and taking croissants and coffee from the tray and putting them on the small table under the window.

'Would you bring another cup?' Mitch lifted the lid on the coffee pot and peered in, 'and another pot of coffee – and bill room 103?'

'Yes, sir.' The waiter left and Mitch closed the door.

Estranged, not knowing what to say to one another, they stood in silence. It was Mitch who spoke first. 'Honey, why are you here?'

Every time he called her honey, smiled at her, or looked into her eyes as he was doing now, Claire felt a sharp pain, like a knife piercing her heart. 'I came to find you!'

'And you've found me, so why are you leaving?'

'Because I *have* found you. I wanted to warn you that British intelligence, Canadian military intelligence, and probably MI6 and the International Criminal Police Organisation are looking for you. Two military intelligence officers searched Esther's house. They took some of your old books away with them. They searched our house while Aimée and I were at Foxden at Christmas. Then two bull-neck guys in civvies turned up at Édith's house in Gisoir asking questions.

'I had crossed the Channel on my old French passport, so when I got to Gisoir, André had my photograph put onto Therese's passport. Two men, similar to the two who came to Édith's house were in the Hotel Central last night, but we gave them the slip.'

'We?'

'I!' Claire said, quickly. She didn't have time to explain how she came to be with Thomas, nor did she want to. It was none of Mitch's business. '*I* gave them the slip.'

'That's my girl.' Mitch took a step towards her, but Claire turned away. She took her hat from the dressing table and put it on. 'Documents proving you are not a traitor, but your psychiatrist in Canada is, will be delivered to Guillaume Cheval at the weekend.'

'I don't understand,' Mitch said.

Securing her hat, Claire checked her appearance in the mirror, and then turned to face Mitch. 'I can prove to Commander Landry, and to the authorities in England, that you are not a German agent. You,' Claire said, keeping her emotions in check, 'can do the same. The proof is in here.' She showed Mitch old Doctor Puel's briefcase. 'I was going to leave it in the hotel safe for Thomas Durand, who I know from 1943, from the Paris Maquis. He has been helping me. He was coming back at the weekend to take the briefcase to Guillaume Cheval, but since you're here you can take it.'

'How do you know about Cheval?'

'You'd be surprised what I know,' Claire said, unable to keep cynicism out of her voice. 'But I don't have time to explain now. I'm catching the nine o'clock train to Paris, but first I need to telephone Thomas and tell him not to come up here because you have the documents. Then I am going back to England to tell Commander Landry what I know. So, as soon as he calls off the dogs, you'll be free to get on with your life.'

'Get on with my life? What did Commander Landry tell you?'

Claire gave him a scathing look. '*He* didn't tell me anything. He'd have guessed I knew something when I didn't turn up for the meeting he ordered me to attend the following day. But, like the goons who came to Édith's house in Gisoir, I gave him the slip too. By the time he realised I wasn't going to show up for the meeting, I was halfway across the Channel.'

Claire's eyes began to smart. She swallowed to stop the tears. 'You should have told me about the accusations *Lucien Puel* made against you, Mitch.'

'I didn't tell you because I didn't want to put you in danger.'

'Then it's a damn good job your grandmother told me, or the authorities would be hunting you as they will soon be hunting him.'

Mitch put his hands on his head and exhaled a long breath. 'She got the letter?'

'Yes.'

'And the medical report?'

'Yes. She showed me both.'

'And she's still got them? Military intelligence didn't find them?'

'No. How would they know you'd sent Esther a copy?'

'Because Puel's secretary came back from lunch early and saw me copying them. She said she wouldn't say anything, but she'd be bound to tell Puel.'

'Well, she obviously didn't.'

'No.' Mitch ran his fingers through his hair. 'How is Grandma Esther?'

'She's fine. Commander Landry had her in for questioning while I was away. She saw the same letter that you'd sent to her on his desk and was worried, which is why she showed it to me. And now I can prove that what Puel said about you working for the Germans and being a double agent is a lie. It's Puel, or should I say, Doctor Heinrich Beckman from the Gestapo prison at Saint-Gaudens, who is the German agent. But you worked that out when you were in Canada, didn't you?'

'I wondered, which is why I copied the documents. How the hell did Beckman end up in Canada?'

'He got out of the prison before the Allies went in. He killed the grandson of the retired doctor who saved your leg, took his identity papers and his doctor's diploma. I don't know how he got to Canada. Most Nazis who escaped went to South American, but he travelled cross-country to Switzerland.'

'Who would refuse to help a French doctor?' Mitch said.

'No one. Which meant in just a few years the murdering, mind-meddling, German doctor had become a renowned Swiss psychiatrist. But not for much longer,' Claire said.

Before she could say more, the conversation was interrupted by another tap on the door. Mitch opened it to find the waiter who had brought Claire's breakfast holding a tray with coffee and croissants.

Taking the tray from the waiter, Mitch crossed to the table and sat down. 'Come and have some coffee, honey,' he said, 'I owe you an explanation.'

'That's an understatement!' Claire spat, unable to hide the anger she felt for her husband. Mitch poured coffee and cream into both cups. Claire sat opposite him and while she drank her coffee, she listened.

'We had planned our escape to coincide with a Resistance guy, a *passeur* who would take us over the Pyrenees to Spain. It had to be that day or we'd have to wait another month, maybe longer. The night before, guards took a woman from our hut to the exercise yard. They beat her until she couldn't stand and when they'd finished, threw her to the ground.'

'And the woman? Was she alive?'

'Yes, just.' Mitch's eyes sparkled with anger. 'Those bastards didn't care what happened to her. She was French, a member of the Resistance, and what made it worse for her, she was a Jew. To them, she was less important than a dog. They laughed and joked as if nothing had happened and passed around cigarettes. When they'd finished smoking they stamped out the butts and strolled off as if they were walking back from a dance, or a night out in a bar.

'When they were out of sight, two of us went out and carried the woman back.' Mitch shook his head. 'There was a deep cut by her temple. From when she fell on the cobbles in the yard, I guess. We couldn't stop it bleeding. One of the men said it needed stitching, so we carried her to the hospital block.' Mitch spat out a harsh cynical laugh. 'Hospital? It was more like a torture chamber.' Reminded of the straps across the beds and the bars at the windows of the psychiatric ward that he had been kept in in Canada, Claire wondered if Beckman was still experimenting. A chill ran through her.

'That was the first and only time I met the prison's doctor, Heinrich Beckman.'

'Who we knew in Canada as, Professor Lucien Puel.'

Mitch looked at Claire, his eyes gleaming with anger. 'Right!' He took a sip of his coffee. 'He ordered us to leave so he could patch her up. She'd been gone for hours when two order-lies half carried, half dragged her back to the hut.' Mitch shook his head as if to shake the memory from his mind. He took a deep breath and exhaled slowly. 'As they dragged her along the ground her legs trailed behind her at odd angles.' He cleared his throat. 'She wasn't able to stand so they threw her unconscious onto my blanket. She came to a couple of times during the night, said a few words, I don't remember what, now, but when we asked her what she meant, she didn't know. She had no memory of what happened to her while she was with Beckman.'

'That's how you were after your sessions at the hospital in Canada. You hadn't been beaten, of course,' Claire said, 'not physically.'

'She had been mentally as well as physically hurt. She slipped in and out of sleep. One minute her eyes were open and she was awake, then next they were closed and she was asleep. And all the time she shook uncontrollably. From being fast asleep, her eyes would open and they'd dart around the room. She would look at the window or the door and start screaming. We would calm her down and just when we thought she had settled she would open her eyes again. Once she said she remembered what had happened to her.'

'And?'

'She said *guard* once, and another time *dawn*.'

TWENTY-NINE

'It sounds to me as if she told them that you were planning to leave at dawn when the guards changed over.'

'We thought that too.' Mitch shrugged. 'If she did tell the Germans, it wasn't her fault. She wasn't able to recall anything that made sense. When she tried she became agitated, repeating the words guard and dawn over and over until she passed out again. Her memory had gone, wiped clean by drugs, or hypnosis, as mine had been by Beckman at the Louis Bertrand hospital.

'She woke once and started to scream. We were worried the guards would hear and take her away again and give her another beating, so I laid down beside her to comfort her. I held her in my arms and rocked her until she quietened. She slept fitfully.

'When she woke, she was lucid. She begged me not to leave. She said the only explanation for her loss of memory after being in the hospital was that she had been drugged, and there was no telling what she had told Beckman.

'She begged us not to go, but it was too late. If we were heading into a trap, so was the passeur who was waiting to take us across the Pyrenees. So, at dawn, when the guards were changing from night to day shift we made our escape.' Tears filled Mitch's eyes.

'And the woman?' Claire said.

Mitch hung his head. 'The guards had kicked her so badly...' He took a shuddering breath unable to speak. Tears streamed down his face. 'Her legs—' he said, at last, 'were broken.'

'So, you left her behind.'

'Yes.' He lifted his head and looked at Claire, his eyes searching hers, pleading with her to understand. 'She told us to go. She said we had no choice, that she would slow us down. And she was right. She couldn't walk. We'd have had to carry her.'

They sat again in silence. This time it was Claire who spoke first. 'Did you think about me? When you were in the prison?'

'I tried not to.' Claire shot her husband a hurt look. 'If I had allowed myself to think about you, I wouldn't have survived. Guys who pined for their sweethearts didn't last long. They either went mad, or they caused trouble and were shot. The guards singled out anyone who showed any kind of emotion. They saw it as weakness, a reason to take them out into the exercise yard and use them as a punchbag. I didn't want to die in there, honey, so I compartmentalised the way the SOE trained us to do. I was stuck in that hellhole for the duration of the war – however long that was going to be – or until I escaped.' Mitch leaned forward and looked into Claire's eyes. 'But you were always with me, China,' he said, his own eyes glossy with tears. 'Safe in here.' He patted his chest next to his heart. 'Safe in a compartment where no one could hurt you, but beyond my mental reach.'

Claire looked at her husband, trying her best to understand. 'Honey, you were fighting with the Resistance. The few times I allowed myself to think about you, I drove myself insane with worry. After I was taken to Gestapo Headquarters, I knew nothing about the outside world. I didn't know if you'd been arrested too. I felt sure that when the SOE got word I'd been captured they'd recall you. I didn't know if you'd stayed in England or come back to France and were still working with the Resistance. For all I knew you could have been shot or blown up sabotaging a troop train, as Marcel was.

'Putting all thoughts of you as far away from that vile place as I could, was how I survived.'

'I understand,' Claire whispered. 'I'm sorry I asked. I did the same every time I went on a mission. I couldn't allow myself to worry about you for fear it would affect my work, so I put you in that *no man's land* compartment. And when Aimée was born...' Tears ran down Claire's cheeks. 'I did the same with her. I daren't think about her or you. If I had, and I'd lost concentration, I'd have been a danger to myself, and to the others in the cell.'

Mitch reached across the table and took hold of Claire's hands. 'We're going to be okay, aren't we, honey?'

With every fibre of her being, Claire wanted to say yes. She wanted more than anything to fall into her husband's arms and for their life together to go back to the way it was before he became ill, but there was still one question she needed to ask. One question she needed him to answer, truthfully, before she could say yes.

'Part of the reason I followed you to France was to clear your name. I didn't believe a word of what Beckman said in the letter he wrote to your commander. And, after meeting the doctor who saved your life when you were shot and finding out that the doctor treating you in Canada was the German doctor from the prison where you were held in the war, I'm glad I did. Now you won't be dishonourably discharged and sent back to Canada as a traitor.'

Mitch started to speak, but Claire put up her hand. 'Let me finish, it's important that you know the other reason, perhaps the real reason I came looking for you.'

Claire was not given to jealousy, but she knew if she didn't ask Mitch about Simone now, she never would. Then his past would become her present, her future, and it would eat her up inside. 'I came to France to find out if you were having an affair with the woman you talk about in your sleep; the woman you dream about. Was the woman you dined with last night the woman from the prison at Saint-Gaudens? Was she Simone?'

Mitch buried his head in his hands. 'Yes,' he whispered.

Claire held her breath. Her suspicions had been confirmed. The idea of the man she loved lying with another woman, holding her while she slept, comforting her... 'Did you love her?'

'Yes.' Claire gasped. She put her hands up to her mouth to stop herself from crying out.

'But it wasn't how you think,' Mitch said.

'No? Then how was it, Mitch?'

'I loved her, yes, but I was not *in love* with her,' Mitch said. 'I was in love with you.' Claire could see Mitch was struggling to find the right words. 'We gave each other comfort. Men and women, our friends and comrades, were being killed every day. We didn't know when it was going to be our turn. Once, for no reason at all, the guards chained me up in the yard and left me there for an entire day. It was early January. Even when it wasn't blowing a gale and snowing, it was freezing. I had never before felt cold like it. It was beyond bearable. I thought I was going to die. When the guards took my chains off, I couldn't stand. I crawled back to the hut and fell onto my blanket. I was shivering so much I was convulsing. That was the first time Simone came to me.

'She brought her blanket and wrapped herself and the blanket around me. There was nothing of her, she was skin and bone, but she laid and held me all night. So, when they beat her, tortured her, or abused her—' Claire's head shot up and her eyes widened in horror. 'Yes. They raped her. So, when she needed someone to hold her, I held her, I comforted her.'

'And now?' Claire asked.

'Now? Although I haven't seen her for many years, there is still a bond between us, still the closeness we felt for each other. Maybe in different circumstances, at a different time?' Mitch lifted and dropped his shoulders. 'Who knows?'

Mitch's words, like a tidal wave, crashed down on her, taking her breath away and tearing at her heart. She wanted to scream but was saved from doing so by someone knocking the door. She put on her coat and picked up her handbag, suitcase, and the briefcase. Without looking back at her husband, she crossed to the door. Mitch leapt out of his chair and got to the door first. Barring Claire's way, he said, 'Please stay? I want you to meet her.'

'Meet her?' Unable to look at Mitch for the rage she felt inside, she said, 'You want me to meet your—?' A louder tap on the door was followed by, 'Your taxi is here, Madame Belland.'

'Excuse me,' Claire said, without looking at Mitch. He moved out of her way, she put down the suitcase and opened the door. Taking ten francs from her handbag she said, 'Would you give this to the driver?'

'You're not going?' Mitch said, relief smoothing the lines on his face.

'Not today.' The porter, like a spectator, looked from Mitch to Claire. 'I promised the real Doctor Puel that I would take the documents he entrusted to me to Guillaume Cheval, which I now feel able to do.' Claire turned to the porter. 'Would you ask the taxi driver to come back in an hour to take me to the Chateau Je Reviendrai?'

When the porter left, Claire handed the briefcase to Mitch. 'The documents Doctor Puel gave me are in here. Read them while I telephone Thomas. If I am going to see Guillaume Cheval today, there is no need for him to come up at the weekend.'

Mitch opened the case, took out a handful of papers and

gasped with shock. 'Good God, where did the old doctor get all this?'

'He has had most of it since just after Beckman murdered his grandson. He had no idea that Beckman has been impersonating his grandson until I told him the name of your psychiatrist in Canada was Lucien Puel. Until then, I think he thought Beckman had used his grandson's identity to get out of France and back to Germany. I'm going to telephone Thomas,' Claire said, heading for the door. 'I won't be long.'

'You can telephone him from here, I'll take these to my room and read them.'

'I'd rather you didn't. I promised the old doctor...'

'They'll be safe enough with me.' Mitch looked shocked that Claire didn't trust him.

'I said no! I promised Doctor Puel. Please respect that and do not take them out of this room.'

'Okay!' Mitch put his hands up. 'The documents and I will be here when you get back.'

Claire left Mitch reading and went down to the foyer. There was only one public telephone, which was in use, so she waited. When the phone was free she called Thomas. There was no reply. He was probably on his way to work at the University. She pressed the coin return button, fished the coins out of the narrow metal drawer and replaced the telephone. A second later she put the money back into the money box and called Antoinette.

Assuming Thomas had told Antoinette about Doctor Puel and the documents he had given her, Claire related briefly what had happened that morning. 'I don't have much time. I've booked a taxi to take me to see Guillaume Cheval. I'll ring you when I get back and let you know what happened. Would you get in touch with Thomas? Tell him there will be no need for him to come up here at the weekend, because I am taking the documents to Guillaume Cheval, today.' Antoinette assured

Claire she would pass on the message and the two friends said goodbye.

'So,' Mitch said on Claire's return, 'Doctor Heinrich Beckman became the psychiatrist, Professor Lucien Puel. The twenty-six-year-old became a thirty-six-year-old – and the German National became French-Swiss.'

'That about sums it up.' Claire took the papers out of Mitch's hand, put them in the correct order, and returned them to the briefcase. 'The taxi will be here soon. Are you coming?'

'Yes.' Mitch's eyebrows rose in surprise. 'I didn't think— Hang on, I'll run and get my coat.'

'I'll be in the foyer.' Picking up her handbag and the brief-case, Claire took the lift down to reception. 'I'd like to stay for another night. Would that be possible?' she asked the manager.

He consulted the booking diary. 'Your room is free tonight and tomorrow, so you can stay where you are if you're happy with the room, Madame Belland.'

Claire said she was, thanked the man, and as she walked across the foyer to the hotel's main entrance, Mitch ran across the reception area to her and together they went out to the waiting taxi.

THIRTY

As the taxi cruised along the narrow country roads towards Chateau Je Reviendrai, the nerves in Claire's stomach began to tighten. She inhaled and exhaled slowly and told herself to calm down. It didn't work. She looked out of the window. The sky was pale blue, the trees and hedgerows were in bud, and fine mist hugged the earth.

She recognised the crossroads where Thomas had taken the turn to the chateau. They were close. Claire began again to doubt her decision to take the old doctor's documents herself. She would have to meet the woman her husband felt so strongly about. The woman who, after seeing her with Mitch last night, Claire had decided not to meet.

Perhaps she should have waited for Thomas to take them at the weekend. She closed her eyes. No! she said to herself. She was doing the right thing. The sooner Heinrich Beckman was arrested and put behind bars the better. And the sooner she met and got 'Simone' out of her system the sooner she would be able to move on with her life.

'He's in love with you, you know?'

'What?' Claire had been deep in thought and only caught the words *love* and *know*.

'Thomas Durand. He's in love with you.'

Her heart thumped against her chest. She had intended to tell Mitch that she'd kissed Thomas and that she'd had feelings for him, but now she didn't need to tell him anything. What she did, or had done, was none of his business. Even so, she felt she needed to deny this revelation. 'Don't be ridiculous.'

'He made it quite clear on the telephone.' Claire held her breath. Would Mitch tell her what Thomas had said? She knew her husband, knew he wouldn't be able to resist telling her. All she had to do was appear disinterested. She did, and it worked. 'He telephoned me at the hotel in the early hours, told me you were leaving in the morning. He said, if I had any sense at all I would tell you how I felt about you. Tell you that I loved you before it was too late, or I'd regret it.'

'Well you did stop me leaving, and you have told me how you feel.'

Mitch laughed. 'Sometimes you can be so naive, Claire. Thomas Durand wasn't telling me to tell you how I feel about you, he was telling me that he should have told you how he felt about you when he had the chance. He was saying that it was too late for him, and now he regretted it.'

'This is not the time to talk about how I— *we* feel, or what we regret. I have a job to do, so do you, we'll talk about who kissed who later! We're here,' she said, as the taxi turned off the road and began the slow drive up to Chateau Je Reviendrai.

The cab pulled up at the bottom of a set of steps leading to the chateau where the Cheval's lived. The driver jumped out of the vehicle and opened Claire's door. Mitch let himself out and paid the fare, while Claire stood and marvelled at the elegant building.

'Beautiful, isn't it?' Mitch said, at her side.

'It is,' she said, deciding there was no need for Mitch to

know that she and Thomas had seen the chateau before, albeit from a distance. She followed him up the steps and he rang the bell. The door was answered by the tall distinguished looking man who Claire recognised from the day she was with Thomas.

'Welcome, Alain,' the man said. He shook Mitch's hand before wrapping his arms around him. Then, turning to Claire: 'Madame Mitchell?'

'Darling,' Mitch said, 'this is Monsieur Guillaume Cheval. Guillaume, this is my wife, Claire.'

'I am delighted to meet you, Claire,' Guillaume said, shaking Claire's hand. Claire felt her cheeks redden. She wasn't sure whether it was because Mitch had called her darling, or because Simone's father called her Madame Mitchell, which meant he knew who she was. He hadn't looked surprised when Mitch announced her as his wife either. Claire wondered how recently her husband had told the Chevals about her. 'Come in, please,' Guillaume Cheval said. Smiling as if he was welcoming old friends into his home, he opened the door wide to allow Mitch and Claire to enter.

'Alain tells me you have important documents that will help us to track down the criminal Heinrich Beckman, Claire?'

Claire shot a look of surprise at Mitch. 'I telephoned Guillaume from the hotel room when you went down to reception.'

'I have, sir,' Claire said, handing the briefcase to Guillaume Cheval.

He looked at her and then at the case. Then he lifted his head to Claire again, and said, 'Thank you. I want to open it now,' he said, clutching it as if it was a priceless piece of art. 'But I must wait. The doctor who treated your husband in Canada is the doctor who tortured my daughter when she was in prison. She is a lawyer now, and she is desperate to see the contents of this case. Come and meet her,' he said, leading the way across a large entrance hall.

As the trio reached the far side of the hall, Claire stopped. 'Someone is playing the piano.'

'My daughter Eleanor,' Cheval said.

'She plays beautifully, monsieur.'

'Yes, she does.' The rhythmic sound of the piano grew louder as they neared the end of a short corridor. Guillaume Cheval opened a door. 'The music room,' he said, 'and my daughter, Eleanor.'

Eleanor, who Claire had only ever thought of as Simone, lifted her head from the music score she was reading and gave Claire a bright welcoming smile. 'Come in.' she called, from behind the piano. 'I shall reach the end of this piece in one second.' Running her fingers along the keys until she came to the last one, she lifted her hands. 'That's it!'

'Beautiful, darling,' Eleanor's father said, applauding his daughter, 'truly beautiful.'

'You are not biased at all, are you, Father?'

Laughing, Guillaume Cheval motioned Claire to come further into the room. He pointed to a pair of matching settees on either side of a long table that was placed sideways on to the fire. As Claire reached the middle of the room, Eleanor Cheval appeared from behind the piano, in a wheelchair.

Claire stopped in her tracks. The beautiful woman who she had seen in the restaurant the night before, was still unable to walk. Trying not to let Eleanor see how shocked she was, Claire said, 'You are a wonderful pianist.' And as Eleanor neared the settee, Claire sat down.

Eleanor Cheval, pushing hard on the wheels of the wheelchair came to a halt beside her. 'I don't know the piece you were playing,' Claire continued, 'it is French, of course—'

'"Daphnis et Chloé". It was composed for Sergei Diaghilev by Maurice Ravel. It's a ballet, but Ravel calls it a *symphonie chorégraphiqué.* Very exotic, and very exciting.' Eleanor laughed. 'Would you believe, before the war, I trained to be a ballet dancer?' Eleanor looked down at her legs and laughed again. This time the laugh was sharp with cynicism. 'Now I am a boring old lawyer.' Claire swallowed hard but couldn't stop her tears.

'Claire, please do not be upset.' Eleanor put her hand on Claire's arm. 'There are many people much worse than me. I don't like being in a wheelchair, but I am alive. There were many times in the prison, especially after Alain and the others left, that I could have been killed.

'But here I am. I may never be a ballet dancer, but I make a difference. My job is important, fulfilling – and I get to see men like Beckman hang, or go to the guillotine. And thanks to you, Heinrich Beckman will be punished for what he did to me, and to the other courageous people in the prison.'

Claire smiled a sad smile acknowledging Eleanor Cheval's gratitude. She didn't say anything in reply; there was nothing to say except she was sorry, futile words that could never express how she really felt. She was sorry for the feelings she'd had before meeting the remarkable woman too.

She looked across the table at Mitch. He turned his head slowly from listening to Eleanor and looked at her. He smiled and Claire nodded that she understood what he meant when he talked about loving this extraordinarily brave woman. Before guilt engulfed her, Claire said, 'What your father has in that briefcase will prove beyond any doubt that Heinrich Beckman is a murderer and an imposter.'

'Let us go to my study,' Guillaume Cheval said to his daughter.

Eleanor pushed on one wheel until the wheelchair was facing the door. 'Coming, Claire?' she called, over her shoulder.

When Claire was at her side, Eleanor's father took hold of the handle on the back of his daughter's chair and began to push her across the room. 'No, Papa!' Guillaume Cheval let go of the handle and stepped back. Eleanor looked up at Claire. 'It is part of my physiotherapy that I wheel myself as much as I can. It builds up the muscles in my arms and back.' She looked back at her father, smiled and shook her head. He shrugged good heartedly in reply.

Claire opened the door and walked along the corridor to the entrance hall with Eleanor. Outside what Claire assumed was the study she and Eleanor waited for the men to catch up with them. When they had, Guillaume Cheval opened the door and held it for Eleanor to wheel herself into the room. Claire and Mitch followed.

The room was oblong with a polished wood-block floor and floor to ceiling panelling. A large desk stood between two sash windows overlooking the gardens and a huge round table dominated the centre of the room. It reminded Claire of the tables used by the WAAF when they were posted out to the coast to plot the whereabouts of enemy aircraft.

Guillaume Cheval laid the briefcase on the table, opened it, and took the documents out one at a time. He placed them around the edge of the table and Eleanor began to read.

Claire had read each of the documents several times and moved out of the way so those who had not seen them had a better view. She looked out of the window. It was noon and the pale sun had a more defined edge. She watched a pair of blackbirds picking at dead leaves, lifting them and flicking them away when they found nothing to eat beneath them. A robin flew out of a nearby bush, his chest more brown than red, a sign that spring was around the corner.

Hearing her name being called brought Claire out of her reverie. She looked back at the table. Three piles of paper now replaced the single row that ten minutes before had circled the table's perimeter.

'This Claire,' Guillaume said, pointing to the documents of

the real Lucien Puel, murdered on the day Heinrich Beckman escaped from the prison at Saint-Gaudens, 'is the proof we need to put the sadistic creature behind bars.'

'And my testimony,' Eleanor said, 'might get him hanged.'

Guillaume excused himself, saying he needed to make a telephone call. When he returned it was with a triumphant smile on his face. 'A manhunt for Heinrich Beckman and Nurse Bryant, the nurse who assisted him at the Louis Bertrand hospital, has begun.'

'The nurse?' Claire said, surprised. 'She couldn't have been at Saint-Gaudens, she is too young.'

'She wasn't at Saint-Gaudens. She isn't German. She's Canadian.'

'Then why are the authorities after her?'

'The police think she murdered Beckman's secretary.'

'What?'

'The police told my associate that Beckman's secretary was killed on the day Alain was due to fly back to England. You were probably the last person to see her alive,' he said, turning to Alain. 'Initially, because you missed the plane, the authorities thought it was you who had killed her.' Mitch gasped. 'She was stabbed. They haven't found the knife, but they found a nurse's fob-watch under the dead woman's body. They searched the staff lockers, looking for the knife, and found Nurse Bryant's uniform with a hole where her watch had been ripped from it. They think Beckman's secretary must have grabbed the watch when she was attacked, it came off the nurse's uniform, and somehow the secretary ended up lying on it.'

Mitch looked at Claire. 'I find it hard to believe Nurse Bryant could kill anyone.'

'I agree,' Claire said, 'Nurse Bryant seemed like a kind, sensitive, woman. Why would she kill her work colleague, someone who she knew and probably liked?'

'People have done worse things for love,' Eleanor put in.

'Whether she was involved or not, there's an alert out for her too. The police are stopping and questioning everyone, irrelevant of age or gender. The docks and passenger ports, railway stations and airports are on high alert. It's a vast country, but I'm told it is only a matter of time before they are caught.'

'Beckman is ruthless,' Eleanor said. 'He'll kill the nurse if she gets in his way.'

'And he'll get a false passport and any other document he needs,' Mitch said. 'He knows what he's doing and he must have enough money to pay for a passage to anywhere. Those guys at the hospital, particularly the specialists, are at the top of the tree when it comes to salaries.'

Guillaume grinned. 'It doesn't matter how much money he has, it won't help him. His bank account has been seized. As soon as he or anyone else tries to draw money out of it the Montréal police will be alerted.'

THIRTY-ONE

Everyone applauded the news of the manhunt – except Mitch. Claire knew her husband would be blaming himself for the murder of Heinrich Beckman's secretary. She reached out and took his hand.

'I think we should come back to this lot after lunch,' Eleanor said.

'Excellent idea. That Beckman's reign has come to an end has given me an appetite,' Guillaume said. 'I hope you're hungry, Alain? This morning, after you telephoned, I told Cook we hoped you and Claire would stay for lunch and she took a ham out of the refrigerator in celebration.'

Claire followed the others out of the study. Guillaume walked at his daughter's side and Claire with Mitch. The dining room was the second room off the main hall. It was as plush as the other rooms but lighter. The windows were wider and faced south. A woman in her late fifties, as round as she was tall, with greying hair and an olive complexion, welcomed them as if it was her house, her dining room.

'Esme, I would like you to meet Claire, Alain's wife.'

'Pleased to meet you, madame.'

Claire returned the greeting.

'Nice to see you again, sir,' Esme said to Mitch.

Esme pulled out the chair at the top of the table for Guillaume. She then pulled out chairs on his left for Claire and Mitch. Eleanor wheeled herself to the right of her father, where at least two dining chairs had been removed.

Lunch was delicious. The ham was succulent, large potatoes had been roasted in their jackets and there was a selection of small pastries stuffed with spicy meats and cheeses. In the centre of the table were dishes of pickled cabbage, onions and gherkins, and a large basket of crusty bread rolls, still warm from the oven.

When they had finished eating, Eleanor beckoned Claire with a flick of her head. 'If you'll excuse us?' Both men said they would. 'You'll be going back to the study, Papa?'

'Yes, but first I shall smoke a cigar while I tell Alain what happens now we have Beckman in our sights.'

'Let us leave the men to it, Claire. You and I shall take the documents that I need to study before the trial to the music room.' Claire thanked Guillaume, and then Esme, for the delicious lunch, got up from the table and followed Eleanor out of the room.

On the way to the study, Eleanor said, 'While my father is not watching my every move, I shall show you my gymnasium, as he calls it.' She laughed. 'It is where I have my physiotherapy treatment. Come,' she said, pointing to a door on her left. Claire opened the door and entered the room first, holding it open for Eleanor. When she had negotiated the doorframe and was safely inside, Claire let go of the door and it closed automatically.

At one end of the gymnasium was a thick padded mat that looked about ten feet square. There were weights on one side of the room and two parallel metal and wood rails on the other. Claire ran her hands along the top of the nearest rail.

'They are for me to hold on to when I stand up,' Eleanor said, 'but I'm only allowed to stand when my physiotherapist and his assistant are here. I need two people to catch me if I fall.' Eleanor laughed and wheeled herself to the beginning of the rails. 'What they don't know,' she said, with a mischievous glint in her eyes, 'is that I stand at these rails as often as I can when they are not here.'

Eleanor manoeuvred the wheelchair as close as she could to the nearest rail, put on the brake and pulled herself up. 'Ta dah!' she said as she stood and gripped one of the rails. She reached out and lunged towards the other rail, 'Got you!' she said, breathing heavily. 'Now, what do you say to that, Claire?'

Claire wanted to say *petrified*. Instead, she applauded and stepped behind Eleanor in case she fell. 'I'd rather you didn't stand at the back of me, it puts me off my stride. If you know what I mean.' Claire moved to Eleanor's left. 'I am quite safe. All the pushing myself about in the chair has made my arms very strong. They won't let me down. Oh!' she said, 'but my legs might. Would you take the brake off my chair and push it nearer, so the seat is against the back of my legs? I think I need to sit down.'

Claire did so with relief and when the chair was in place behind Eleanor, she put the brake on again. Eleanor took her hands off the rails and dropped onto the seat of the wheelchair. 'Damn!' she said. 'I managed twice as long yesterday.'

'I'm sorry,' Claire said.

'Don't be. I didn't stand for long today, but I did yesterday, and I shall tomorrow.'

As she moved to let Eleanor pass her, Claire noticed a ballet bar. It ran along the four walls, two with floor to ceiling mirrors on them. She gazed at it wondering why Eleanor hadn't had it taken down. Tears threatened and Claire cleared her throat.

'I won't let my father take the bar down.'

Claire was miles away. 'Sorry?'

'The ballet bar. Papa wants to take it down, but I plan to walk around the room one day. And when that day comes, the bar will come in handy to hang on to. Come on, let's look at the documents. I think I've had enough exercise for one day.'

Claire carried Eleanor's pile of papers from the study to the music room. Eleanor wheeled herself over to the piano and took a notebook and pen from inside the piano stool, before joining Claire by the fire.

Claire on one settee and Eleanor in her chair at the end of the settee opposite, looked through the papers that Heinrich Beckman had killed for. As she read each of them, Eleanor tutted and made noises of disgust. She asked Claire how the papers had come into her possession and Claire told her about meeting the murdered doctor's grandfather. She omitted to say she was looking for her at the time. She told Eleanor how she had first met Thomas Durand in Paris, and how he had driven her to the prison and together they had met the late Lucien Puel's grandfather and namesake.

Remembering the broken-hearted old doctor's tears, Claire told Eleanor how he had found his grandson in the road, dying, after the beating Beckman had given him on the day the camp was liberated, the day Beckman had escaped.

Eleanor sat for an hour hunched over the documents, reading and making notes. Then she sat upright, stretched, and rolled her shoulders.

'I'm so sorry you had to read them,' Claire said, 'they must have brought back horrific memories.'

Eleanor looked up, her eyes sparkling with anger and revulsion. 'Day after day this monster, Heinrich Beckman, had me taken out of my hut and paraded in front of a dozen men; mostly Resistance members, patriots from our colonies – and occasionally a woman.' Eleanor shook her head. 'I was made to watch them as they were executed. The guards,' she caught her breath, 'showed no mercy. They would make the prisoners stand against the wall for sometimes as long as ten minutes while the firing squad laughed and joked and smoked cigarettes. They sneered and taunted them when they prayed, or they cursed them. Sometimes men wet themselves before they were executed – and the guards would ridicule them, or shout obscenities at them—' Eleanor paused and clenched her fists.

'There were a couple of guards who put black bags made of coarse sacking over prisoners' heads, but others, the more sadistic among them, made the prisoners look at me. I was an unwilling spectator at their cruel games, Claire.

'Some weeks before the Allies liberated the prison, I was dragged out of my hut and propped up against the wall with half a dozen other prisoners. This time they did put black bags over our heads. The sergeant in charge of the firing squad ordered them to take aim, then fire! I braced myself and began to pray. When the firing stopped I heard the bodies of the men on either side of me falling to the ground while I was still propped against the wall.

'That was the latest game. Ordered by Heinrich Beckman as a punishment because, although he was sure that I was a member of the Resistance and he suspected a Jew, I wouldn't confirm either. I wouldn't tell him anything, except under the influence of one of his mind-meddling drugs.'

Eleanor spat out a harsh laugh. 'But that wasn't good enough for Doctor Beckman. He was an egomaniac. He needed to personally break me, not have a truth serum do it for him. So that was the torture he designed for me. Propped up against the wall, in agony from legs already broken, not knowing if I would be executed that day or the next, or in a week's time.'

'You said women were executed?'

'Yes, there were only a few women in the prison. Some, like me, were members of the Resistance. Each hut had at least one woman in it. It was another way to break the men. Most of the prisoners had spouses or sweethearts back home – the women too. They missed their loved ones, so the Germans put temptation in their way. Two or three years in a place like that can make the most faithful man lonely for a woman.' Eleanor shook her head. 'Relationships between prisoners was a breach of discipline, punishable by death. If two people were caught together, or even suspected of having an affair, they were taken out and shot.

'Thankfully, most of the men were like Alain, able to control their needs. But then Alain knew you were waiting for him. Never doubt that he loved you then, Claire.' Eleanor sighed. 'Alain is the best of men. I owe him my life.'

Eleanor looked into Claire's eyes. 'Without Alain, I would not have survived the torture Beckman dished out to me. I think if I hadn't had Alain to go back to, Beckman would have broken me. But every time the guards dragged me back to the hut, Alain would wrap me in his blanket and hold me, taking care not to do more damage to my broken body.'

Guilt and shame swept over Claire. She couldn't help herself, and said, 'Last night I saw you in Le Restaurant du Parc and I thought—'

'You thought I was in love with him?'

Claire lowered her eyes, her cheeks red with embarrassment. 'Yes. I'm sorry. Can you ever forgive me?'

'There is nothing to forgive. I was in love with him in the prison, but Alain was in love with you. As for last night?' Eleanor reached out and took Claire's hands. 'Last night I felt the warmth and love of a big brother. I want to always know him, and always feel that love. I shall do nothing to risk losing it.'

'Thank you.'

'No. Thank you.' Letting go of Claire's hands Eleanor stacked the documents one on top of another. 'With these,' she said, 'we've got the devil.'

'We have the proof, but how do we get him to a court in France for a trial?'

'The Canadian police will find him, and when they do they will bring him to France and turn him over to the French authorities. Or, two of our investigators will fly to Canada and bring him back.

'It is usually investigators working for the lawyers who find the proof to put war criminals away – and that can take time.' Eleanor lifted the documents and waved them above her head. 'But with all this, Beckman won't know what has hit him,' she laughed.

Eleanor Cheval was ready for the fight. Claire too was ready. Full of admiration for this courageous woman whose enthusiasm was rubbing off on her, Claire was laughing when the door of the music room crashed open.

Mitch rushed in, his face was as white as a sheet. 'Heinrich Beckman is holding my father and stepmother hostage. Guillaume is taking me to Orly airport, I'm flying to Canada tonight.'

'I'm coming with you,' Claire said. She reached over the arm of the settee and grabbed her handbag. Ripping a page from her notebook, she scribbled down Antoinette Marron's name and telephone number. Beneath it she wrote Thomas Durand and his telephone number. 'Would you telephone my friend Antoinette? Tell her what has happened. Tell her we won't be coming to Paris now, and,' Claire took a panicky breath, 'ask her to let Édith Belland and my sister Bess know? She has their numbers.'

Eleanor assured Claire that she would telephone Antoinette Marron as soon as she and Alain left. 'And Thomas? What do I tell him?'

'Tell him to meet me at Orly airport.' Claire thought for a second. 'I don't know what time we'll arrive, but Thomas will work it out if you tell him what time it was when we left here. And, tell him to bring me a *key kit*.'

Eleanor knew, as Thomas would know, that a key kit was for picking locks. She nodded that she understood. 'Thank you, Eleanor,' Claire said, and kissed her goodbye.

'*Jusqu'à ce que nous nous réunissions de nouveau.*'

'Yes, my friend. Until we meet again.'

Guillaume was in his car with the engine running and the doors open. Mitch kissed Eleanor goodbye, grabbed Claire's hand, and together they ran out of the chateau and down the steps. No sooner had they jumped into the car than Guillaume put his foot on the accelerator. Eleanor, from her wheelchair at the top of the steps, lifted the sheet of note paper that Claire had given her with one hand and blew kisses with the other.

Claire opened the window and waved back. 'Thanks for everything. See you at the trial.'

THIRTY-TWO

'How did you find out Beckman was at your father's house?'

'I telephoned Commander Landry to tell him you had documents that would prove my innocence and that Puel was really Heinrich Beckman, and he already knew.'

'He did?'

'Yes. He said you sent him a telegram.'

'I wrote a telegram, and I tried to send it, but the guy in the post office had shut shop for the day and wouldn't open up for me. I pushed it through the letter box and when he ignored it, I called him a bastard and kicked the door.' She bit her bottom lip. 'He must have come back, looked at the address, and because it was an RAF aerodrome realised its importance.'

'Thank God he did.' Mitch sighed. Claire looked at her husband. He had dark circles under his eyes and his face was set in a heavy frown.

'How did the commander find out Beckman was keeping your parents prisoner?'

'Dad rang our house, on Beckman's orders. I expect Beckman blames me for the situation he's now in. Anyway, when Dad couldn't get hold of me he rang Grandma Esther and asked her if she knew where I was. She said she didn't, but could find out, and asked Dad to telephone her again the next day. She knew from your phone call that I was in France, but she didn't know how to get in touch with me, so she had no choice but to telephone the commander and tell him what was going on in Canada.'

'Thank God she did.'

'Landry said when he got your telegram, he contacted the War Crimes Committee. They gave him Guillaume's telephone number and the rest you know.'

Claire nodded, then smiled at Guillaume Cheval who was looking at her in the reverse mirror. 'Where are we going, Guillaume?' she asked, when they turned right at a T-junction that was signposted *Paris left*.

'To the hotel to pick up your suitcases and from there to Orly Airport. There's a Trans-Canada Airlines flight at five-twenty to Montréal.'

Alain looked at his watch. 'We're cutting it fine. Will we make it?'

'We should. But, if you miss the Trans flight, there's a Canadian Pacific plane due out at 6.30. Both planes have to refuel in Northern Ireland and again in the USA, so...'

'When you land in Montréal you'll be met by Canadian military intelligence. The Chief of Police may, or may not, be there. It depends on the situation at your parents' house as to whether Chief Jacobs will be at your hotel when you arrive. He might leave it until the morning. You'll be taken to the hotel, where someone will brief you. Have something to eat and I suggest you have an early night. It may be the last night's sleep you have for a while. Negotiations in these kinds of situations can take a long time. In the morning, you will be taken to your father's house.'

'And Claire? What time does she leave?'

'Not sure. I'm sorry, Claire, there wasn't time to organise a flight for you. There is a plane to London-Croydon this evening, at around eight o'clock. We'll book you a seat as soon as we've seen Alain off. Commander Landry has already dispatched a car to collect you. One of his officers will meet you from the plane and drive you to Oxford.'

'I'm going to Canada with my husband,' Claire said to Cheval's reflection in the reversing mirror. 'I'm going to Canada!' she said again, this time to Mitch.

'Honey, it's too dangerous. I need to know that you and Aimée are at home and safe. If anything should happen to me—'

'Nothing *is* going to happen to you.' Mitch took hold of Claire's hand. 'No, Mitch!' She snatched her hand away. 'I promised Aimée I would find you and I would bring you home, and that is what I am going to do!'

'But if we are both—'

'Stop it! Nothing will happen to either of us, because I intend to keep my promise to our daughter!'

Claire was first through the door of Le Petit Château Hotel, and first to reach reception. She was not going to be left behind in France or sent back to England, she was going to Canada. Mitch would need her, and she needed to be with him. When the manager appeared, Claire asked for the keys to both their rooms. When she was given them, she passed them to Mitch. 'My suitcase, as you know, is already packed and is just inside my room. When you have packed your case pick mine up. I'll pay our bills. Don't be long,' she called after him, 'I'll see you in the car.'

Claire, a worried expression on her face, explained to Thomas's old Resistance friend that she and her husband had been called back to London because her mother had been taken ill. Sympathetic to Claire's plight, he didn't ask her to pay for the coming night, or the following night, which she had only booked that morning.

Claire paid, thanked the man for his kindness and hightailed it out of there to Guillaume Cheval who was waiting in the car.

'How are we doing for time?' Mitch asked, throwing their suitcases into the boot of Guillaume's car and leaping into the back seat next to Claire.

'We are in good time. We should reach Paris-Orly airport in just over an hour.'

Guillaume dropped Claire and Mitch off at the entrance to Orly airport. With only time for a brief goodbye, he shook Mitch's hand and gave him a customary hug. 'Be careful,' the Frenchman said, his voice hoarse with emotion. Mitch nodded but couldn't speak. Guillaume hugged Claire. 'Take care.'

'I will.'

As they entered the Departure Hall Claire spotted Thomas leaning against the Trans-Canada Air Lines desk. She waved, and he walked quickly to the centre of the hall. Claire ran to meet him. 'There's no need for Mitch to know about the keys,' she whispered, hugging her friend.

'Okay.'

'Thank you,' she said. She knew what Thomas had to do and held him until she felt the weight of the lock picking keys in her coat pocket. Mitch joined them with Claire's ticket. 'Darling, this is my friend Thomas Durand.' Mitch put down the suitcases and shook Thomas's hand.

'Thank you for looking after her,' Mitch said, 'and thank you for telephoning me at the hotel.'

Thomas gave Mitch a friendly nod and looked at Claire. 'No problem.'

While they were talking two airport officials arrived, asked Mitch and Claire their names and after a quick look at their passports, each picked up a suitcase. 'The plane is on time,

Captain,' the older of the two men said, 'we would like to get you on board before the rest of the passengers.'

The plane to Montréal left on time. Once they were settled in their seats, Claire and Mitch slept.

Claire woke to the sound of a stewardess asking passengers if they would like tea or coffee. 'Coffee for me please,' she said and nudged Mitch. 'Do you want a coffee, darling?' He nodded sleepily.

When the stewardess moved on, Mitch rubbed his eyes. 'It's my fault Beckman's secretary is dead.'

'How do you make that out?'

'I told you she came into the office while I was copying my medical report and Beckman's letter and she didn't try to stop me. It's hard to explain, but she looked at me as if she agreed with what I was doing. When I'd finished she took the original papers from me and put them in another envelope. It appeared to be identical to the one I had ripped open, but Beckman must have noticed there was a difference because it got her killed.'

'By Beckman's nurse?' Claire queried, more to herself than to Mitch.

Mitch shook his head. 'Doesn't ring true, does it?'

'No, it doesn't,' Claire agreed. 'But if she loved him—?'

The stewardess brought their drinks and Claire relaxed back in her seat to enjoy her coffee.

'What did Thomas Durand put in your pocket?'

Claire choked. 'This coffee is hot!'

Mitch rolled his eyes. 'I'll ask you again. What did—?'

'All right!' It was pointless lying to Mitch, he knew her too well. 'Lockpicking keys.'

'Lockpicking—?'

'Keep your voice down.' Claire put her coffee cup on the tray in front of her and reached into her coat pocket. 'These,' she said, showing him a leather pouch with a pattern of the fleur-de-lys embossed on it. The small red case looked like a lady's purse, or a manicure set. Opening it, she jangled the long needle-like keys in front of him.

'I wish I hadn't asked.' He put out his hand and Claire whipped them away.

'Do you know how to use these?'

Mitch didn't answer.

'Well I do, so they're staying with me.'

'Why do you want— No! No way!' He looked around to see if anyone was listening. No one was. He lowered his voice anyway. 'You are not getting involved in the situation at Dad's house.'

Claire returned the lockpicking keys to her pocket. Her argument was, the years he had spent in the prison in France were the years she had spent working with the French Resistance, and, although she didn't want to say it, she could probably handle herself better than him in a hostage situation. She could open locked doors better. André Belland taught her, and he had taught her well.

She was saved from saying anything when the stewardess arrived with their meal.

'Ladies and Gentlemen, this is your captain speaking. Today the weather in Montréal was bright and sunny, though a little colder than in Paris, France. If you haven't already changed your watches to conform to the time difference, I suggest you do so now. We are now making our descent. I won't be speaking to you again as we will soon be in our landing pattern. It was a pleasure to have you aboard. We hope to have you with us again, soon. Thank you.'

Claire looked at her watch. It was 3.30am. The flight, with landings to refuel in Northern Ireland and Detroit had taken

ten hours. They both wound their watches back six hours to
9.30 in the evening. Mitch buckled his safety belt and leaned
back in his seat. 'Are you all right, Mitch?'

'Yes, honey. I'm just worried about Dad and Marie.' Claire
held his hand, as she always did when they took off or landed.
She liked flying, she just didn't like taking off and landing. The
rise and fall in altitude hurt her ears and made her deaf. She
was deaf now and would be until she was on the ground. She
swallowed a couple of times, hoping her ears would pop. They
didn't.

Claire felt the aeroplane land, the wheels bump as they
touched down, and the pull of air from the reverse thrust. She
looked out of the window. As the plane taxied towards the
airport building the sprinkling of tiny lights she saw from a
distance grew bigger until she could see they were lights to
guide the plane towards the arrivals building of Montréal
Dorval Airport.

CANADA

SPRING 1950

THIRTY-THREE

A waft of fresh spring evening air gusted into the aeroplane as the exit door at the front of the cabin opened.

'If you would like to follow me, sir, madam?' a stewardess said. 'Two RCAF officers are waiting to escort you from the plane.'

Mitch stood up and stepped into the aisle. Claire edged out of her seat sideways until she was able to bend down and pick up her handbag. She joined Mitch and the stewardess in the narrow passage between the door and the galley kitchen. Mitch took Claire's hand, letting go only to salute the two officers at the exit.

'Officer Boucher, sir,' the female officer said, saluting Mitch.

'Officer Lloyd,' the male officer said, following Officer Boucher's lead.

Then the officers turned and saluted Claire. She returned the gesture. It had been six years since anyone had saluted her – and then it was only when she was wearing her WAAF uniform, which, once she had been recruited by the SOE, wasn't often.

Officer Boucher escorted Claire down the steps, while

Officer Lloyd walked alongside Mitch. 'We need to pick up our cases,' Claire said, when they were on the tarmac.

'Already in the car, Mrs Mitchell,' Officer Boucher said.

Claire looked over her shoulder at Mitch. He winked and she gave him a nervous smile. 'Where are we going?'

'To a hotel, Mrs Mitchell.'

Claire sighed. She wasn't going to get anything out of the female officer. She probably hadn't been told the name of the hotel or its location, Claire thought.

The car, a standard RCAF six-seater black saloon, was waiting for them when they came out of the airport. The driver, standing at the back of the car, opened the boot and stowed the suitcases. Claire and Mitch got into the back of the car, the driver took up position behind the steering wheel and waited for his fellow officers. Lloyd sat in the front next to the driver, Boucher in the back next to Claire. When everyone was seated, the driver pulled into the stream of traffic leaving the airport. Claire, leaning forward, looked past the officer and out of the window. There were vehicles on either side of them. In a slow-moving convoy, they were heading into Montréal.

When they arrived at the hotel, they were met by a police sergeant who, after introducing himself, ushered Mitch and Claire into the hotel and, bypassing reception, pressed the button for the lift. As the lift rose to the sixth floor, Claire took hold of Mitch's hand. She gave it a squeeze to reassure him everything would be all right. Whether it would or not remained to be seen. She tried to imagine how she would feel if it was her mother, or one of her sisters and their husbands, being held prisoner by a madman like Beckman, but she couldn't.

The hotel suite was modern and spacious. There was a sitting room, double bedroom, and a reasonable sized bathroom. No sooner had they taken off their outdoor clothes than there was a knock at the door. Officer Lloyd opened it and Montréal's Chief of Police entered with the sergeant who had met them.

'Let's get down to business, shall we?' Chief of Police Sam Jacobs introduced himself, then pulled out a chair from beneath the dining table. Mitch pulled out another. When Claire took the sofa, sitting on the end nearest to the table, the men sat down.

'Your parents' house is surrounded. I've got armed police on the ground and an elite task force of specially trained officers with snipers in the upstairs windows of the neighbouring houses. The German won't get away this time,' Chief Jacobs said.

'Has Beckman said anything about my father and mother? Has he made any demands, other than wanting to talk to me?'

'He told the police negotiator that the hostages were in the basement. We have no proof of that, but we can't see them in the room where Beckman and the woman are.'

'Nurse Bryant, who worked for him?'

The Chief of Police nodded. 'We haven't seen much of her in the last four hours. I guess she's either in another room or she's keeping out of sight.'

Claire was visualising the layout of the house, where the basement door was in reference to the sitting room and the dining room, which were both at the front of the house, both with big windows. 'Which room is Beckman in?' she asked the chief. 'When you look at the house, is he in the room on the right of the front door or the left?'

'The right.'

'That means he's as far away from the basement door and the kitchen as he could possibly be, Mitch.'

'That's what I was thinking.'

'He seemed happy to talk to the police negotiator,' Chief Jacobs said. 'In fact, our guy thought he had Beckman's confidence, was getting through to him, but—' the Police Chief shrugged, 'the next time the negotiator spoke to him, Beckman said he was bored and wasn't going to talk to anyone but you, Captain Mitchell.'

'Beckman was playing with your negotiator.'

'I should have got someone else, someone more experienced,' the chief said.

'Don't beat yourself up, Chief. And don't blame your negotiator. Beckman's a controlling liar. He's an expert confidence trickster. When do I get to talk to him?'

'Tomorrow. The negotiator will brief you on his findings.'

'I meant when do I get to talk to Beckman?'.

'As soon as it's light. Once my men have changed shifts – when the guys on duty tonight have left and the day shift is in position – it will be safe for you to negotiate.'

'Negotiate? I'm going in. I want my father and mother out of there.'

'We would rather you didn't go inside the house,' Chief Jacobs said. 'Our experts think it will be too dangerous. We can't protect you if we can't see you.'

'And I can't see any other way of getting my parents out. And, since it is because of me that they are in this situation, I shall do what Beckman wants.'

'What are you suggesting?'

'A trade. Me for them.'

Claire heard Chief Jacobs suck his teeth. 'Once Alain is inside he'll be able to separate Beckman from the nurse,' she said.

'How?'

'Accuse the nurse of killing Beckman's secretary.'

'She'll deny it,' Alain added, 'but played right, she'll turn against Beckman.'

'But she did kill the secretary. We found—'

'My wife and I have met Nurse Bryant, and neither of us believes she is capable of murder. We think Beckman killed his secretary and planted the watch and uniform. Then, when the secretary's body was found, the evidence would point to the nurse and not to him.'

'And the only thing Beckman would be guilty of was having an affair with a nurse who was obsessed with him, jealous of his secretary, and killed her,' Claire said.

'A woman scorned, huh?' The chief shook his head.

'The nurse would hang and Beckman would have got away with murder.'

'Again!' Mitch said.

'But when Nurse Bryant finds out the man she loves has framed her for the murder of his secretary – who we, Alain, will hint he was also having an affair with – she will turn against him.'

'And once she knows he's a murdering Nazi she'll testify against him in court.' Chief Jacobs' broad red face lit up at the prospect. 'Let me discuss it with my negotiators, Captain. I'll be back in the morning to take you to your parents' house.' He looked at the two air force officers. 'Someone will stand guard outside the door all night?'

'Yes, sir,' they both said.

'Right! Then I shall leave you. You need to eat,' he said, looking from Claire to Alain. 'I would rather you didn't leave the suite. Order food from room service and get an early night. Tomorrow looks like it's going to be a long day.'

Claire fell onto the settee and Alain went over to the telephone. 'What do you want to eat, honey?'

'Whatever you're having, I don't care,' Claire said, resting her head on the back of the settee.

'Officers, can I get you anything?' Alain said, picking up the telephone.

'No, sir. Thank you, we—'

'I'll order for four. If you're going to be here all night you need to eat... Hi, this is room 642. Can I get chicken and French fries for four? Bread, cheese and some pancakes with bacon and maple syrup. A pot of coffee and a bottle of Canadian Club. Could you bring the coffee and the CC up straight away? That's great.' He returned the receiver to the telephone's base. 'The drinks are coming up now. The food will be half an hour.'

The coffee and the whisky arrived within a few minutes. Claire poured four cups of coffee and Alain poured the whisky. 'No alcohol for us,' Officer Boucher said, 'but a coffee would be welcome.'

When they were seated with their drinks, Claire and Officer Boucher in two armchairs by the window, the men on dining chairs at a small table, Alain asked Officer Lloyd if he could get some money changed from French francs into Canadian dollars. The officer said he was sure the hotel would change the money. If they wouldn't he would go to the bank first thing in the morning.

Officer Boucher asked Claire if there was anything she needed. 'Yes,' Claire said, 'clothes.' She jumped up and went over to her handbag, which she had dropped next to her suitcase when she arrived. She grabbed the bag and returned to her chair. 'I have been living out of a suitcase, rotating the same clothes for months. Is there anywhere near here where I can buy a couple of skirts and blouses, a suit or a thin sweater?' She took her purse from her handbag and counted her money. 'For a hundred and twenty francs.'

'I know just the place,' Officer Boucher said. 'What's your dress size?'

'In England I'm a twenty-two-inch waist. I have no idea how that translates over here.' Claire took a step back and looked at the young Canadian officer. 'We're about the same dress size. If it fits you, I'm sure it will fit me.'

'Colour preference?'

Claire could see a wisp of light brown hair poking out from under Officer Boucher's hat. 'Whatever suits you will be fine.' She gave the officer a hundred francs. 'I'll keep twenty in case there's an emergency. Unless you need more—' The officer put up her hand.

While they waited for the food to arrive, Alain and Officer Lloyd talked about the changes to both Canada and Europe since the end of the war, and Claire opened the suitcases. Alain's clothes were crumpled because he had thrown them into the suitcase without folding them. On closer inspection, she could see they were clean and only needed a shake before she hung them up.

Her clothes, on the other hand, although folded neatly, had been worn several times while she had been in France. They all needed to be washed or taken to a commercial dry-cleaning shop. 'Do you think the hotel will have these cleaned for me?'

Officer Boucher stood up. 'They will, Mrs Mitchell. I'll go down and get a couple of laundry bags from reception. If you'd like to give me your francs, sir?' she said to Alain. 'I'll see if I can get them changed for you while I'm down there.'

Alain took a wad of notes from his pocket, and Officer Boucher counted them. 'Two hundred and eighty francs.' She put the money in the breast pocket of her uniform and buttoned it. 'I won't be long.'

Officer Boucher returned as a waiter was wheeling in the evening meal. She quickly went over to the two piles of clothes that Claire had put outside the bathroom door, put garments to be laundered in one bag and those needing to be dry cleaned in the other. 'I'll pop these down to reception,' she said to Officer Lloyd. 'I shan't be long.'

By the time Officer Boucher returned, her male counterpart had eaten and was standing guard outside the door. Officer Boucher snacked on bread and cheese, drank a cup of coffee and then joined him.

THIRTY-FOUR

The telephone extension in the bedroom rang, waking Claire from a deep sleep. Eyes barely open, she squinted at Mitch. He was nearest to it. She nudged him but he didn't wake. She turned over, reached out and took her wristwatch from her bedside table. It was eight o'clock. They had overslept. She leapt out of bed, went round to Mitch's bedside table and picked up the telephone. 'Hello? Yes. Let yourself in, will you? Thanks.' She put down the receiver. 'Mitch,' she said, shaking him by the shoulder. 'Mitch, darling,' she said again, 'it's time to get up.'

'Where's the fire?' he said, turning over and pulling the sheets over his head.

'It's gone eight. Come on.'

Claire dragged on her dressing gown and opened the door. Officer Boucher stood in the sitting room with navy blue slacks and jacket, and a pale blue sweater over her arm. In her hand was a paper bag. 'Shoes,' she said. 'Navy to match the pants. It all fits me. Fingers crossed it will fit you.'

Claire took the trousers and jacket from the officer and held them up. 'They're lovely. How on earth did you get a shop to open for you at this hour of the day?'

'The owner of the shop is a friend. Ex-air force. I called her when I took the washing down last night and she opened up for me at seven.'

'Thank her for me, will you?' Claire tried on the new clothes. 'They fit perfectly,' she said. 'I can't keep calling you Officer Boucher. What's your Christian name?'

'Céline, but I'm not sure it's protocol to—'

'Céline it is.'

The young RCAF officer laughed. 'The car to take Captain Mitchell to his father's house will be here at nine.'

Claire returned to the bedroom to wake Mitch. He was in the bathroom. 'A car will be here at nine,' she said, standing beside him as he cleaned his teeth.

'Huh-huh!'

'I'm coming with you.'

Mitch put down his toothbrush and spat out a mouthful of toothpaste. 'You are not!'

Claire followed him out of the bathroom and into the bedroom. 'I'll stay out of your way. You won't know I'm there.' He didn't answer. 'Mitch?'

'No, Claire!' he shouted. 'It's out of the question. Jacobs won't allow it, you know damn well he won't. And I don't want you there either. I don't want to have to worry about you.'

'Okay, okay.' Claire put up her hands. 'There's no need to shout! Damn!' Claire said, as the door closed. After using the bathroom, she dressed in the clothes Céline Boucher had brought her, put on her make-up and left the bedroom.

They ate breakfast in silence. When they had finished, Claire said, 'I'm sorry, darling. I was only trying to help.' She reached across the table to take Mitch's hand. At the same moment he picked up the napkin to wipe his mouth. Her hand dropped to the table.

'I know you want to be there,' he said, looking into her eyes, 'part of me *wants* you there, but—'

Dare she hope her husband was coming round to the idea of her going with him? She needed to tread carefully. 'A man and a woman holding someone hostage needs a man and a woman to go in—'

'And, you have had more experience dealing with guys like Beckman.'

Claire wasn't going to remind him of that, but it was true. During the war, when Mitch had been captured and imprisoned, she had worked solidly with the Resistance. She poured them both a cup of coffee. 'I'll see what the chief says, honey.' Claire knew the Chief of Police wouldn't like the idea. She also knew asking him was the best her husband could do.

She was right. Chief Jacobs didn't like the idea. His reply to Mitch when he mentioned Claire going with him to his parents' house was a categorical *No!*

'It's time we left,' Chief Jacobs said, walking to the door.

Claire threw her arm around Mitch's neck. She kissed him on his lips and cheek, before burying her face in his neck and kissing him again, loudly. It had the desired effect. Out of the corner of her eye, she saw the chief turn to his sergeant and shake his head.

'I shan't be far behind you,' Claire whispered. Mitch sighed. She couldn't tell whether he was sighing because he thought it was good that she was going to follow him, or bad. She let her arms drop to her sides, took a step back, and looked into his eyes.

A faint smile played on Mitch's lips and he said, 'See you later, China.'

'My husband agrees I should go with him,' Claire told Officer Boucher, when Mitch and Chief Jacobs had left. Officer Boucher listened. Her forehead was lined and her eyebrows seemed close together, but she didn't comment. 'A hostage situation, where a coldblooded murderer is calling the shots, is beyond dangerous for one person to try and defuse,' Claire went on. 'It will take two people if everyone is to get out alive.

'Mitch's only concern,' she said, her voice almost a whisper, 'is what will happen to our daughter if we were both—'

'Killed?' Officer Boucher said.

'The chances of that, Céline,' Claire purposely used the officer's first name to show friendship and solidarity, 'are almost nil when two trained—' She stopped. Should she tell Officer Boucher about her and Mitch's jobs in the war? She decided for the moment, not to. 'As I was saying, Mitch was worried about our daughter if anything happened to me— or both of us.' Officer Boucher nodded sympathetically. 'What worries me,' Claire said, 'is Mitch going into a hostage situation on his own with a Nazi killer and a woman who loves him – worships him – and I expect would do anything for him; a woman who might already have killed for him. That makes it a very dangerous situation and is more likely to get Mitch killed.'

Officer Boucher nodded, again. Claire couldn't read what the nodding meant. She was wasting time by trying.

'I'm going to Mitch's father's house. I am not having my husband risk his life with that monster Beckman when I know a sure way of helping him.'

Céline Boucher stood up and crossed to the door. 'I'm sorry, Mrs Mitchell, my orders are not to let you leave the room.'

'Then you'd better restrain me because if you don't I *will* leave. Céline, I love my husband, we have been through a great deal together.' She left her seat, walked over to the door and stood next to the officer. Careful not to stand too close in case she felt intimidated, Claire decided it was now time to tell Céline Boucher about the work she and Mitch had done in the war. 'Mitch and I were members of the Special Operations Executive. We were dropped into German-occupied France and from forty-two to forty-five worked undercover with the

French Resistance. Mitch was captured by the Gestapo and put in prison. Heinrich Beckman was the doctor in that prison. He will, if he gets the chance, kill Mitch. You see, Mitch recognised him and has exposed him. And Beckman knows, if he doesn't get out of the situation he's in, he'll be taken back to France, tried for murder, and hanged.'

'Good God, I—'

'No one knows the relationship between my husband and Beckman except Chief Jacobs and your commanding officer.' Claire returned to her chair and Céline Boucher followed. 'I don't want to get you into trouble, Céline, but I intend to leave here, with or without your help.' Claire liked Céline Boucher and hoped it was going to be with her help.

Céline gave Claire a wry smile. 'I know for a fact that my superior at St Hubert, Captain Hillier, is in a meeting all morning. So, I am going to ring his office and when his secretary tells me he is in a meeting and is not to be disturbed, I shall apologise. When she asks me if she can take a message there will be a problem with the telephone. So, since I am the senior officer here and I can't get in touch with my superior, whether you follow your husband or not is up to me.'

Claire reached out and took Céline Boucher's hands. 'You could get in trouble, couldn't you?'

The young officer raised her eyebrows. 'I'll be court marshalled for disobeying orders, so you'll have to overpower me and tie me up,' she said, with a glint in her eye. 'First, let me call my superior officer.'

Céline Boucher picked up the telephone on the table by the window and asked to be put through to St Hubert Air Force base. When she was connected, she asked to speak to Captain Hillier and was put through to his secretary. 'Miss Elliott, it's Officer Boucher here. Would you patch me through to Captain Hillier? Oh, he's still in the meeting, is he? What? Oh, but there's—' She looked at Claire and bit her lip. 'Sir? Yes. I'm sorry to disturb you while you're in a meeting, but Captain Mitchell's wife has given me the slip. She— Yes, sir... No, sir... Yes, straight away. Thank you, sir.' Officer Boucher put down the telephone, put her hand up to her mouth and giggled.

'He said I was to go after you and when I caught up with you I wasn't to let you out of my sight. "Stick to her like glue!" were his exact words. Well, what are you waiting for, Mrs Mitchell? If we're going we'd better look sharp. We'll hail a taxi in the street.'

THIRTY-FIVE

The taxi dropped Claire and Officer Boucher off several streets away from Alain and Marie Mitchell's house. It was the nearest the taxi could get. 'Sorry I can't take you any further,' the driver said when Claire paid him. 'Some guy has gone nuts and is holding an old couple hostage. Everyone around here has been evacuated.' He offered her fifty cents change.

'Keep it,' Claire said. The two women made their way to Mitch's father's house. Claire had been there more than a dozen times during the three months that she, Mitch and Aimée had lived in Canada.

Claire was conscious of the heels of her shoes clip-clopping along the pavement of the empty streets. 'It's like a ghost town,' she said. Turning the corner into the long road where her in-laws lived, she stopped. Fifty yards ahead armed officers and air force personnel were crouched behind a dozen police cars and military vehicles.

She quickly took the paved path to the back of the first house. Céline Boucher followed.

'Damn! There's no way I can climb over all these fences,' she said, 'it would take me forever to get to the Mitchell house.'

'Look!' Céline pointed to a narrow lane running along the side of the garden. 'That, if I am not mistaken, is the beginning of a service road.'

Claire followed Céline out of the garden and turned right onto the narrow strip of tarmac. Keeping low, they ran until they were at the back of Alain's father's house. 'Céline, I appreciate you coming with me, but now I think you should go,' Claire said. 'I'm going to try to get close to the house, have a look through the windows. I can't do it if I'm worrying about you.'

'I'll wait here.'

'No. It would be more helpful if you went back to the road and approached the house from the front. Make sure Mitch sees you, then he'll know I'm here. Stay there ten, fifteen minutes and then come back. But stay on the service road, we can't risk Beckman looking out of an upstairs window and seeing you, or my plan will be blown.'

Céline thought for a moment, then said, 'Okay. But be careful.'

'I will.' The two women embraced, then went their separate ways.

Claire waited until Céline had reached the end of the service road before opening the back gate. Making herself as small as she was able, she crept into the garden. The trees and shrubs, only just coming into bud, gave little cover. She moved swiftly from one shrub to another until she came to the garden shed. Suddenly aware that she had been holding her breath, she relaxed and exhaled. Standing upright, with her back pressed against the wall, she sidestepped along the length of the shed until she arrived at the front. She stopped and poked her head around the corner.

The back door of the Mitchell house was on the side, accessed by a paved path. She had a clear view of it. She looked at the upstairs windows – one bathroom and one landing. You would have to stand in the bath to look out of the bathroom window – and then you'd only see the rooftops and chimneys of the neighbouring houses. The same with the tall window on the landing.

A movement in an upstairs window of the house opposite caught her eye. A glint of something metal was all she needed to see to know snipers were in place. She looked at the bedroom windows of the house next door. The same. She wasn't sure whether she felt safer knowing trained marksmen were focused on Beckman or not. But she needed to trust they knew what they were doing, the way she had trusted her comrades in France.

In the muffled discussion coming from the road at the front of the house Claire heard Mitch's voice, speaking into a loud hailer. 'You wanted to talk to me, Professor Beckman?' There was no reply. 'Let my parents go and I'll come in.'

Claire held her breath and inched forward. She looked to the left, then right. There was no cover on the left, but on the right there was an ornate wooden trellis. It stood six feet tall and masked the garbage bin from the street. From where she was standing she could see a space at the back of the bin where she could hide, where she would be near enough to see and hear Mitch. She crossed the narrow gap between the shed and the trellis and crouched down behind the bin.

'Beckman? Can you hear me?'

'Yes!' The professor shouted, his voice sending shivers down Claire's spine.

'Let my parents go, and I'll come in.'

'If I let them go I have no bargaining power. Do you think I am stupid?'

'No. I never have. But this is between you and me. My folks have nothing to do with it.'

Claire could hear a hushed conversation between Mitch and several other men. She got to her feet and peered through the diamond-shaped pattern of the trellis. The police chief was speaking animatedly. Listening to him was a high-ranking air force officer and two older men in civilian clothes who, Claire assumed, were from the Jewish Council.

She looked back at Mitch. His attention was suddenly taken by someone in the crowd. He looked, and looked again, then for the briefest moment he smiled. He has seen Céline, Claire thought. He knows I'm here. Claire's heart began to hammer in her chest and the butterflies in her stomach took flight. She loved her brave husband as much today as she did when she first fell in love with him a decade ago. But, she told herself, if I am going to be any use to him, I need to use my brain not my heart.

'I need to see for myself that my parents are alive,' Mitch shouted. 'Just bring them to the window.'

'I cannot do that, Captain Mitchell. They are not in this part of the house,' Beckman said.

There was a pause in the negotiations. Mitch consulted Chief Jacobs, then said, 'How can I be sure they're alive if you won't let me see or speak to them?'

'Because I give you my word.'

Mitch handed the loudhailer to Chief Jacobs and put his hands above his head. 'Yes. Okay, I'm coming in.'

The 'yes' was for Claire. She watched Mitch walk up the drive towards the front door. Without looking in her direction, he coughed, looked down, and put his left hand to his mouth. She saw that his forefinger and middle finger were straight while the others were slightly bent. That was what she had hoped to see. Two fingers, two people. He looked down, which meant below floor level. Mitch had told her his family were in the basement, and she was to get them out.

When Mitch disappeared from view, Claire returned to the back of the shed and slipped unseen to the back door. She took out the set of lockpicking keys that Thomas Durand had given her in France and set about unlocking the door. She heard a click, turned the doorknob and pushed. It didn't open. She put the picks in again and turned them again. A second click. The door opened.

Without making a sound Claire moved through the kitchen to the basement door. It was locked, but the key hung on a piece of string on the doorframe. She opened the door and with as much stealth and speed as she had ever had she flew down the stairs. Mitch's father looked up and blinked rapidly. His wife looked as if she was going to cry. Claire put her forefinger to her lips. 'Shush...' She tiptoed across the stone floor. They were each tied to a chair by their wrists and ankles with strong garden twine. Claire untied Marie first. She put her forefinger to her lips again, indicating not to make a sound. She then took the twine from around Mitch's father's wrists and ankles. He was bound tighter than his wife. His wrists were bleeding where the twine had cut into the skin.

Claire beckoned them to follow her. Marie was shaky on her legs so between them, Claire and Alain Senior helped her across the room. The steps leading from the basement were wooden but they were new and they were solid. With Marie sandwiched between them, Claire and Mitch's father left the basement without making a sound. Once they were in the kitchen, Claire closed the door, locked it, and returned the key to the nail on the doorframe. If Beckman walked past the door, there would be nothing different for him to see.

Claire took her handkerchief and a small revolver from the inside pocket of her jacket. She looked around the kitchen, wrapped the gun in the hankie and placed it in an earthenware jar with flour written on the front.

Satisfied that Beckman was not likely to bake a cake anytime soon, so he would have no reason to look in the flour jar, Claire pushed it back in line with several other jars and directed her father and mother-in-law out of the house. Using the keys she had used to unlock the door, Claire double locked it. Again, if for any reason Beckman came into the kitchen he would neither see nor find anything amiss.

'Someone is waiting for you on the other side of the garden gate,' Claire whispered. 'She will take you to our hotel. Walk down the right side of the garden,' Claire instructed, 'and stay behind whatever foliage you can. When you reach the gate don't look back; go through it quickly and quietly.'

Marie leant forward to kiss her. 'No time,' Claire whispered. 'I'll see you at the hotel when this is over.'

THIRTY-SIX

Claire leaned against the side of the house and closed her eyes. She inhaled deeply and exhaled slowly and calmly. Mitch's folks were safe. Now all she had to do was go back into the house without being seen. She visualised the interior of the rest of the house. Could she go in through the kitchen and get to the front door via the hall? She could, but she couldn't risk Beckman seeing her, or he'd guess she'd freed the hostages. On the other hand, if the living room door was shut... No! Claire shook her head. A stupid idea. It was too risky.

She would have to go in by the front door. She couldn't use the service lane and approach the house from the road because Chief Jacobs, or someone in authority, would stop her. She had no choice. She would have to make a bolt for it. The door was seconds away. Once she was inside the porch neither the police nor the military could do anything about it.

She ran her hand over the lockpicking keys in her pocket. If necessary she could use them as a weapon. Then she thought better of it. Beckman would more than likely search her – and it wouldn't take a genius to guess why she had them on her. She took the keys from her pocket and forced them into a narrow gap between a regular house brick and a blue airbrick. She looked at the bricks from the left and the right; the keys couldn't be seen. To be on the safe side she plucked a small plant from a patch of garden further along the wall and placed it in front of the airbrick, pressing the soil around it with the toe of her shoe.

It was time she made her move. She didn't want Mitch to persuade Beckman to let his parents go. The last thing she needed was for the mad Nazi to go down to the basement and find Alain and Marie Mitchell had gone.

Staying close to the side wall, Claire edged her way to the front of the house. She took a deep breath, put her hands up, in the hope she wouldn't be shot by a sniper, and ran like a hare around the corner of the house. Within seconds she was in the porch hammering on the front door with her fists.

The door opened. Beckman gave her a cursory glance and barked, 'Don't move!' Holding a gun on her, he patted her down on the right side of her body. 'Turn round,' he said. When she turned he did the same to her left side, checking her pocket and then thrusting his hand between her legs. Claire gritted her teeth and tensed.

She looked out at the sea of faces watching from behind a couple of dozen cars, and she prayed there wasn't a trigger-happy cop looking through the sights of his rifle. If there was, and he fancied himself as a hero, he'd have to be a bloody good shot not to hit her. Beckman pulled her round to face him, grabbed her by the collar of her coat with one hand, and held his gun to her head with the other. 'Come!' he ordered. 'Nearer!' Claire stepped over the threshold. Almost touching Beckman, she could smell an overpowering fragrance of sweet cologne, feel his chest rise and fall as he breathed, and taste his stale breath. She held her own.

Now only his head would be visible above hers as he scanned the upper windows of houses on the other side of the road. Damn, she had given him an opportunity to see what he faced, or at least some of it. 'Get in!' he ordered, backing up and dragging Claire with him. He spun her around again, so she was facing the posse of police and military officers who, hands on their guns, looked considerably nearer than when she had watched them from the side of the house. Chief Jacobs, his face white and lined with worry, lumbered across the path as if he was going to storm the building.

'Shut the door!' Beckman shouted. Claire slammed it as fast as she could, lest Beckman put a bullet through the Police Chief. It would have been easy for him to do, but then he would probably have caught one himself.

The curtains at the small windows on either side of the front door were drawn, making the entrance hall dark, but the door to the living room was open. A beam of light shone out of it illuminating the polished block-wood floor of the hall. Beckman pushed her into the sitting room. The curtains at the bay window were drawn, a precaution against a sniper's bullet.

With the gun still aimed at her head, Beckman gave Claire another shove and she staggered into the middle of the room. She took her time regaining her balance so she could survey her surroundings. Beckman standing behind her, Nurse Bryant sitting on the sofa, and Mitch in an armchair with his back to the window. It would be Mitch who took a bullet if— Claire shook her head to rid the image of her husband being shot in the back of the head. 'Thank goodness those two are safe,' Claire said, to Beckman, nodding as if to reaffirm the nurse and her husband's safety. Beckman didn't reply, but Mitch cleared his throat, which told Claire he understood it was his parents who were safe.

'Silence!' Beckman lifted his gun. Mitch leapt out of the chair, but he wasn't fast enough. In a second Beckman had the gun pointing at him. 'Sit down!' Without taking his eyes off Claire, Mitch backed off and returned to his seat next to the window. 'You too,' he said, bringing the gun back to

Claire. She held her hands up and sat on the settee next to the nurse.

'What are you doing here, Claire?' Mitch said, feigning an emotion between worry and anger.

She looked at Beckman, waiting for him to shout Mitch down, or order her not to speak. He did neither. Instead, he said, 'Yes, Mrs Mitchell, what are you doing here?'

'The same as your woman is doing,' Claire said, 'I am supporting the man I love.' Beckman's eyes flitted from Claire to Nurse Bryant. He said nothing. Claire turned her back on him and smiled at the nurse. 'You were very kind to me on the day my husband had to stay on the ward.' Nurse Bryant looked up at Beckman doe-eyed. Claire smiled. 'You love your boss very much, don't you?'

'Yes.'

'You're a lucky man, professor.'

Beckman grunted.

Claire looked across at Mitch and raised her eyebrows. She needed his help. Her plan to stir up trouble between Beckman and the nurse wasn't working.

'So?' Mitch said, 'what is it you want, Beckman?'

Beckman pulled in his stomach and stood tall. 'A new passport and two tickets to Argentina.'

'Don't you mean, two passports?' Mitch said.

'No. One passport, but two tickets – one single and one return.' He looked at Mitch and grinned. 'You will use your own passport.' Mitch's mouth fell open. 'Oh,' Beckman said, laughing, 'didn't I say? You, Captain Mitchell, are coming with me. That way I will be guaranteed a safe passage.'

'That wasn't part of the agreement.'

'No?'

'You know it wasn't. We agreed that you'd let my parents go if I got you a passport and a ticket to a pro-Nazi country—'

Nurse Bryant looked from Mitch to Beckman. 'What about me, Lucien?'

'You?' Beckman set his jaw and looked at the nurse with distaste. Then his face softened. 'I will send for you when I am settled.'

'But you promised to take me with you,' Nurse Bryant said, near to tears. 'You promised we would go to Argentina together, and when you had proved you were innocent of these— false charges, you would take me home with you to meet your family in Switzerland.'

Beckman laughed. 'You are deluded, woman.'

'But— I love you, Lucien. Haven't I proved that to you?'

Claire glanced at Mitch. He pressed his lips together and raised his eyebrows as if to say, maybe we were wrong, perhaps the nurse did kill Beckman's secretary. 'He can't afford to take you with him now you have killed for him,' Claire said. Beckman looked at her, his eyes blazing with anger.

'What? I haven't killed anyone,' Nurse Bryant cried.

'Silence!' he shouted to Claire. 'And you,' he said, pointing the gun at the nurse, 'stop whining. No one has killed anyone.'

'Your secretary was found on the floor of her office the morning after you left. She had been murdered.' Claire looked at Nurse Bryant. 'And your fob-watch was found under her body,' Claire said. 'How could it have got there? Perhaps Doctor Beckman's secretary loved him and wanted to go to Argentina with him, too. Is that why you killed her?'

'I didn't kill your secretary, Lucien. And who is Doctor Beckman?'

'Enough!' Beckman said to the nurse. 'Keep your mouth shut. Don't say another word.' He turned to Claire. 'You think you're so smart, don't you?' Claire didn't think she was smart. She was scared to death that she had gone too far and Beckman would put a bullet in her.

Suddenly Chief Jacobs voice, deep and slightly muffled,

boomed into the room. 'What is going on in there? What are your demands, Doctor Beckman?' Claire sighed with relief. For the moment Beckman's attention was on the police chief and not on her or the nurse.

'You,' he said, to Claire, 'go to the kitchen and make me coffee and sandwiches. You go with her,' he said, flicking his head at Nurse Bryant. 'And while you're there take a look in the basement, make sure the old folks are still alive.'

THIRTY-SEVEN

Watching Claire all the time, Nurse Bryant crossed to the basement door. The feeling of hot nauseous panic rose from Claire's stomach to her throat. She couldn't let the nurse go down to the basement.

'Nurse?' she said, distracting her. 'What shall I do first?'

'Make the coffee.'

Turning away from the basement door, the nurse went into the larder. This might be the only chance Claire had to retrieve her gun. Her temples throbbed. In one fluid movement she took the lid off the flour jar, took out the gun, unwrapped it, and slipped it into her pocket. Returning the hankie coated in flour to the jar, she pushed it back in line with the other jars.

'Milk,' Nurse Bryant said, leaving the larder and closing the door. She handed Claire the milk and pointed to the spilt flour on the worktop. 'The wrong jar,' she said, 'the coffee is in this jar.' The nurse picked up the jar next to the one containing flour. 'See, it says, coffee!' She stood it next to the milk. 'Lucien likes cream in his coffee,' the nurse said, as if she was imparting privileged information, 'but there isn't any, so he'll have milk. I won't be long.' she said, heading back to the basement door.

Claire flicked the electric switch on the wall behind the kettle, then hastily opened the cutlery drawer and took a knife from it. 'Shall I make a start on the sandwiches while the kettle's boiling?' she asked, waving the knife in the air.

'Give me that!' the nurse shouted. Turning away from the basement again she stomped across the kitchen and grabbed the knife out of Claire's hand. '*I* will make Lucien's sandwich, *you* make the coffee.'

The colour had drained from the nurse's face. Claire could see fear in her eyes. 'I wasn't going to hurt you, Nurse Bryant,' she said. The nurse gave her a sideways glance and flicked her head back. 'I'm sorry if that's what you thought.' Had Claire wanted, she could have overpowered the nurse half a dozen times since they'd been on their own in the kitchen. But she needed the nurse onside. She wanted her to see what a murdering animal Beckman was.

'You are innocent, I know you are.' Claire switched off the kettle and busied herself putting out cups and saucers. 'The police think you killed Beckman's secretary, but Mitch and I think it was Beckman who killed her. You *know* he killed her, don't you?'

'I know no such thing,' the nurse said, giving Claire a defiant look.

'Well if he didn't kill her, and you didn't kill her, who did?'

'I only have your word that Lucien's secretary is dead. How do I know what you're saying is true?'

'Because she knew from the recordings of Mitch under hypnosis, which she typed up after each session, that Mitch had recognised his doctor from the war. The man you know as Doctor Lucien Puel is an imposter.' Claire saw a flicker of fear cross Nurse Bryant's face, so she carried on. 'The man you are in love with, who has manipulated you and made you believe that he is in love with you is a Nazi, a criminal by the name of Heinrich Beckman.'

The nurse put her hand over her ears and shook her head. 'I don't believe you. Lucien is a kind man. He's a clever doctor. What you are saying is lies. Lies, lies, lies.'

'I am telling you the truth, Nurse Bryant. Heinrich Beckman is a Gestapo doctor who drugged women, men too most probably, experimented on them, and then had them beaten and executed.' The nurse stopped making the sandwich and looked out of the window. She was gripping the handle of the knife so tightly her knuckles were white. 'During Mitch's treatment,' Claire persisted, 'while he was under hypnosis, the years he spent in the prison came back to him. He began to remember things that happened to him – and to other prisoners – and he remembered the doctor in charge of the prison, Heinrich Beckman.

'That's why he went back to the hospital on the day he was meant to leave Canada. Mitch knew Beckman would write a report to his commanding officer in England, and he wanted a copy of it. And it's a good job he did go back. Beckman had written a fictitious account of what Mitch had said under hypnosis. He tried to destroy Mitch's reputation by saying he was a traitor.

'If I hadn't been given proof that your Doctor Lucien Puel in Canada was an imposter, by the real Doctor Lucien Paul's grandfather in France, Mitch would have been court marshalled by now and...'

'What has that to do with me? I'm not German, I wasn't in the prison – if there was a prison – and I didn't kill Lucien's secretary.'

Claire threw her hands up in exasperation. 'His name is *not Lucien Puel!* He murdered the real Lucien Puel, killed him and stole his identity papers. That man in there, who you love and admire, is a murdering Nazi by the name of Heinrich Beckman! He had God knows how many people killed in the prison. Beckman murdered an innocent young doctor named Lucien

Puel. And if you didn't kill her, Beckman murdered his innocent secretary too!'

'I didn't kill her,' Nurse Bryant whispered, her eyes
pleading with Claire to believe her.

'Mitch and I know you didn't,' Claire said, sympathetically.
'But the way things stand at the moment, all the evidence points
to you. Your fob-watch was found under the secretary's dead
body and your uniform had a hole where the watch had been
torn from it. Don't you see? The only way your watch could
have found its way under the body of Beckman's dead secretary
was if he put it there. Nurse Bryant, if you don't help us put this
monster away, you will hang for the secretary's murder.'

'Where is the coffee?' Both women jumped at the sound of
Beckman's voice booming along the passage from the sitting
room.

Nurse Bryant looked at Claire and gasped. 'Oh my God.'
She put her hand to her mouth. 'Lucien told me to check the
basement and I haven't.' She ran across the kitchen, grabbed the
key from the hook, opened the basement door, and froze.
Turning on the spot and breathing heavily, she held on to the
doorframe, Claire watched the colour drain from the nurse's
face. She looked in the direction of the passage and grimaced at
the sound of Beckman's heavy footfall on the wood floor.

As he entered the room Claire turned her attention to
making the coffee. She gripped the edge of the worktop to
steady herself. Pouring coffee into four cups she added milk and
stirred.

'Are the hostages *comfortable*?' Beckman asked, laughing.

Nurse Bryant didn't answer but laughed with him. Her
laughter sounded forced, Claire thought, still stirring the coffee.
She heard the nurse pull the door shut, lock it, and put the key
back on the hook. Then there was silence. 'I'll take the coffee
through to the sitting room, shall I?' Claire said, turning and

seeing Nurse Bryant with the knife still in her hand. 'Nurse?' Claire called, bringing the broken-hearted woman out of whatever labyrinth of unhappy thoughts she was lost in.

Her reply – a quick nod. 'I'll make the sandwiches,' she said.

THIRTY-EIGHT

Had the penny dropped at last? Had Nurse Bryant finally realised that Beckman had set her up to take the fall for murdering his secretary? If she hadn't, Claire reasoned, she would have told Beckman that Mitch's parents weren't in the basement. Balancing four cups of steaming hot coffee on her mother-in-law's best silver tray she left the kitchen and walked along the passage praying Nurse Bryant didn't try to use the knife she was holding on Beckman. He would turn it on her and stick it into her as easily as he had his secretary.

As she approached the sitting room door, she became aware that Beckman and the nurse were behind her. 'Were they all right down there?' she heard Beckman say.

'I, err,' the nurse stuttered. Claire held her breath. 'Yes,' she said, at last, 'they were all right.'

Claire entered the sitting room and pressed her lips together. Mitch raised his eyebrows as if to ask if there was a problem. Claire responded by lifting her shoulders and shaking her head very slowly, which told him she wasn't sure. She put the tray on the sideboard, took Mitch a cup of coffee and, doing her best not to look worried, helped herself to a cup.

Nurse Bryant came into the room ahead of Beckman and put a plate of sandwiches on the sideboard next to the coffee tray. Taking one of the two remaining cups, she sat on the settee. Beckman appeared. He didn't come into the room, he stood in the doorway staring at Nurse Bryant. He made no attempt to cross the room to retrieve his coffee, the only cup left on the tray. Instead, he kept his cold steel grey eyes on the nurse. Waiting for her to jump up and get his drink for him, Claire thought – and she wished the nurse would. Claire needed the nurse to behave normally towards him. She didn't want Beckman to suspect the poor besotted woman had at last seen him for what he was.

Beckman was many things, stupid he was not. So, suspecting he had noticed the change in Nurse Bryant, Claire put her coffee back on the tray, picked up Beckman's cup and took it to him. He dismissed her with a flick of his hand. She needed to distract him somehow – but how? By the hard stare he was giving the nurse he no longer suspected, he *knew* something had changed since the two women had been alone in the kitchen.

Nurse Bryant must have sensed Beckman was staring at her. She looked up and met his eyes with a stare as hard and as cold as his. She was no longer the gullible fool Beckman had once taken her for. She was a ticking bomb and Claire couldn't risk her exploding.

With Beckman's eyes still trained on the nurse, Claire returned his cup to the tray and picked up the coffee pot. 'More coffee, Nurse Bryant?' The nurse shook her head. 'A sandwich then?' Before the nurse had time to say no, Claire had lifted the plate of sandwiches. She pushed it towards her with a shaky hand. When the nurse held the edge of the plate to steady it, Claire let it go and turned to Mitch. 'More coffee?'

'Thank you.' To the nurse, he said, 'I'd like a sandwich if

you wouldn't mind?' The nurse put down her coffee and got to her feet.

'What are you idiots playing at?' Beckman roared. 'Do you think I am stupid? That I do not know what you are trying to do?' He looked at Claire and grinned. 'You are trying to turn the woman I love against me.'

Claire shook her head in disbelief. Beckman hadn't shown Nurse Bryant one ounce of respect, let alone love, since they'd been there. She glanced at the nurse. Her face was as resolute now as it had been when she returned from the kitchen. Claire's heart was pounding. Had she pushed the situation too far?

Out of the corner of her eye Claire saw Mitch put his cup on the floor at the side of his chair. He gripped the arms. She smiled inwardly. He was preparing to move quickly. She swallowed, took a breath to calm herself, and put her own cup on the sideboard.

'The woman you love?' Nurse Bryant said. 'Oh, Lucien,' she cooed, as only a woman in love would. Beckman's eyes softened and he walked towards her. She threw Claire a scathing look. 'Her?' she snarled, 'turn me against you? She didn't. She couldn't.' Nurse Bryant put her arms around his neck, lifted her right knee and drove it into his groin. 'You did that when you murdered your secretary and put my fob-watch under her body,' Bryant screamed.

Beckman's knees buckled, but he didn't go down. He lifted his hand with the gun in it. He was about to strike the nurse when Mitch, already on his feet, kicked the gun out of his hand. It went spinning across the floor. Both men dived for it. Mitch got to it first. Beckman jumped on him and pushed his face into the carpet. Mitch brought his elbow back and jabbed Beckman in the ribs. He fell backwards, the wind knocked out of him. Mitch rolled over and, making a fist of his right hand, thrust it upwards until it connected with Beckman's jaw.

Beckman howled. He threw himself at Mitch. He put his

hands around Mitch's neck and squeezed. Mitch reached out. The carpet chaffed the back of his hand as he thrashed about in search of the gun. Gasping for breath his fingers found the gun's hand grip. In a frenzy, Beckman grabbed Mitch by the lapels and rabbit-punched him on the nose. Mitch's head shot back and struck the floor. He cried out in pain, lifted the gun, and slammed the barrel into Beckman's ribs.

The German rolled off Mitch. On all fours he scrambled to his feet. He put up his hands and took a staggering step backwards. He lost his balance and shook his head like a man who was drunk. He staggered again, stopping only when his legs met the arm of the settee.

Half sitting, half lying, his nose pouring with blood, Mitch pointed the gun at Beckman.

'All right!' Beckman said, panting.

Without taking the gun off Beckman, Mitch got to his feet.

Beckman lowered one hand, gasped, and clutched his side. Mitch approached him and Beckman screamed in pain. Turning his back on Mitch, Beckman began to lower himself onto the settee.

'Don't sit down!' Mitch shouted. 'Stand up!'

'Okay!' Beckman grabbed the arm of the settee. Then, using it as a lever, he hauled himself upright and toppled forward. Before Mitch could reach him, Beckman seized the nurse. Mitch lifted the gun, then quickly lowered it. Beckman was holding a small, very sharp blade at the nurse's throat.

'So,' Beckman said, turning to face Mitch, holding the nurse as a shield, 'are you going to shoot me?'

'No,' Claire said, 'I am.' She felt Beckman tense as she pressed the cold steel of her small Beretta on the back of his head.

Beckman twitched. He didn't speak. No one spoke. Then Beckman gave a nervous laugh. 'I searched you,' he said. 'You don't have a gun.'

'I didn't when I came in through the front door, but I did earlier when I came in through the back door.' Beckman's top lip curled in a snarl of disbelief. 'When I set the hostages free. Oh, didn't I say?' Claire said, mimicking the German's earlier sarcasm. 'After I'd let them out of the basement I hid the gun in the flour barrel. If you hadn't insisted on coffee, I wouldn't have been able to retrieve it.'

'You lying bitch,' he hissed at the nurse. He tightened his grip on her and pressed the blade of the knife into her neck.

The nurse cried out. It was a shallow cut, but deep enough for blood to trickle down her neck onto the collar of her dress.

'I do wish you hadn't done that,' Claire said, and shot him in the back of the knee.

Beckman roared. His head jerked back, his hands flew up, and the knife fell to the ground. Mitch picked it up. Claire, keeping the small gun aimed at Beckman, pulled the nurse from his grasp.

Beckman's face was running with sweat and contorted with pain. He took a stumbling step towards her. 'Don't come any nearer,' she warned. Lifting the gun, she aimed it at his head.

'*Schlampe Frau, ich werde dich töten.*'

'Kill you? Is that what you want? Sorry to disappoint you, *Herr Doktor Professor.*'

Beckman laughed. 'These – games – you English – play.'

'I'm warning you. Don't come any nearer,' Claire said. Beckman ignored her. She tightened her finger around the trigger of the Beretta and began to squeeze. 'If you think I'm going to kill you you're wrong.' She lowered the gun until it was pointing at his groin. 'I have no intention of putting you out of your misery,' she said looking into Beckman's eyes. 'That pleasure will be the hangman's.'

THIRTY-NINE

The sound of hammering on the front door broke Claire's concentration for a split second. It was long enough for Beckman to throw himself at her. He grabbed the gun and forcing it up, pointed it at his stomach. Using all her strength Claire tried to push the barrel of the gun down. Even with a bullet in him he was stronger than her. She brought her foot up and kicked him in the shin. She heard the bone crack, but he didn't let go.

He wanted her to shoot him, but she was damned if she was going to let him off a trial and the punishment he was due. She held on to the gun. Mitch took his shot. And Beckman went down from a bullet from his own gun.

Claire and Mitch were helping the hysterical nurse from the settee when there was an almighty crash. The front door burst off its hinges. Men in uniform were suddenly everywhere. Chief Jacobs stormed into the room followed by representatives from the Jewish Council.

'Take her downtown,' Jacobs ordered.

'Chief?' Mitch said, holding onto the sobbing nurse's arm.

'Nurse Bryant was instrumental in the escape of my parents, and—'

'What? The hostages aren't here? Where the hell are they?'

'At the hotel,' Claire said.

Chief Jacobs looked at Claire in disbelief. He took off his cap and scratched his bald head. 'So, she let the hostages go?'

'No. I let the hostages go. Nurse Bryant covered for me. She knew they had gone, but she told Beckman they were still in the basement.'

The chief seemed to physically sag in the middle making him appear even more thickset than he was. 'We still have to take her downtown, Mrs Mitchell.' He pulled himself up to his full height and looked squarely into Beckman's face. 'She is not only a material witness to everything this Nazi murderer has been doing in my city, while he's been living the life of Riley,' he bellowed, 'she's wanted for murder herself.'

Claire put her hand on the chief's arm. 'Chief, you might want to—'

'Want to what?' he barked.

'Consider Beckman for the secretary's murder. Nurse Bryant didn't kill her.'

'What?' Chief Jacobs said, again.

'She didn't know the secretary had been murdered until I told her.'

Beckman mumbled something inaudible and grunted.

The Police Chief threw his hands in the air. 'Okay,' he huffed. 'But we still have to question her. She was complicit in Beckman's escape.'

'Except she didn't know Beckman was escaping until it was too late,' Claire said.

'Whether she was aware of what she was doing or not, is another matter. She stayed with him knowing he had taken your husband's parents hostage.'

Mitch looked at Nurse Bryant. 'Under duress?' She nodded.

'All right, all right,' the chief said, shaking his head. 'But we will have to take you to Police Headquarters, Miss Bryant. If, as Captain and Mrs Mitchell believe, you are innocent of the secretary's murder, you won't be charged.'

'Thank you,' Nurse Bryant whispered, sniffing back her tears.

'You will, however, be charged as Beckman's accomplice in the kidnapping of Mr and Mrs Mitchell.' The nurse's body went limp and her eyes rolled and closed. She looked as if she was about to faint. A policewoman leapt to her side and held her upright. Chief Jacobs looked at her sympathetically and sighed. 'Because Captain and Mrs Mitchell have said you helped them, I shall have a word with the judge; ask him to take into account that you were instrumental in capturing the war criminal. Okay?'

'Thank you,' she said, again. 'And thank you,' she whispered to Claire.

'Good luck,' Claire said. Police officers on either side of her armed her out of the room. Nurse Bryant didn't look back.

'And you, *Herr Doctor!*' The Chief of Police put on his hat. He was on surer ground now. 'You will be facing a very different judge. Cuff him!' the chief ordered.

'Are cuffs necessary, Chief?' the policeman asked, looking down at the disabled German.

Chief Jacobs flashed the young policeman a look of fury. 'Reptiles don't need legs, they crawl on their bellies!'

FORTY

The chief looked from Mitch to Claire. 'Thank you, both of you,' he said with admiration. He put out his hand to Mitch who shook it, and then turned to Claire. Holding the chief's hand, she said, 'And Nurse Bryant? You will put in a good word for her, won't you?'

'You can do that yourself. You two are heroes. Just wait until the citizens of Montréal hear what happened today. I shall call a press conference tomorrow.' Claire opened her mouth to interrupt the chief, but he put up his hand. 'Go to the hotel and see your folks. Have a well-earned rest, I'll send a car for you in the morning.'

'No!' Mitch said.

The chief physically jerked. 'No? What do you mean, no?'

'No, we are not going to attend a press conference. We are not heroes, and we are not taking the credit for what happened here today. The Montréal Police Force caught a Nazi criminal while defusing a hostage situation. The family kidnapped are anonymous – and must remain so. The glory, Chief Jacobs, is all yours. We don't exist,' Mitch said.

'But what about the guys who were here? They saw you.'

'So, they saw me. It was my mother and father who were being held hostage. That's all they need to know.'

'Only a handful of your people saw me,' Claire said. 'If anyone asks who I am, tell them I'm a British copper working undercover. I'm sure they'll accept that. Especially as they will be taking the credit.'

At the front door, the chief shook Mitch and Claire's hands, again. 'We could do with a *copper* like you in Montréal. You too, Captain Mitchell. Are you sure you don't want to stick around?'

'Sounds tempting,' Mitch said.

'No!' Claire playfully punched Mitch's arm. 'Thank you, Chief, but our home is in England with our daughter.'

'Well, if you ever change your mind— I'll get a car to take you to your hotel.'

'Thank you, but we're going to get some fresh air. We'll pick up a cab on the way.' Mitch took Claire's hand. 'We'll leave by the back door, if that's okay with you, Chief?'

Chief Jacobs shrugged. 'Would it make any difference if I said it wasn't okay?'

Claire and Mitch laughed. 'If you give us a five-minute start before you go out?' Mitch said, saluting Montréal's Chief of Police. Claire kissed him on the cheek and thanked him.

Leaving the chief at the front door, Mitch and Claire walked down the passage to the kitchen and left the house by the back door. Claire bent down and took the lockpicks from behind the airbrick, waved them at Mitch, and together they fled across the garden.

Once they were through the back gate, they walked swiftly down the service lane to the road. 'Well?' Mitch said.

'Well?' Claire said, linking her arm through his and strolling along at his side.

'Good shooting, China.'

'Thank you. You weren't so bad yourself,' Claire replied, laughing.

288   MADALYN MORGAN

Mitch took a deep breath and sighed. 'You know, honey, you were the only person who believed me incapable of treason.'

'Esther didn't believe you were a traitor. Nor did any of my family. Édith, André and Therese laughed at the suggestion, so did the guys who were in the Resistance with you. No, darling,' Claire said, leaning her head on her husband's shoulder, 'it was only Commander Landry who doubted you after reading Beckman's letter.'

'Huh!'

'What?'

'Commander Landry doubted me. My own commander thought I could be turned by a German spy. Me, a German sympathiser, an agent? How long has he known me?' He cuffed a tear. Without speaking they walked on through the suburbs. Then Mitch said, 'There might be something in what Chief Jacobs said. Maybe I'll leave the air force and become a cop.'

Laughing, Claire looked up at her husband. He wasn't laughing. 'Are you serious?'

'About being a cop? No. About leaving the air force? Yes. Once the legal stuff is over and my name has been cleared – and after Beckman's trial – I shall resign my commission.'

Claire put her head on her husband's shoulder. 'Whatever you decide to do, Aimée and I will back you all the way.'

'Mmmm... Aimée,' Mitch said.

'She'll be pleased I kept my promise.'

'What promise?'

Claire looked up into Mitch's face. 'I promised her I would find her daddy and bring him home to her.'

Mitch pulled Claire close. 'She'll be pleased? I'm pleased you found me.' Leaning forward he kissed Claire hungrily. 'I've missed you, China.'

'I've missed you too, darling. Shall we hail a cab?'

'Good idea.' Mitch put up his hand and the first cab that approached stopped. 'We'll telephone Aimée from the hotel's lobby. It will be quieter.' He gave the driver the name of the hotel and jumped into the back of the cab with Claire. 'We could ring Dad and Marie from the lobby too; tell them it's over and we're on our way back. We could say we're walking some of the way. Then...'

'Then?'

'We could book a room for a couple of hours. What do you say?'

Claire looked into Mitch's eyes. Her heart was pounding and the butterflies he always woke in her began to stir in the pit of her stomach. 'We'll telephone Aimée first,' she said.

A LETTER FROM THE AUTHOR

Dear reader,

Huge thanks for reading *Reckoning*. I hope you enjoyed meeting Claire and Alain again in their personal battles for truth and justice. If you enjoyed Claire's journey, and I hope you did, perhaps you would like to sign up for my newsletter along with other readers to hear about my new releases and bonus content.

www.stormpublishing.co/madalyn-morgan

If you enjoyed *Reckoning* and could spare a few moments to leave a review, I would really appreciate it. Even a short review, when it is positive, can make all the difference in encouraging other readers to discover my books for the first time. Thank you very much!

The inspiration to write *Reckoning* came from the story and the characters in *Betrayal* and later from Mitch's behaviour in *Legacy*. The main story in *Betrayal* was resolved, as were the lives of Claire and Mitch. The story of the beautiful French spy and the POW camp doctor remained open.

Halfway through writing *Legacy*, I suddenly realised that, although Mitch was with Claire at the Foxden Hotel in the new year, I hadn't given him anything to say or do. Being uncharacteristically quiet and thoughtful, coupled with dark mood swings, were symptoms of shell shock. In *Foxden Acres*, Bess

Dudley had seen her brother Tom go through something similar when he came home from Dunkirk. And, so, the seed was sown.

Having established that Mitch had shell shock, I had an idea that the Nazi doctor from the prisoner-of-war camp where Mitch was held in WW2 escaped when the Allies liberated the camp. He could set up a medical practice in another country. Fake papers were easily bought, and post-war Europe was desperate for doctors. It would make sense for him to go to Austria, as Germany borders Austria – and although the language is not the same, the differences would be easy for a doctor to pick up. Mitch came from Canada, so the doctor became a phoney Austrian, specialising in post-war disorders practising in Canada.

Mitch was an intelligent guy. If he became suspicious of the doctor, and the doctor caught on to him, Mitch could disappear. And, if Mitch didn't return to England, questions would be asked about wartime treachery. Claire wouldn't believe Mitch was a traitor, but why hadn't he gone home to her? So many questions needed answers. Claire knew there had been a French woman, a spy, who he'd become close to when they were prisoners of war. Had he gone to France to be with her? Had they been more than comrades? Claire hoped not. But even if it meant confronting the French woman, Claire was determined to find her man.

Thank you for being part of my writing journey. I hope you'll stay in touch, as I have many more stories and ideas to share with you!

Best wishes and happy reading,

Madalyn x

www.madalynmorgan.wordpress.com

facebook.com/madalyn.morgan1

twitter.com/ActScribblerDJ

instagram.com/madalynmorgan1

pinterest.com/madalynmorgan

ACKNOWLEDGMENTS

Thanks to my mentor Doctor Roger Wood. Thanks also to Rebecca Emin, Cathy Helms and Maureen Vincent-Northam for their advice and support.

Maureen Vincent-Northam for proofreading and to writer and poet Fiona McFadzean, my beta reader. To my family and friends for their love and support, to author friends Theresa Le Flem and Jayne Curtis, and to readers and writers on Facebook and Twitter. Thanks also to the authors of the Leicestershire RNA chapter – The Belmont Belles – for their friendship and encouragement. Thanks to W.H. Smith and Hunts Independent Bookshop in Rugby, and to the libraries in Lutterworth, Rugby and Markfield.

Printed in Great Britain
by Amazon